UNICORN
RESCUE

ISLAND OF FOG LEGACIES #1

UNICORN RESCUE

by Keith Robinson

Printed in the United States of America
This Edition: March 2019 (formerly *Unicorn Hunters*)
ISBN-13 978-1091792081

Cover design by Keith Robinson

Visit www.UnearthlyTales.com

UNICORN RESCUE

ISLAND OF FOG LEGACIES #1

KEITH ROBINSON

Chapter 1
Poachers from Old Earth

Travis moved through the trees, whistling tunelessly, hands in pockets, his eyes on the narrow trail because it had a habit of tripping him the moment he looked elsewhere. He normally headed straight home across the fields, but today he wanted inspiration. This longer, far more scenic route always managed to surprise him with its hidden wonders.

Birds chirped high above. A dragonfly the length of his forearm buzzed past his face, causing him to jerk backward and look left. As it happened, he then spotted two glowing will-o'-the-wisps circling a tree trunk. The tiny creatures were smaller than faeries and with fuzzy blue fur.

When he moved on, an ugly squonk shuffled off the trail ahead and into the bushes, its folds of fat wobbling. About the size of a dog and with four spindly legs, the pitiful creature sobbed mournfully as it went, leaving a watery trail. It was said that a squonk could dissolve into a pool of tears if too many people stared at it at once.

Travis smiled. He'd been right to come this way. The forest was teeming with fascinating wildlife, magical or otherwise.

Fleeting movement distracted him. He glanced off to the right, squinting through the vegetation. There he saw a tree-colored, man-shaped figure, possibly a dryad—

He tripped on a root and went sprawling.

When he picked himself back up, the dryad was gone. Or if not gone, then absolutely still as it blended into the background and studied him. Wishing he could be the first of his classmates to meet one face to face, he scanned the trees with a keen eye, looking for even the slightest movement, the tiniest blur that would give away the dryad's location.

Nothing.

Sighing, Travis continued on his way. "A dryad," he muttered. "That could work. Not as cool as a wyvern, though."

A wyvern remained at the top of his shortlist. He'd seen one a week ago, and its slender orange-and-blue reptilian body and blood-red wings had awed him. Though not much bigger than a man, they had razor-sharp teeth and barbed tails. To be able to transform into one . . .

He heard the cracking of a twig to his left and paused. A bush quivered, and he tensed, waiting to see what would emerge. To his relief, a tiny childlike female moved into view— tan-colored skin, large mischievous eyes, oversized pointed ears, long black hair, dark-brown tunic and pants, and fine leather boots. She stood no taller than his waist.

"Oh, it's *you*," Travis said. "Can't believe you followed me out here, Nitwit."

"What did you expect?" she said in her squeaky voice. "I'm an imp. It's my job to annoy you."

"And *only* me," he murmured. "Nobody else."

Nitwit grinned. "Is school over already?"

"Yep." He felt a renewed surge of excitement. "And guess what? I got approved."

The imp frowned as she joined him on the trail. "For what?"

"To be a shapeshifter!" Travis said, unable to contain his joy. "Dad filed the paperwork with Lady Simone, and she presented it to the committee, and they approved. No big surprise, really. Both my parents are shapeshifters, so it's in the blood." He paused. "Well, not *literally* in the blood, otherwise I'd be half dragon and half faerie. How would that work? But shapeshifting kind of runs in the family, so the committee didn't have to think too hard about it."

"Because you're a *natural*," Nitwit said, rolling her big brown eyes. "Everyone else has to be nominated by at least two dozen non-family adults before the paperwork can even be filed to the committee. You skipped all that."

"Well," Travis said, continuing on the winding trail, "I can't help it if my parents have friends in high places."

2

"I suppose not."

"They're old heroes, you know, and my dad—"

"Yes, we all know about your dad," the imp mocked.

"What's *that* supposed to mean?"

She avoided the question. "What do you want to be?"

"I'm not sure yet. Maybe a wyvern."

"Why a wyvern?"

"Because they're cool."

She squinted up at him. "You know wyverns can't breathe fire, right? If you want to be a dragon like your dad, why not just—"

"I'm not allowed to be a dragon," Travis grumbled. "There's a whole bunch of things I'm not allowed to be. These days, shapeshifters have to be something safe and nonthreatening."

"In case you turn bad and go on a rampage," Nitwit said, nodding.

Like twenty years ago when scrags stole the top secret formula for creating shapeshifters, Travis thought. *A gang of villains turning into deadly monsters like the chimera, hellhound, dragon, and the massive simurgh. Not good.*

"Yeah, but also we have to be something *useful,* something that can contribute to society. Like a dryad. My dad knows a dryad shapeshifter, and she makes medicines. And his friend Robbie's an ogre who builds houses."

Nitwit frowned. "So what use is a wyvern? They're vicious things! They don't breathe fire, but they have a nasty, poisonous barbed tail."

"But they're cool."

"And how is being cool useful to society?"

"I don't know."

"Are they even allowed? They seem pretty dangerous to me."

"Sometimes the committee will make exceptions if—"

The roar of an engine sounded from outside the forest ahead. The sound was so unexpected that it took a moment for Travis to register what it might be.

He picked up speed, muttering as he went. "Sounds like Old Earthers. They shouldn't be driving around in these parts. Come on, let's see what's going on. Probably joyriders again."

He didn't care much for Old Earthers in general, though he had to admit some were okay. There were a few in his class. Twice a week they stepped off the yellow bus, one of the few vehicles allowed to rumble into Carter on a regular basis. Those kids couldn't get enough of New Earth; they stared wide-eyed at literally *everything*, even the mundane stuff, always expecting something magical to happen. They couldn't wait for the Friday field trips.

Travis had tried Alter-Education a while back. He'd gone to an Old Earth school once a week until he'd had his fill of it. The other world was impressive with its massive cities, impossibly tall buildings, flying machines, and super-fast road vehicles. But machines literally left a nasty taste in his mouth, and he'd dropped out.

The forest ended, and the trail opened out into a lush meadow. Normally it was peaceful here, nothing but the buzz of bees. Today, however, four mud-splashed off-road vehicles shattered the serenity as they spun about and left deep wheel marks in the grass surrounding a small thicket.

Travis felt a surge of anger at the Old Earthers. Did they have nothing better to do than tear up his beautiful countryside? Why couldn't they stay in their own world instead of fouling this one?

Then he froze as a flash of white bolted from the thicket. A unicorn!

The vehicles roared after the creature, one of them hot on its heels. Unicorns were larger than horses and much faster, but the open-topped Jeeps were built for scrambling on rough terrain, and they quickly matched the frightened equine's speed. With unerring precision, the four vehicles pressed in tight on both sides as well as in front and behind. The one bringing up the rear looked like it might clip the unicorn's hooves at any second.

The leading driver jammed on his brakes, and the startled unicorn leapt into the air, clearing the entire length of the vehicle in one bound. It came down hard just ahead, then bucked and caved in the front of the Jeep with a savage backward kick.

The unicorn galloped away with three Jeeps in pursuit, leaving the fourth to halt with steam pouring from its radiator grille. But the other hunters seemed more determined than ever now, and they quickly closed in despite the frenetic pace. Travis watched in amazement as the unicorn danced about and frequently changed directions, trying to shake off the drivers. They spun and tore up the grass, leaving a crisscrossing mess of tire tracks and a haze of noxious exhaust fumes.

Travis wrung his hands and hopped from foot to foot. "They can't *do* this! It's illegal to hunt unicorns! It's illegal to hunt *anything* without a license! They're not even supposed to be *driving* in New Earth!"

He realized after a moment that Nitwit had disappeared, and he clicked his tongue with annoyance. She had a habit of showing up when not wanted and disappearing when he needed her. Not that an imp could help in this situation.

"I wish my dad was here," he growled. "He'd chase them off."

The unicorn grew desperate and began ramming the moving Jeeps. It lunged and stuck its horn deep into a side door, briefly tilting the Jeep to one side before wrenching loose. The driver of that vehicle yelled and then started laughing at his lucky escape. Meanwhile, the unicorn shook its head and bucked wildly as the hunters once more closed in and began driving circles around it.

A flock of rocs flew over. Travis imagined them glancing down at the ruckus and most likely not caring one bit. If he were a roc shapeshifter, he'd use his massive talons to pick up the Jeeps one by one and take them off into the sky, then drop them from a great height. At the very least, he could easily slam down and break up the hunt in short order.

What other kind of shapeshifter would help? A wyvern could lash out with its barbed tail and inflict a few well-aimed bites. An ogre or troll could stomp on the Jeeps and tip them over. A manticore's poison-tipped quills could easily find their mark and take the drivers out.

But Travis was no shapeshifter, at least not yet, and he watched helplessly as the unicorn grew weary, its eyes wide and nostrils flaring. As big and fast as the creatures were, they weren't much for fighting and were easily shocked. The Jeeps maneuvered into formation around the poor equine and herded it down the grassy slope. It tried to veer off once or twice but lacked the energy to leap away.

Where were the hunters taking it? Travis scanned the way ahead, looking for—

Ah! There it was on the fringe of the sprawling forest opposite: an inky-black dome of smoke twenty feet across, protruding from the ground and pulsing rhythmically, growing larger one second and sucking inward the next, breathing in and out. His old-fashioned parents still called them holes, but Travis and everyone else of his generation knew them as portals. This one was pretty big, and it definitely hadn't been there last time he'd come this way. The hunters must have created it recently.

"That's illegal, too," he growled, clenching his fists. "If my dad were here . . ."

The three Jeeps disappeared through the smoky portal and vanished, taking the unicorn with them. Just like that, they were gone, their noise cut off.

Travis started running down the slope after them, then changed his mind and headed for the fourth Jeep. It remained motionless, the hood up, steam drifting from its radiator. The driver rummaged in a compartment at the rear, produced a large can, and unscrewed the lid as he hoisted it around to the front. When he poured water into the radiator, more plumes of steam erupted. Even from a distance, Travis could see the water running straight out the bottom of the radiator, but it probably helped cool things down a little.

Panting, he hurried closer, fearing the man would turn and see him at any moment. Travis's luck held, and he darted to the back end of the Jeep while the driver slammed the hood down. Then it was a case of keeping the vehicle between them, hiding behind it while the man threw his half-empty can onto the passenger seat and climbed in. When the engine roared into life and the twisted radiator fan screeched in protest, Travis clambered into the back seat and ducked low, still amazed he hadn't been spotted.

"Come on, baby," the driver grunted as he swung the steering wheel around and made the Jeep spin. "Just down the hill, okay? Don't overheat on me yet."

No more steam erupted from the radiator, probably because its contents had already poured out into the grass. It was running dry now. But the smoky portal was just down the hill, a short ride in a speeding, bouncing Jeep.

Travis remained low on the back seat, looking up at the wispy clouds. When blackness filled his vision for a second, he knew the Jeep had just passed through the portal. The sky returned immediately, now deeply overcast, the air ten degrees cooler and somehow thinner. He felt sprinkles of rain on his face.

He'd crossed into Old Earth.

Fear gripped him. *What am I doing?*

Chapter 2
Unicorn Rescue

The Jeep skidded to a halt almost straight away, and the engine died. The screeching fan cut off, too. "We hoofed it outta there," the driver shouted with a laugh. "My ride's a wreck."

"Bagged us a cool fifty, though," another replied. "Ran straight up onto the truck."

Travis identified three or four more voices as he lay there squeezed into the smallest form possible. After half a minute, he twisted around to peer between the front seats and through the windshield. He saw the other three Jeeps parked alongside a gigantic, dark-blue semi-trailer truck. Its rear doors were open and a ramp down, but just inside the trailer was a sturdy metal gate, through which Travis could see the unicorn.

It stood panting, sides heaving and tail swishing. It started to turn around but stopped when the ivory-colored, spiral-indented horn caught on the wall. The unicorn stamped and whinnied, then let out a deep-throated growl before resuming its frantic panting.

The hunters—a group of six men in all—stood on the very end of the ramp, looking up at their prize. "So are we going back for another or not?" one asked.

"I'm game."

"We only have three Jeeps now, though."

"I still think it would be safer to tranq the unicorns. Safer for us, safer for them."

"Yeah, and then what? We drag their sleepy butts out of New Earth and onto the truck?"

Trying to calm his nerves, Travis took in his surroundings. The terrain was vaguely familiar, with open hills all around, only this version of the world had a smooth road stretching to the horizon. The truck had pulled over onto the hard shoulder, its rear end facing the smoky-black portal. There was no way this gateway between Earths had been there already. It was brand new, created by poachers for their dastardly expedition.

"This portal might be closed by tomorrow," one of the men said, "And Portal Patrol will be watching for us. Right now we have the advantage of surprise. I say we go in again now, while we can, and nab a couple more."

"Another hundred thousand?" another said, and let out a low whistle. "I'm in."

"We got lucky with this one. The herd is spooked now, so it won't be as easy next time. Maybe we should take a foal."

They kept arguing, and Travis grew angrier by the second. He looked over his shoulder. The portal, a dome of black smoke, stood fifty yards away on the roadside. He'd seen dozens in his lifetime and would never get used to them. Some floated above the ground, others high in the air or even deep underwater. All were carefully monitored these days, but there was a time when such a task had been impossible. Thousands of portals had exploded into being twenty years ago, pockmarking the landscape and bridging the two worlds, unifying them. Travis's own dad had been responsible for that event. It had been a time of awestruck wonder as people from a virus-stricken Old Earth had wandered across into a magical land filled with creatures they'd always believed to be the stuff of myth and legend.

The novelty had never worn off. Naturally, everyone wanted to see unicorns and dragons and other so-called exotic creatures, and some rich Old Earthers paid handsomely for private zoos filled with the most exciting beasts, dangerous or otherwise.

The poachers came to an agreement. Five of the men climbed into the three vehicles while the sixth sauntered back to the truck's cab, which seemed far away. As engines roared into life, Travis laid low and waited, thankful that his driver had left his crippled Jeep alone and gone off with the others.

He glimpsed the vehicles tearing past as they headed back to the portal. Craning his neck, he watched as, one by one, they vanished into the blackness—and as they went, the noise of their engines cut off until an abrupt silence fell.

The truck driver climbed up into his cab and slammed the door shut.

Travis leapt out from his hiding place and hurried to the back end of the trailer. The unicorn turned its head and banged its horn on the metal wall. There just wasn't room for it to spin around. It was, however, able to watch him out of one eye.

"It's okay," Travis whispered. "I'll get you out of here."

Up close to a unicorn like this, he couldn't help feeling intimidated. Horses had always made him nervous, and this was no ordinary horse, standing at least a foot taller than most and packed with twitching muscles across its flanks. He'd never seen such pure white hair. Even its mane, long and flowing, gleamed like it had been thoroughly shampooed. The unicorn's horn had to be over three feet long.

He unlatched the gate and paused, wondering how this was going to work out. "Now, when I open this," he said, trying not to sound so nervous, "I need you to run back through the portal and hide. Okay? Do you understand me?"

The unicorn merely stared back at him, unmoving.

"Don't get yourself caught again," he added. "Go find your herd and stay with them. Warn them."

As far as he knew, unicorns were no smarter than horses, which meant his words were futile. This was where being a shapeshifter came in handy. If he were a unicorn shapeshifter like one of his dad's friends, it would be a simple matter to transform and help this poor, dumb creature understand. He sighed and pulled the gate all the way open, keeping his fingers crossed that all would go well.

"Shoo!" he urged, stepping off the ramp and around to the side of the trailer out of the way.

The unicorn backed up in a hurry and swung its head around—too early. Again it banged its horn on the side. But it was halfway down the ramp the second time it tried to turn, and it cleared the end of the trailer and spun about in obvious excitement. Then it was off, galloping away as fast as its legs could take it.

In the wrong direction.

Travis's jaw fell open at the sight of the unicorn tearing across the field toward the trees, completely ignoring the smoky portal. Or perhaps willfully avoiding it.

"Whoops," he muttered. But at least the unicorn was free.

"Hey!" a voice yelled.

The driver had witnessed the escape in the side mirror and jumped down from the cab.

Travis turned and ran, heading for the portal, aware that his only chance was to outrun the middle-aged man until he could lose himself in the forest. What if the Jeep drivers abandoned the unicorn chase and came after him instead? Could he make it home? Not with those Jeeps tearing after him! But if he was going to run and hide, he'd rather it was in New Earth than this unfamiliar place.

He made it to the portal without breaking a sweat and had time to glance back and see the hunter's angry face—and then Travis was plunging through blackness and out the other side. The temperature rose, and everything brightened considerably. Even the air smelled sweeter.

The noise of Jeeps filled the air. In the distance, the three of them had spread out around a herd of a dozen unicorns, some of them foals. Travis kept running, glad they were so far away but upset they were closing in on one of the younger creatures. One Jeep tore ahead, and the foal reared and darted sideways—exactly as the hunters had intended. Now cut off from the herd, the foal found itself galloping alone with noisy, frightening vehicles pursuing it.

As the rest of the herd stampeded away, one of the adult unicorns paused and looked back, then let out a screeching whinny and went after her foal.

Travis kept running, panting as he climbed the grassy hill. Glancing back, he saw the truck driver emerge from the portal and pause to look around. Travis concentrated on his own two feet, knowing he had a good lead and could probably keep his distance as long as he didn't trip and sprain his ankle. The truck driver already looked ready to give up the chase.

The next time Travis looked back, the three Jeeps had herded the foal almost all the way down the hill to the portal. But the drivers hadn't noticed the much larger unicorn bearing down on them from behind. It moved with purpose, head low and horn jutting forward, and Travis stopped to watch with a sense of dread as the furious equine closed the gap.

This couldn't end well. He imagined the horn ramming into the rear end of the Jeep, snagging on the metal, and the unicorn tumbling and twisting, being dragged along and severely injuring itself in an effort to save its foal . . .

But at the last second, the Jeep at the rear suddenly veered away from the danger. The unicorn swung its head in vain but missed, saving itself from serious injury in the process.

Flanking the foal on either side, the men aboard the two remaining Jeeps either didn't notice the charging unicorn or didn't care. But they shouted in alarm when it inserted itself between the fast-moving vehicles and swung its head viciously to one side. The horn pierced a windshield, and fragments of glass flew everywhere. Then the horn swung the other way and nearly took out a driver. Both vehicles split off and peeled away, their tires spinning and sending up clods of dirt.

The unicorn and her foal ran on side by side, now free.

"Yes!" Travis yelled.

Then he, too, hurried on his way. Maybe the poachers would give up the hunt now. They seemed pretty shaken and fed up judging by the way they slowed their Jeeps to a halt and threw up their hands in disgust. Maybe the news of the escaped unicorn would dash their resolve once and for all.

Or infuriate them further.

He made it to the brow of the hill and slowed, out of breath. Looking down into the valley ahead, he could see his home nestled in a stand of trees. He'd lived there all his life, and he loved it despite it being so far outside Carter. His parents had moved here long ago when the village had expanded well beyond its perimeter and become a town. In fact, most of the shapeshifters had left around the same time, preferring the solitude. Travis knew their reclusive nature had something to do with a sheltered upbringing, a life on a lonely, foggy island.

Whatever the reason, he enjoyed being well away from the busy, bustling town.

He started down the hill—and at that moment heard the sudden roar of an engine as one of the Jeeps rumbled up the slope toward him.

Sagging at the knees, he knew he'd never make it home. The hunters would be on his tail in less than ten seconds. Still, he broke into a sprint and yelled until he was hoarse.

"Mom! Dad! HELP!"

The Jeep hurtled over the hill, bumping and sliding as it circled around in front and skidded to a halt. Two men leapt out, their faces screwed up in anger. One hunter held a rifle.

"You just cost us a fortune, kid!" the driver snapped.

"Hunting unicorns is illegal," Travis said shakily, looking past the men toward his home. It seemed so close yet so far away. If only his mom or dad would look out the window.

One of the men laughed and spoke sideways to the driver. "You hear that? Hunting unicorns is *illegal*. Man, I feel so bad right now."

"They're just horses with spikes on their heads," the other snarled. "Never saw the fascination. What's so great about them? They're bigger and faster, but so what? Are they magic? I didn't see any fireballs or rainbows. What's the big deal?"

"They're sensitive," Travis said, trying to remember everything his dad had told him. The one and only unicorn shapeshifter, an elusive lady named Ellie, had learned a lot about them over the past two decades. "They can make poisoned water drinkable. They can heal sickness. They're just really gentle and harmless, and they scare easily—"

"Yeah, they do," the second man said, laughing again. "We were just getting the hang of it, herding them straight through the portal into the back of the truck. We shoulda left the foal alone, though." He glared at his colleague. "I *told* you."

"Lesson learned," the driver admitted.

Travis remained still and quiet, hoping they would grow bored and leave *him* alone, too. What could they do to him anyway? Being paid to hunt unicorns was one thing. The murder of a twelve-year-old human boy was something else entirely.

Unfortunately, they had other plans. The driver waved him closer. "Come on. Get in."

"Wh-what?" Travis stammered. "Why?"

"Because you know stuff. Unicorns can heal? My boss is gonna want to know everything about that. So come on, get in."

Travis backed away. "No way!"

"Get in, kid." The man raised his rifle. "I won't ask nicely again."

Both men watched Travis with narrowed eyes, and he looked from them to the rifle, his heart thudding. Whether they would actually shoot him or not didn't matter. Even if he turned and ran, they could easily climb into their Jeep and catch up to him, then reach out and grab him. He had no chance.

But he smiled, a wave of relief flooding through him. "I'm not going anywhere. But you'd better run before it's too late."

"Huh?"

Travis pointed behind them. Both men swung around—and gasped.

Soaring toward them from the direction of his home, with massive leathery wings beating hard and steady, came a giant adult dragon with a hard, knobby spine and club-ended tail. With claws flexing and casual bursts of fire shooting from its jaws, the monster was a terrifying sight for those who didn't know him.

"You messed with the wrong kid," Travis said with a grin. "That's my dad."

Chapter 3
A Very Famous Shapeshifter

The dragon's rapid approach spurred the hunters into action. They yelled and clambered into their Jeep, and moments later the vehicle roared away, tearing up the grass and showering Travis with clods of earth.

Down the hill, the truck driver and the other two Jeep crews must have seen the approaching dragon, because they wasted no time in skedaddling. The whole lot of them vanished through the portal before the third team had made it halfway there.

Travis watched with mounting excitement as his dad—a very famous shapeshifter—flew almost lazily over the hill to catch up with the last remaining hunters. His massive shadow fell across the field, twice the speed of the vehicle and closing fast.

"Go, Dad!" Travis yelled.

While the driver hunched over the steering wheel, the passenger twisted around in his seat and pointed his rifle into the air. A *crack!* rang out, then another, and the dragon veered off. But then a huge sheet of fire leapt from his fearsome jaws toward the Jeep below, and both hunters yelled as flames licked over their heads.

Travis's dad swept by, turned, and thumped down in front of the smoky portal, thwarting any attempts at escape. The driver had no choice but to skid to a halt less than twenty paces away—just a couple of short hops where the dragon was concerned. As the rifle came up once more, a blast of fire engulfed the front of the Jeep and blackened the windshield. Both men cowered behind the glass, screaming with terror.

Their hands shot into the air in surrender when the stream of fire cut off. The dragon thumped closer and leaned over the vehicle, giving another bellow just to make it absolutely clear the chase was over.

Laughing inwardly, Travis raced down the hill, eager to hear the stern lecture his dad was about to unleash on behalf of Portal Patrol. The dragon abruptly shrank down and took the form of a man dressed in silky clothing of varying greys and greens—a knee-length coat, a loose-fitting shirt, comfortable-looking pants, and a pair of finely tailored boots made from the same silky material only much thicker and sturdier.

Smart clothes, the magical garments that adapted to fit a shapeshifter's form. With Travis's dad, they became a strap around the dragon's throat, rather like reins. When he reverted to his human form, they instantly reshaped around him.

Travis almost lost his footing in his haste to catch up to the Jeep. His dad had already started into his lecture as the two men stared in amazement, one loosely grasping his rifle as though he'd forgotten it was there. Both their mouths hung open. In a moment, they'd get over their shock and probably rise up in anger, but for the moment they listened like meek schoolboys.

". . . Creating a new portal," the shapeshifter scolded, counting off on his fingers, "entering New Earth without a permit, hunting without a permit, bringing a vehicle through without a permit, tearing up the countryside, harassing the wildlife, *capturing* the wildlife, firing a weapon at a dragon—" He broke off and frowned. "So stupid. Wounding a dragon will always result in a deadly attack on the assailant and probably wider retaliation on a nearby settlement."

"You're not a *real* dragon, though," the driver argued. He rose out of his seat and leaned over the windshield. "You're a shapeshifter."

Travis's dad raised an eyebrow at him. "And that's better how? Do you think I won't roast your hides in a heartbeat?" He waited a half-second, then added, "In fact, firing on a shapeshifter is an even worse crime. Last time I checked, killing a human is murder."

"Yeah, well, whatever," the driver grumbled. He scowled. "So what now? You gonna arrest us?"

The other hunter hung out of the passenger seat with his rifle still hanging loosely. Travis sidled alongside the Jeep and reached for the weapon. "I'll take that," he said nervously. As he clamped his hand around the barrel, the man jerked in surprise and yanked it away.

"Hand the rifle to my son," Travis's dad warned from up front. "Don't make things worse than they already are."

To make his point, he let out a quick belch of fire.

The driver gasped. "H-how did you do that?"

Travis reached for the rifle again, and this time the passenger released it.

"Now, both of you out of the vehicle, face down on the ground, hands behind your back."

The hunters moved slowly, their eyes darting about, obviously looking for a way out. Travis watched nervously, holding the rifle but doubtful he could shoot anyone with it even if he knew how. His dad was unarmed but amazingly calm.

"Son, take the keys out of the Jeep."

Travis hurried to the driver's side and removed the keys. He tossed them to his dad, who caught them deftly.

At that moment, one of the men jumped up and shouted, "Now!"

Both sprinted off in exact opposite directions, not looking back.

Travis's dad sighed. "They always run. Go on home, Travis. I'll have to take these men straight off to jail instead of waiting for backup."

"But there's a unicorn, Dad. They took one earlier, and I followed it through that portal into the back of a huge truck. I let it escape, and it ran off—but it's stuck in Old Earth!"

His dad looked at him with raised eyebrows. Then he smiled. "I'll have to call Ellie, then. She'll track the unicorn down, don't worry." He hurried over to the portal and disappeared into it, then reappeared after a few seconds. "The truck's gone. I'll go look for it in a minute. First, let me catch those two men and drop them at the jail. Back soon."

Once more, he transformed and took to the sky, his massive wings beating hard and his tail swinging around. Travis watched with glee, wishing he could be a dragon just like his dad. Of course, even if he were allowed, he wouldn't be *that* big. Not yet, anyway. But it wouldn't take long. As a human youth on the cusp of adulthood, he might only gain another ten or twelve inches in height, but his dragon form would grow three or four yards in length and probably put on a few thousand pounds of weight.

As his dad flew off after one of the hunters, Travis wondered for the umpteenth time how a human could transform into such a monstrous animal. Where did all the extra mass come from? Lady Simone had always dismissed this mysterious aspect of shapeshifting as "too difficult to explain," probably because she had no clue herself.

In fact, the reverse was true of his mom. She could grow faerie wings and remain at five and a half feet, but she could also shrink down to faerie size, about six inches tall. Where did the surplus mass go?

He watched as his dad descended and snatched the frantic hunter off the ground. Soaring high again, he swept around in an arc and headed back to fetch the other. By now, that hunter was nearly at the line of trees . . . but the dragon got there first, casually grabbing the man by the scruff of the neck and yanking him into the air.

With a hunter dangling from each of his front paws, Travis's dad headed off to the town.

Travis turned to look at the portal, anxiety growing. The others would get away if his dad didn't hurry back. Right now they had to be still in sight. Maybe his dad just hadn't seen them on the horizon. Still holding the rifle, he edged past the silent Jeep and toward the pulsing cloud of black smoke.

Steeling himself, he plunged through, walking fast. The ground under his feet felt the same all the way through, nothing but long grass, but the air temperature changed again, and everything looked dingy. He raised the rifle, half expecting to face a crowd of hunters.

But nobody came at him. The massive semi-trailer truck had gone, and the three Jeeps had disappeared with it, including the one with the smashed-in front. Maybe they'd towed it away.

He looked all around, puzzled. He could see for miles. Surely he should be able to see the tail end of the slow truck in the distance? How could it have driven over the horizon so quickly?

He shook his head. Maybe it had taken longer than he realized dealing with those other two escapees, and the rest of the crew had wasted no time making themselves scarce. It was a shame they'd gotten away. Though two men down, they would probably be back some other time.

He returned to New Earth and started up the hill toward home. If his dad hadn't gone off with the keys, Travis might have been tempted to try and drive the Jeep home, too!

* * *

"All taken care of," his dad said when he returned home a little later and walked into the living room. "Those two hunters will be in the town jail today and then moved to the Prison of Despair for a week. The council is contacting Portal Patrol to get that hole secured and shut down, but it might take a while. Apparently, there's been a spate of poaching in the area—seven new holes to deal with!"

Travis's mom jerked upright on the sofa. "Seven? Wow! What's happening around here?" She pushed her dark-brown hair away from her face and frowned. "I don't like it. We've had poachers before, but this is different."

"Yeah, more organized. Abi, these people are serious. Well funded and professional. Someone is paying big money to nab our wildlife." He turned to Travis. "So those men are in jail, and the goblins came and took their Jeep away. There's no sign of the others anywhere, not even that truck you mentioned."

Travis shook his head. "I can't believe they got away so fast."

"I flew up high and looked, but I didn't see anyone for miles. I would have spotted a convoy like that from the air. They must have hidden somewhere."

Travis smiled. "If only I had wings of my own . . ."

"Oh, there he goes again," his mom said, throwing up her hands. "Hal, your son wants to be a dragon just like you. So he can work for Portal Patrol and deal with illegal visitors."

Travis had always liked the sound of Portal Patrol, and not just because "Portal" was an anagram of "Patrol," something he found amusing. To be a shapeshifter assigned to policing the gateways between Old and New Earth? It was his dream job. Of course, he had to finish school first, but he could be an apprentice until then. And who better to train with than his dad?

"Well, it'll be your turn soon, son," his dad said, coming over to squeeze his shoulder. "Now, is that dinner I smell?"

Travis's mom looked stern. "Yes, but you have to earn your keep if you want to eat, Hal Franklin. All you've done today is sit around in caves with nasty white-tentacled monsters."

"Just one cave, Abi, and one nasty white-tentacled monster. And someone has to do it."

She rolled her eyes. "Feeding the brain? Sitting there daydreaming under the pretense that you're providing information to a giant being under the ground?"

"It likes its regular updates."

"It gets plenty of fresh news from everyone else who visits the hundreds of sites you've unearthed across the land—"

"*Eighteen* sites."

"—And now it's going to drain the brains of two hunters in the Prison of Despair."

"It doesn't drain their brains, it just reads their minds and makes time slow to a crawl."

Travis had heard this routine many times. He smiled, almost tuning them out. Many people already thought his dad was crazy without him going on about the weird white tentacles and what they were supposedly attached to. Most scientists believed they were simply plants of some kind, growing wild like ivy, completely smothering a cave or ceiling but always originating at a thick, treelike trunk in the ground. His dad insisted those trunks were merely the tips of massive arms reaching out of the Earth from deep within, part of a colossal underground brain, and he had a huge following of devoted believers offering their services as daydreamers.

Yes, his dad was crazy—but in a good, lovable way.

Chapter 4
Lady Simone's Warning

Just as Travis was sitting down to dinner with his parents, a visitor came knocking.

His dad frowned and went to see who it was. When he opened the door, his voice floated along the corridor. "You're just in time. It's beef and potatoes tonight."

A woman's voice answered. "Sorry to intrude, Hal. I just wanted a quick word with you all."

"Come on in."

Lady Simone swept into the dining room, and Travis swore her presence chased away the shadows. She was pretty amazing for someone in her fifties, though she did have mermaid blood running through her veins. She threw off her silky green cloak, pulled out a chair, and perched sideways with one elbow on the table. "Hello, Travis."

"Hi, Lady Simone," he mumbled, awed. He'd seen her a million times in public, and she'd visited the house as well, but she rarely sat down at the same table, two feet away, smiling and speaking directly to him!

His mom had already fetched an extra plate and silverware. She pushed the plate toward the visitor and said, "Please help yourself. There's plenty."

"Oh, no, thank you, Abigail. I really didn't mean to invite myself to dinner. Besides, I ate a late lunch. No, I just wanted to talk to you all about Travis's shapeshifter application."

His mom absently reached back to fiddle with her ponytail as she often did. "Is this what you normally do? Visit applicants at their homes?"

"Only those of particular importance," Lady Simone said, her piercing blue gaze still trained on Travis. "Have you decided what you want to be?"

The steaming beef and potatoes, not yet served onto plates, lay forgotten while Travis squirmed in his chair. His dark-haired mom had a quizzical look and a slight smile on her freckled face, while his dad stood behind her with a raised eyebrow and folded arms.

"Um, well," Travis said, "I was thinking of a wyvern."

Lady Simone looked off to one side of the room, obviously giving his choice some thought. She nodded slowly. "Not bad. Capable of flight, a poison-tipped tail, quite vicious at times . . . You'd definitely be able to defend yourself."

Travis's mom frowned and stared at her. "I thought wyverns were classed as dragons."

"They are. Small ones."

"But dragons aren't allowed."

"Well . . ." Lady Simone waved a hand airily and smiled at her. "The committee can make exceptions for certain young people." She returned her gaze to Travis. "After all, young man, the Shapeshifter Program might not exist if not for your parents."

Travis felt a swell of pride. "I know."

She reached out to pat his knee. "And all because a gorgon turned your dad to stone."

"Molly, yes," Travis said, nodding.

Though as stiff and lifeless as a lawn statue for two weeks, his dad's consciousness had ended up in a strange world full of dead souls. There, a so-called Lady of Light said it was not his turn and released him back to the living. But during his dreamlike visit, he'd met a boy named Chase who knew the whereabouts of the long-lost sphinx twins, Bo and Astrid, and it was Astrid's amazing power of knowledge that resulted in an improved method of creating shapeshifters.

"It used to take years to create shapeshifters," Miss Simone mused. "Your parents were born with shapeshifter blood, and so was I before them. It was a very long process, and it had to be that way—a slow, eight-year transition from human to full-fledged shapeshifter, at which point the young student could be trained to switch back and forth at will. The only place the program could take place was in Old Earth, with its lower oxygen content and lack of magic."

"The island of fog," Travis whispered. He'd heard *this* story many times.

Lady Simone cocked her head. "Well, not just the island— but yes, certainly for your parents. The fog was there to filter out the virus that struck the world just as the Shapeshifter Program started, but the fog worked a little too well, dulling the effects longer than anticipated. Your parents were twelve before they experienced their first transformation." She suddenly frowned and shook her head. "But the point is, that overly complicated system is no longer necessary. These days we can create shapeshifters just like *that*."

She snapped her finger and thumb, and the noise made Travis jump.

"So, Travis, you'd like to be a wyvern? Is that your choice?"

He paused. "I think so, yes."

"So you can come along tomorrow morning for the procedure?"

"Whoa," Travis's mom broke in. She leaned across the table and touched Lady Simone on the elbow. "What's the hurry? I know the forms were approved yesterday, but isn't there normally a whole series of induction meetings and training sessions? Counseling and advice?"

"We may not have time for that, Abigail," Lady Simone said quietly, her face darkening.

Travis's dad came around the table so he could face her directly. "What's going on?"

She sighed. "I had a visit from the soothsayer yesterday. He warned me of today's poaching incident and said something worse would follow, something involving a burning house, a crowd of angry monsters, and Travis begging them to calm down. Since the old man's prophecies always come true, he strongly suggested—and I agree—that Travis should at least be prepared to defend himself should he find himself in trouble.

Travis featured in the dream, but whether he was a shapeshifter or not is unclear—so that's something perhaps we can control by making sure he *is* one before trouble brews."

A long silence fell.

Then his mom said, "That's it. Travis is staying home from school tomorrow."

"And the next day?" Lady Simone asked, arching her eyebrow. "And the day after that?"

"As long as it takes."

"Abigail," Lady Simone said, rubbing the bridge of her nose, "I understand, really I do. But since you've already agreed that Travis will be a shapeshifter, and his application is approved, and he knows what he wants to be, why not just cut through the red tape and get it done?"

Travis's mom and dad looked at one another.

Finally, his dad nodded. "Fine. If Travis is ready to do this, I'll bring him along to the laboratory tomorrow morning. That good with you, son?"

Travis nodded eagerly, his heart thumping. It was really happening! He'd dreamed of this for years, and now here it was. In just over twelve hours from now, he'd be waking up at dawn and heading to Lady Simone's laboratory for a quick procedure involving wyvern blood and a healthy dose of magic. When it was over, he'd be able to transform into a small dragon creature . . . and fly!

The idea of soaring around in the sky thrilled him. He'd been up in the air countless times with his dad, but to zip about on his own . . .

"Can't we just go now?" he begged.

Lady Simone smiled. "We need to allow a few hours for the procedure—putting you to sleep, allowing you time to wake, then keeping an eye on you afterward. We don't want to rush it through this evening and have you transform while you're asleep in your bed tonight. No, tomorrow morning will be fine. First thing, okay? I'll arrange an excuse note for your school teacher."

With that agreed, she stood and gestured at the table.

"Sorry again to disturb you. I'll leave you in peace."

"It's no trouble," Travis's dad said. "Thanks for the warning. Where *is* the soothsayer? I'd like to talk to him, see if I can jog his memory and get some more details."

"He's probably in his shack on the hill, but I doubt he'll remember anything more. He would have said."

"I'll ask anyway."

Travis detected a growl in his dad's voice, probably accompanied by a rising surge of heat. That happened a lot with him, his inner dragon trying to break free.

After Lady Simone had left, the three of them started into their dinner in thoughtful silence. Travis stared hard at the table as he chewed, thoughts of flying buzzing through his mind.

"Worried?" his mom asked. "Look, whatever the soothsayer was talking about—"

"Oh, I don't care about *that*," Travis assured her. "Never gave it a thought. All I can think about is being a shapeshifter! I'll be the first of us."

"If by 'us' you mean the offspring of our shapeshifter friends," she said with a smile, "then you're right. And I'm pretty sure Melinda will be next, then Mason."

Travis hadn't seen Uncle Robbie and Aunt Lauren for months. They weren't *really* his uncle and aunt, just close enough friends to warrant the titles. Their eleven-year-old daughter Melinda and seven-year-old son Mason likewise called Travis's parents Uncle Hal and Aunt Abigail.

The other shapeshifter friends were scattered far and wide. Travis idly gave them a passing thought: Fenton and his wife Hailee lived in the east near a family of massive lizards; Darcy and her dryad husband Gresforn dwelled in the forest near the Lake of Spirits with their three small children; Dewey was still in the same sad, futile relationship with a girl who demanded everything from him and gave nothing in return; Thomas was on a personal lifelong mission to encourage manticores to step foot outside the woods; and Emily was a miserable old spinster who still couldn't decide between her human and naga clans.

Well, maybe not a miserable old spinster, he corrected himself. His mom had admonished him about that several times before. Emily wasn't miserable, and thirty-three was not 'old' by any means. "Old to me," Travis usually responded under his breath.

His dad pushed his plate aside and leaned back. "There's still some speculation about people like us."

"People like us?" Travis repeated. "What do you mean?"

His mom rolled her eyes. "Don't listen to your dad. Some people say that the child of a mom and dad who are *both* shapeshifters would surely be born a shapeshifter. But that's never, ever turned out to be the case. And that's probably a good thing. Imagine a cross between a dragon and a faerie! How would that work? No, there's some truth to the theory that shapeshifter blood is passed down, but not a single child has ever been born a ready-made dragon or whatever. The important magical element is missing."

Travis's dad tapped the table with a finger. "The offspring does inherit a better immune system, though. That's a fact."

"No, Hal, it's a theory."

"How can you say that? A kid with two shapeshifter parents has a *fantastic* immune system." He nodded slowly and looked at Travis. "All the times you've avoided a common cold. And chicken pox. And measles. All the other kids in the class would catch something and pass it around, but you never did. You may not be an actual shapeshifter, but you have a shapeshifter's immune system—passed down by your mom and me, double the strength!"

Travis grinned. "Sure, Dad. Melinda's the same. Last time we saw her, she was complaining because most of her class had taken the day off sick, and she felt fine so had to go to school. It wasn't fair."

"Exactly. I rest my case."

His mom stood up and pushed her plate aside. "Well, whatever. I believe you, actually. I'm just saying it's not scientifically proven."

"You sound like Simone. She used to refute everything she couldn't prove. There was a time she didn't even believe in magic. Shapeshifting is an ancient art, and she firmly believed it was pure science even though she couldn't explain how it could possibly work."

Travis's mom nudged him. "Anyway, it's your turn to wash up, Mr. Franklin. I cooked, so I'm done."

"I've been out working all day!" he protested.

"No, *I've* been out working," she countered. "While you've been sitting around in a cave feeding a giant tentacle plant, I've been running a dozen errands in town. I'm worn out. If you loved me, you'd jump at the chance to let me put my feet up and rest." She reached slowly for the plates. "But I see how it is. I'll just collect these and take them to the sink and wash them. You go sit by the fire and relax some more while I slave away in the kitchen again. It's okay, I know my place. I'm just a faerie, while you're a magnificent, powerful dragon . . ."

Travis watched with glee as the mock-argument ended the way it always did—with his dad rolling his eyes and giving in. "All right, all right, I'll do the dishes. Quit bugging me, woman."

Chapter 5
Fatherly Advice

The sun's early-morning rays stretched across the room as Travis's mom kissed him on the cheek and hugged him. "I'll see you there, all right?"

He nodded and headed out the door. On the lawn, his dad was already in full dragon form, his leathery wings spread wide. He was thirty feet long from the flared nostrils on his snout to the clublike tip of his tail. Thick muscles bulged everywhere, and his dark-green scaly hide was almost impervious to damage. Almost. He still had a tiny bullet hole in one of his wings from yesterday. In his younger days, that injury would have healed almost instantly. Now that he was in his thirties, his regenerative abilities were ebbing. Lady Simone was in her fifties and still had a scar on her leg from fifteen years ago.

But Travis had a lifetime ahead of him, maybe thirty years of happy shapeshifting before he had to worry about his healing abilities beginning to fade.

His dad grunted, and Travis climbed aboard, clinging to the silky material around the dragon's throat. In about an hour from now, he would be presented with similar garments, a rite of passage for all new shapeshifters. He gripped the fine material and tried to contain his excitement.

It's really happening!

His dad launched, and Travis flattened himself against the knobby spine, holding on for dear life. Launching was always the hardest part for a passenger, when his dad was stretched upright and beating his wings hard. Once in the air, he flattened out and soared gracefully.

The dragon grunted again.

"Sure, Dad," Travis said. "About as comfortable as can be."
He grinned. "Hey, this might be the last time I need to sit on your back—cuz I'll be flying alongside you!"

His dad remained silent at this.

Travis finally figured out that he might have hurt his dad's feelings. "When I say 'the last time,' I just mean for a little while. I'll come ride with you again when I get lazy and need you to carry me."

He heard a huffing sound, and he smiled. That was his dad's dragon laugh.

Rather than go straight to the laboratory in town, his dad took him out to the fields where the unicorns roamed. The herd would be moving on in a few days, so Lady Simone said, but right now the equines were content to graze on the fringes of the forest. The tire marks from yesterday's attack were a mess of vivid lines in the grass, but the unicorns seemed to have forgotten the incident judging by the way they fearlessly spread out.

The dragon landed near the smoking black portal. Travis dismounted and waited for his dad to revert to human form. The silky smart clothes magically arranged themselves around him before the reptilian bulk had finished morphing into human flesh, and the weird plastic boots appeared out of nowhere.

The shapeshifter eyed the triangle of posts erected around the smoky mass. "Like that'll help," he muttered. "Poachers wouldn't *dare* come through with those terrifying posts there."

Yellow tape had been wrapped all around, sporting the words DO NOT CROSS. The tape was one of many small imports from Old Earth. The vivid color seemed out of place in this world, but it made it clear that the portal was under strict surveillance by Portal Patrol.

Except it wasn't. Portal Patrol in this region was a small operation, a handful of shapeshifters including Travis's dad, and there were too many illegal portals at the moment to post guards around them all. Similar posts and tape had probably been set up on the other side for the time being, but poachers would simply laugh if they stopped by again.

Still, the portal would be closed in a day or two. Sometimes it just took a while for the centaurs to get around to things even though Lady Simone had probably escalated its importance. There was only one portal deactivation system in the local area.

"Why are we here, Dad?"

His dad turned to him. "Just doing my duty as a Patrol Officer. Plus I wanted a little chat, father to son. I want to make sure you understand that this choice you're making—to be a shapeshifter—is not to be taken lightly. Everyone dreams of being one, but very few are really serious about it. You don't choose this life because it's cool to transform into a monster, or because one or both of your parents are shifters. You choose this life because you're willing to work hard, make good decisions, and take responsibility very seriously. And you need to be aware how dangerous a shapeshifter's life can be. Especially for dragons."

"I know, Dad."

"Do you?" He moved closed. "Son, you want to be a wyvern. I get it. You want to be a dragon but aren't allowed, so you're choosing something close. But that means you'll be tasked with meeting other wyverns, putting yourself in danger, literally flying into their nests to study them. And if there's a problem with rogue wyverns attacking villages, *you'll* be the one called on to deal with the situation."

"I know."

"And then there's *this*." His dad nodded at the cordoned-off portal. "I don't know how many illegal holes have popped up in recent years, but it's an ongoing battle. They were all over the place when I blew up the mine twenty years ago, but that was in a time when Old Earthers needed help. People were different then. They were desperate. And yes, some were dangerous, the scrags especially. But mostly they were just grateful for a chance at a normal life without that virus hanging in the air."

Travis had heard this tale many times, and not just from his dad. He'd heard various sides of the story. Some said his dad had gone crazy, a twelve-year-old kid using dynamite to cause an explosion at Bad Rock Gulch, a known hotspot for enormous amounts of magic. The explosion had set off a chain reaction, and thousands of smoky portals had opened up across the land. He'd done this after being turned to stone by a gorgon and waking a couple of weeks later. He'd lost his mind, or so the story went.

The portals had joined two very different Earths, and this sudden unification had been met with mixed feelings. Stepping into a magical new world with clean air had certainly excited the Old Earthers, and the variety of equally intelligent creatures had humbled them. But New Earthers had unanimously complained about the huge influx of human refugees. The naga and manticores had fought hard for their forests; the elves had largely retreated to the mountains; and the centaurs—well, they'd dutifully kept quiet since they'd caused the virus in the first place.

New Earth humans, along with their close goblin allies, eventually began to see the benefits of such a massive merger thanks to advanced medical knowledge and plenty of safe, useful, environmentally friendly technology. And as the years had rolled on, respect and understanding had gradually settled into a blanket of peace.

But there were always bad eggs. Illegal hunting had become a problem, and a high percentage of portals had been closed in an effort to police who came and went.

"It's been twenty years," Travis's dad said, looking off into the distance, "and we've surpassed the future I saw when Molly turned me to stone all that time ago. Here in New Earth, people watch their manners and get along. Everybody is happy. Everybody knows their boundaries, respects their neighbors, and have never forgotten that this world is not theirs to trash. Unlike Old Earthers, who are still at war." He shook his head and sighed. "We've closed a lot of portals in the last decade,

32

quietly shutting doors and increasing security. I see a day when the two worlds will be separate once more . . . and then Old Earthers will probably destroy themselves. The Gatekeeper was right."

Travis felt a chill at the mention of that mystical being, the powerful Lady of Light. His dad never talked about her, which was probably for the best. He already had a reputation for being weird. After all, he spent his spare time sitting with white-tentacled plantlike creatures that supposedly thrived on human company.

"Poachers are a scourge," his dad said bitterly. "But what sickens me more are the Old Earthers who give the poachers a reason to keep doing what they're doing. They pay to see magnificent creatures they might not otherwise get to see up close—trolls, griffins, manticores, minotaurs, dragons, and of course unicorns. And if they're not paying to see these things in cages, they're buying skins or tusks or claws to show off to their friends. It's expensive business."

"It's sick," Travis agreed. He'd heard quite a few brutal stories that made him queasy. "Our teacher said one single dead ogre could make a whole bunch of knee-length coats or really big living room rugs."

"A hot favorite at the moment are manticore stingers," his dad growled. "They fetch a fortune. It's said they still produce venom even when severed, but that's a dumb myth that only very stupid people buy into."

Across the field, something spooked the unicorns, and they galloped for the safety of the trees. An enormous roc bird sailed overhead with wings outstretched. It wasn't uncommon for a roc to snatch up a horse, but unicorns often proved a little too dangerous with their spiral horns.

"Being a fierce wyvern shapeshifter," his dad went on, "will probably mean getting involved with poachers somewhere along the way, and if not poachers, then just unruly types who come through and cause mischief. Old Earthers police their world with helicopters and guns. Shapeshifters look after ours.

Portal Patrol. It's part of our job. And it'll be part of *your* job, Travis."

"I'm ready," Travis said, drawing himself up. "If I'm a wyvern, I'll be able to handle poachers the way you do."

His dad pursed his lips. "Well, I'm much bigger. And I breathe fire. Besides, poachers *always* carry guns, and a well-aimed bullet could be fatal. Never assume you're invincible just because you're a shapeshifter with the ability to heal whenever you shift back and forth. "

Travis nodded. "Can we go now? Lady Simone is probably getting impatient . . ."

"Ha! *You're* getting impatient, you mean. All right, hop on."

A few seconds later, Travis was clambering up onto the back of the dragon again. He clung tight to the silky reins during launch, then grinned with anticipation as they left the unicorns behind and flew low over the town of Carter.

Lady Simone's laboratory complex sprawled on the fringes of the woods at one side of town. The main building fronted a dusty road, and a dozen small workshops stood out back, some connected with outdoor wooden corridors thrown together by goblins and overhung by trees.

Travis's dad thumped down in the middle of the road and reverted to his human form the moment Travis had dismounted. "Well, here we are, son. You'll walk into this building a human and walk out a shapeshifter. Who knows, maybe you'll *fly* out." He placed a hand on Travis's shoulder and pointed upward. "I smashed my way out of this place once. Rocs landed out back carrying scrags from Old Earth—immune virus survivors bent on getting hold of Simone's secrets. They did, too. Flew off with one of the doctors and made her talk. We tracked them to a castle—"

"Dad, I *know*," Travis broke in, hopping up and down despite the hand on his shoulder. "Tell me later, okay? C'mon, I want to get this done."

Chapter 6
Creation of a Shapeshifter

Travis started feeling drowsy less than a minute after he drank the weird-smelling liquid. "Sleep tea," the doctors called it. He sank back into his pillow and watched the ceiling spin. His mom and dad leaned over him on one side of the bed, Lady Simone on the other. As far as he knew, the busy woman rarely supervised a procedure even though the Shapeshifter Program was close to her heart. "You should feel honored," his dad had mumbled in an echoing, booming, strangely distant voice as she'd entered the room just moments ago.

Lady Simone's eyes shone, dabs of vibrant blue in an otherwise dreary room. She wore a white lab coat like a couple of other doctors who moved about in the background. "Rest," she said, smiling. "When you wake, you'll be a shapeshifter."

The last thing he remembered was a doctor behind her holding aloft a syringe filled with blood. *Wyvern blood*, he guessed. *They're gonna stick it in me . . . and then . . .*

Very few people knew the process involved in creating a shapeshifter. It certainly wasn't just sticking a needle full of blood into his arm. Magic was involved, and timing was everything. It only took twenty minutes or so, but the recovery took longer, two hours or more.

"Sleep," Lady Simone whispered, her voice reminding him of a wave rushing up a sandy beach. As it receded, he drifted off with it, totally relaxed . . .

* * *

"How do you feel?" his mom asked, leaning over him and pressing the back of her hand to his forehead.

Travis blinked and squinted. "Huh?"

"It's all over, son," his dad said. "All went well, no problems. You've been out for just under two hours. It'll be lunchtime soon. Bet you're hungry."

He was. Skipping breakfast was mandatory for the procedure. He struggled to sit up, his vision swimming. But he felt fine. No sickness, no headaches, nothing. "So I'm a shapeshifter?" he asked, hardly able to believe it.

"You're a shapeshifter," his mom said, nodding. He realized she'd been holding his hand the whole time. "The first local wyvern in a very long time."

Travis knew this already. Research was part of the decision process. There was no point choosing an overly common creature and being one of many similar shifters. Wyverns were in short supply around these parts, though mainly because they were technically dragons, and very few applicants were granted that privilege.

"When will I be able to . . . you know, *change?*"

His dad shrugged. "That's up to you. Some change right away, others take longer. But don't worry about that right now. Let's get you fed and then home."

Laboratory staff brought him a thick sandwich, which he ate hungrily, his mind buzzing. While his parents talked with the doctors, he finished his plate and slid out of bed in his clinical gown.

"Where are my clothes?" he asked.

His dad turned to face him. "Well, if you can wait a second, Lady Simone will be along with a gift."

He already knew what the gift was. He sat on the side of the bed and fidgeted, barely listening to his mom as she explained that he could take the day off school but would be fine to return in the morning. All he could think about was the wyvern blood in his system. He would never truly believe he was a shapeshifter until he actually transformed. But though his dad had explained many times how such a feat was done, doing it was another matter entirely.

Lady Simone showed up at last, and she presented him with a neat pile of silky garments—two pairs of pants, some boxer shorts, and three shirts, all greens and greys in faint, mottled patterns, a patchwork of pieces with fine stitching. Resting on top of the pile were two pairs of weird, plastic shoes the same as his parents wore. His dad had an antique pair at home that clung to the soles of his feet and barely wrapped up over his toes. Modern smart shoes reached to the ankles, though they worked the same way. The material was actually the same as the clothing, multiple layers of woven silk stuck together and hardened with some secret ingredient. The silk itself was very special, full of magic.

"Cool!" he exclaimed, hurriedly pulling on a pair of boxer shorts and pants before throwing off his clinical gown so he could put a shirt on. The material felt warm and comforting. He'd tried on his dad's shirts before, but these smart clothes were *his very own*.

"There's something you should know," Lady Simone said. She sounded serious.

Travis slid into one of the smart shoes. At first it yielded, then slowly tightened around his bare skin, a perfectly snug fit. He knew it would remain the right size for years to come no matter how much he grew. Smart clothes easily adapted to fit.

"Listen up, Travis," his mom said.

His ears pricked up, and he paused midway through putting on the second shoe. "Uh, okay," he said. His parents stood together, clearly in on whatever it was.

Lady Simone seated herself on the end of the bed. "Travis, your blood is a little different to most. You're the first of a kind, though by no means the last."

He listened, saying nothing.

"Both your parents are shapeshifters," Lady Simone went on. "We've created many right here in this room, but you're the first whose parents are also shapeshifters, passing genes from one generation to the next."

Adults these days were generally prohibited from participating in the Program because their bodies wore out too quickly. Like the villainous scrags, who had stolen the secret and vials of blood and gone on a rampage twenty years ago. While they'd successfully transformed into all manner of creatures, five years later they'd all lost the ability and been reduced to haggard wrecks. Only one had lasted well—a youth named Seth, who'd showed up years later fighting fit.

Becoming a shapeshifter earlier in life was the key to longevity. The younger body adapted better, embracing rather than rejecting the foreign blood and infused magic.

Lady Simone picked her words carefully. "The old way was to create shifters from birth. The new method is easier, but you could argue that it doesn't stick as well."

His dad cut in. "Think about when I cook thick slabs of meat with my dragon breath. A quick blast of fire for a few seconds blackens the outside really quickly but doesn't always cook it properly on the inside—"

"Which is why we prefer to roast it slowly at a lower temperature," his mom added.

Travis nodded. *Whatever*, he thought, thinking about being a wyvern. He was ready to go home and practice transforming. Instead, his mom and dad were giving him cooking lessons.

Lady Simone said, "Your parents, Travis, are from the original program, and they're the first double-parent shapeshifters with a shapeshifter child of their own. The results are interesting. Your immune system is far stronger than theirs ever was, and stronger than mine. You—"

"It's a double-whammy," Travis broke in. "I know. But so what? That's good, right?"

Lady Simone raised an eyebrow. "Well, up to a point, yes. But the stronger your immune system, the more likely it is that your body will revert to its former state."

Travis stared at her. "Wait, what? Its former state?"

"Its former *non-shapeshifter* state, yes."

The silence in the room deepened.

"What—what do you mean?" Travis asked, not liking the sound of things.

She looked troubled. "I'm not entirely sure, but I believe your body will fight to reject your shapeshifter blood. It will treat the ability like a virus and eradicate it, and after that you'll no longer be able to shift. You'll become *ordinary* again."

Travis gritted his teeth and clenched his fists. *I don't want to hear this, I don't want to hear this.*

"I'm fine," he said rather foolishly. "Can I go now? I feel a change coming on, and I want to be outside when it happens."

His mom sighed and rolled her eyes, but it was his dad who spoke. "Son, I'm not sure you understand the significance of this. It means that you—"

"You're saying I won't be a shapeshifter forever!" Travis cried out, jumping to his feet. "I get it! That's why I don't want to sit around any longer. Please, Dad, can we go now?" He swallowed and, shaking, turned to Lady Simone. "Thank you. I'll . . . I'll try to do some good work as a wyvern before I turn back to normal."

She gave a rueful smile and nodded. "I know you will, Travis. If you're anything like your mom and dad, I expect great things of you."

Leaving his spare smart clothes and old garments for his mom to pick up, Travis hurried toward the door. He paused and looked back. "How long do I have as a wyvern? Twenty years? Ten?" Seeing no immediate reaction, he whispered, "Five?"

Her eyes downcast, Lady Simone frowned at the floor for a moment before looking up. "Maybe a week or two."

Travis sucked in a breath. The bottom had just dropped out of his world. His mouth opened and closed a few times, but the words stuck in his throat.

His dad edged closer. "Simone watched a blood sample under the microscope and said it was pretty aggressive, the antibodies swarming in to smother your shapeshifter ability like it's some kind of nasty flu. But Simone has already agreed to start over with a new procedure when—"

"You mean I can keep having this done?" Travis interrupted, hope flaring. "So it won't last forever, but I can keep starting over?"

Lady Simone shook her head. "Not exactly."

* * *

Travis burst out of the front doors of the laboratory into sunlight, his head spinning. Elation at being a wyvern shapeshifter had turned to bitterness.

"Son," his dad called, hurrying out after him. "Don't run off. Let's talk about this."

"She said a week or two!" Travis yelled, and several goblins glanced his way. "And I can't ever be a wyvern again, because my body will be *immune* to that shapeshifter blood!"

"Yes, rather like fighting off a common cold. The same strain never gets you twice—not that you ever get ill. The point is, a wyvern is just one creature. If and when you lose that ability, you can pick something else and start over. Look at the positive side. I often wish I was something else. It gets old being a dragon sometimes."

"It's true," Travis's mom said, appearing behind him. She smiled. "Hal often tells me he wants to be faerie."

"Not funny, Mom." Travis angrily kicked at a rock. "So I'm supposed to keep coming here every couple of weeks and get stuck with needles and sleep for hours? And whatever I choose will only last a short time? How am I supposed to do my job as a shapeshifter? How will I have time to *do* anything? What's the *point?*"

Chapter 7
Travis the Wyvern

Travis stormed away from his parents. "I'll see you at home."

"Hey, it's not a good idea to go off on your own," his dad called after him. "Come back here, please. We need to stay together. I don't want to let you out of my sight until you're a full wyvern shifter."

"But I'm not!" Travis protested, turning back to face his mom and dad. "I'm a screw-up."

His mom frowned. "You're acting crazy. Your dad's right— we need to stay together. You heard what Simone said about the soothsayer's vision. So stomp about in a circle if you want to, but don't go too far. We'll wait for you on that tree stump over there."

While his parents went to sit on one of a few thick stumps outside the laboratory building, Travis paced about the grounds, crossing the path multiple times and drawing the attention of more goblins as they plodded past.

He calmed himself within a minute, already feeling a little ridiculous for his outburst. And sorry, too. It wasn't his parents' fault his promising shapeshifting career had come to a grinding halt.

"What's bitten *you?*" a small voice asked.

He turned to see Nitwit hiding among the bushes just behind the nearest tree. Her large eyes blinked at him, and her oversized pointed ears twitched.

Travis sighed and shuffled toward her. "I'm a wyvern shapeshifter now, but it turns out I can't stay one for long. It'll wear off in a week or two, maybe sooner."

Nitwit stuck out her bottom lip. "Sorry. Better enjoy it while you can, then. Can you transform yet? Or are you too busy throwing a hissy fit?"

Travis felt his face heat up. "I haven't tried yet."

"Well, try now. See if you can change."

He glanced toward his parents. They were watching him, both with frowns on their faces. Realizing they probably couldn't see his impish friend where she hid in the bushes, he pointed at her and shouted, "Nitwit's here!"

"Shh!" she hissed, ducking down. "Don't let them see me."

"Why?" He clicked his tongue. "When are you gonna get over this? You can't hide forever. Come talk to my parents. They're really nice. You'll like them. My mom's a faerie shapeshifter, and my dad—"

He paused and reconsidered mentioning that his dad was a ferocious dragon. Nitwit knew already, but she didn't need to be reminded. She was nervous enough as it was.

"Come on out," he said, leaning toward her. "Here, I'll hold your hand."

Nitwit shook her head and lowered herself even more so that only one ear and part of one large eye were visible.

Travis glanced toward his parents. They'd gotten up and were heading his way, curiosity written all over their faces. But when he looked back at the bushes, Nitwit had gone.

He scowled and hurried into the trees. "Nitwit! Come back! Why are you running away?"

Sometimes he wondered if she truly ran anywhere. She had a habit of appearing out of thin air and disappearing just as quickly, though of course that couldn't be so. As far as he knew, imps were just very fast on their feet. She came and went on her own terms, and he'd never been able to track her.

Until now.

He sniffed, picking up a scent he'd never noticed before. He couldn't quite place it, but somehow he knew it was her. He leaned close to the ground behind the bushes where she'd been standing, then raised his head and sniffed the air. To his surprise, her escape route was blindingly obvious. She'd headed *that* way, weaving in and out of the trees toward the outskirts of town. He could almost taste the scent.

Noting that his parents were hurrying after him, he told himself it was okay to nip into the woods and go after Nitwit. Just this once, it would be nice if they actually caught a glimpse of the elusive imp.

He pursued her, scurrying through the trees, wondering why he hadn't done this before. She smelled strongly of . . . what? A kind of damp, musty scent? That made sense. Didn't imps hide out in caves? Nitwit had mentioned that before.

He picked up speed, aware that his mom had started calling his name. "Travis!" she yelled, sounding pretty angry now. The buzz of her faerie wings filtered through the trees as she came after him. His dad's deeper voice seemed farther away, lagging behind.

Something had taken ahold of Travis deep inside. The urge to track his impish friend, to hunt her down, was too strong to resist. He wouldn't hurt her, just catch up and hold her until his mom arrived. Nitwit would hate him, but she'd get over it.

Travis hurdled a clump of brambles and zigzagged around trees, suddenly aware that he felt different. When he looked down, he gasped and almost stumbled and fell. His feet were still his own, complete with new smart shoes, and his legs were still covered with silky material . . . but his upper body had changed, and his arms were lengthening into scaly appendages with flaps of leathery, blood-red webbing. The top half of his silk shirt peeled open to allow more room for his new orange-and-blue reptilian torso and arms.

He took all this in with one quick glance, and he let out a gasp of amazement as he burst out of the trees and into a clear meadow beyond. The dazzling sunlight blinded him momentarily, and he threw up his hands to block the glare— only they weren't hands but orange reptilian claws on the ends of long, sinewy arms that stretched at least six feet. A single vicious-looking claw projected from each of his elbows.

The webbing snapped taut and caught on the breeze, halting him. Trembling with awe and fright and excitement, he watched as his lower body shortened and changed, his smart clothes seeming to dissolve though they didn't really. The material, including that of his shoes, would follow him everywhere in some form or another—perhaps a cloak, or a belt, or a second skin, or—

"Travis!"

His mom's voice seemed distant now. Either he'd zipped through the woods faster than he'd imagined, or she'd gotten lost. His dad was probably far behind, weaving through the tight spaces of the forest in human form.

Travis would have waited for his mom except the wind tugged at his webbing, and his short, muscular legs seemed eager to launch him upward. He resisted the urge for a moment, but then he sprang into the air, lifting his wings.

It was like the wind snatched him away. With a shout of surprise, he soared upward and spun wildly, curling around and around as he rose. Full-sized dragons always seemed to find it a great effort to launch, but Travis felt like he was *supposed* to be in the air, like it took more effort to cling to the ground. Now he was free, flying like a kite on strong gusts high above the trees.

"I'm a wyvern!" he shouted.

His voice came out as a screech. *I sound like a strangled pig*, he thought.

The stretch of woods he'd run through wasn't huge, just a narrow strip wrapping around one edge of the town. He glimpsed the laboratory's roof before he whipped past. He was already in full control of his spins and turns, beating his wings as though he'd had them all his life.

My arms are wings now, he told himself. His dad retained both his legs and arms and grew wings on his back, but Travis had no arms in this form, and his legs were short and stumpy.

His skin, scaly and orange with swirling blue patterns, was definitely finer and more delicate than his dad's rough hide. His wings and tail were blood red. The length of his tail impressed him, long and skinny with a vicious barb on the end that he knew contained deadly poison.

As for his head . . .

That was one thing he couldn't get a look at. He needed to find a mirror, or perhaps a still pool of water.

When he looked about, he couldn't believe how far he'd flown from Carter. He circled around and started heading back, knowing his mom and dad were probably worried about him. She might be hovering above the trees by now, but she was too far away to see. Was that her? A speck rising from the treetops?

Movement down below caught his attention. Unicorns. He'd wound up back at the illegal portal, and the herd was on the move.

He did a double take. The unicorns weren't just on the move. They were scattering in all directions, trying to get away from three very familiar Jeeps, their tires once more tearing up the grass. One still had a dented front, but it didn't look quite so squashed as before, and obviously the radiator had been fixed. The vehicles spun about everywhere, zeroing in on one particular frightened equine, gradually cutting it off from the herd.

"Not again," Travis growled, noticing that the posts and yellow tape around the portal had been yanked free and tossed aside.

He looked around. His dad had to be back there somewhere. Yes—there he was, swooping low across the trees, looking down, obviously trying to locate his runaway son.

"Over here!" Travis yelled, and his voice emerged as a screech. But he was too far away to be heard, and his dad ignored him, his gaze cast downward.

His mom heard him, though. She spun around and started toward him, painfully slow with her faerie wings. Not that she'd be able to do anything to stop the poachers. Only a powerful dragon could help.

Or maybe a wyvern.

Travis felt his stomach knot up at the thought of taking on these men in the speeding Jeeps, their weapons at the ready. What if they shot at him?

Torn with indecision, he glanced back to find his parents. His mom was at least a minute or two away, and she would be no help. Worse, she'd only put herself in danger. His dad was a distant speck and didn't even realize he was looking in the wrong place. Meanwhile, right below, the poachers were busy herding the terrified unicorn toward the portal.

He dropped out of his circling pattern and plummeted with his wings stretched backward. At full speed, he angled toward the three moving Jeeps. Waiting until the very last moment, he let out the best screech he could muster and spread his wings wide to slow his descent. Most of the men in the vehicles snapped their heads around and looked up at him, and they barely had time to let out squawks of shock before Travis shot overhead.

He'd hoped to cause a knee-jerk reaction where the drivers would yank their steering wheels around and veer off in all directions. The unicorn would have had a moment to bolt to safety before they converged again.

Instead, as Travis spun around in midair and prepared for another flyby, he found himself staring down the business ends of several rifles. The Jeeps hadn't veered at all—they retained their tight formation around the galloping unicorn, one on each side and the third at the rear. The drivers gripped the steering wheels and concentrated on their job, leaving their passengers to deal with the threat from above.

"Oops," Travis muttered, already committed to his flyby. He flapped hard to rise higher as several shots fired. He felt a couple of stings, one in each wing. *Just like dad*, he thought with dismay.

Another volley of shots caught him again, and this time they *hurt*—at least three more stings in his right wing. He suddenly felt a little numb on that side.

Spinning out of control, he yelled with fright as he dropped out of the sky.

Chapter 8
Attack of the Poachers

Travis slammed onto the grassy hillside, his breath knocked out of him. Struggling to suck in air, he flailed helplessly as an engine roared nearby. He looked sideways to see one of the three vehicles bearing down on him. *It's gonna run over me*, he thought with terror. But it didn't. As he finally managed to take a short, stuttering breath, the Jeep skidded to a halt less than ten feet away. The driver stayed put, but the passengers—two of them, one heavyset with a black beard, the other skinny with a high forehead and grey ponytail—jumped out and set to work. Blackbeard grabbed a net from the back while Ponytail approached with his rifle raised.

Now that he had his breath back, Travis ignored the stinging pain in his wings, rolled over onto his belly, and sprang to his feet. To his surprise, Ponytail calmly threw his rifle down into the long grass and reached for another weapon slung around his waist.

Maybe he's out of ammo, Travis thought. He leapt forward, spreading his wings wide and standing as tall as he could while letting out a screech.

But Ponytail seemed fearless, wielding an odd-looking weapon a little larger than a handgun. In one practiced movement, he brought it up and fired.

It made a soft *phut!* sound. Travis barely felt a thing, yet when he looked down, he found a tiny dart sticking out of his chest.

He screeched again, this time pouncing on the man—only Ponytail had already scuttled away, picking up his rifle as he went. The other man, Blackbeard, came running up, dragging the net and yelling as he swung it around.

Travis instinctively ducked as the net flew toward him. Weighted on all sides, it spread out over his head and fell around him. He clawed at it, angry that these men were so easily getting the better of him. Then again, they were experienced hunters while he'd been a wyvern shapeshifter for no more than ten minutes or so.

He struggled to get free, but the net snagged on his scales and claws, and it became far more of a nuisance than he ever could have imagined. He tried to lift his wings, but the claws on his elbows got tangled up. Stepping away from his attackers only resulted in tripping. Swinging his tail proved ineffectual. And roaring did nothing to scare the hunters.

The men circled him. He couldn't watch both at the same time, so he kept his eye on Blackbeard first, then swung around when Ponytail shot him with another dart.

"Leave me alone!" Travis shouted. "My dad'll be here any minute!" But the men didn't understand a word he said. They shouted to each other, manic grins plastered across their faces, their eyes wide. They were *enjoying* this! And all the while, the other two Jeeps—

Blinking, Travis realized they'd gone quiet. *Gone through the portal,* he thought with renewed anger. *They herded the unicorn into a trap.* He imagined the poor thing galloping through the smoky black cloud and straight into the back of a waiting trailer. *Just like yesterday, only this time I can't do anything to help.*

His vision blurred. He felt woozy.

His sense of time failed him after that. At some point he fell flat on his face and became aware of the men running around him with handfuls of rope. He blacked out for a while, then woke when he was dragged through the long grass, the net tight around his upper body while his feet and tail stuck out.

"Mom," he whispered, wondering if she was seeing all this. Even if she were, what could she do? Only his dad could help. He'd catch up shortly, tearing through the portal, and then the hunters would pay.

His body limp and completely at the mercy of the men, Travis felt himself sliding up a ramp. The walls and ceiling of the trailer came into view around him. He heard a gate slam shut, then a door closing, and everything went dark.

The peace and quiet lasted just a second or two before he heard the anxious whinny of the captured unicorn. Then the truck started moving, and the gentle rocking from side to side lulled him to sleep . . .

* * *

He woke a few times, the truck still moving. In near darkness, Travis shook his head and struggled to fully wake up. But the tranquilizers had done a number on him. He kept slipping away, descending back into blissful sleep.

The truck stopped. The silence and stillness alerted him, and once again he fought to rouse himself, forcing his eyelids open and trying to penetrate the gloom—not that there was anything to see except floor, walls, and ceiling. He spotted a bright-white smudge in the darkness and felt a stab of fear at the idea of being confined in the same space as a unicorn. They were dangerous. Those horns could pierce the armor of dragons, and Travis was a mere wyvern, small and skinny in comparison, a weakling without even fiery breath for defense.

But he did have his barbed tail. He knew wyverns could pack a punch, though the last thing he wanted to do was attack a unicorn! If it panicked and charged him, though . . .

He fell asleep again. It was impossible to keep his eyes open.

* * *

Travis blinked awake. This time he had none of the dizziness that had floored him earlier. He felt like he'd woken after a good night's sleep, well rested and surprisingly alert. A quick check confirmed he was still in wyvern form, complete with bullet holes through his webbing.

A feeling of despair seeped through him. He was no longer in the back of the trailer with the unicorn. Instead, he lay in a cage about twenty feet square and twelve feet high, with a concrete floor covered with fresh straw, a full bale in the corner, and a small trough of water in the front left corner. The cage itself stood within a massive room with subdued lighting, some kind of warehouse with a huge roller door at one end. Cages stood to his left and right, and a dozen more lined the wall on the opposite side some forty feet away, all the same size, shrouded in darkness.

With a jolt of fear, he became aware of shadowy figures lurking within some of the cages opposite. Worse, it seemed he had neighbors to his sides as well. He spun to his right and stared into the baleful blue eyes of a red-furred manticore.

Luckily, all the cages were separated by a three-foot clear space between, so even if the manticore turned backward and stuck its scorpion stinger through the bars, Travis was safe as long as he didn't huddle up to the wall on that side. Then again, what if it shot poison-tipped quills at him? He edged away, distancing himself from the forest-dwelling monster.

His parents had a friend named Thomas, a famous manticore shapeshifter. But Travis's caged neighbor was a *real* one, not an ounce of humanity in it. It stared at him with narrowed eyes, its mouth hanging open slightly, needlelike teeth visible behind its black lips. It sat on its haunches, clearly tense, its segmented tail arced up over its head, the stinger oozing venom—

Wait a minute, Travis thought, doing a double take. In fact, the stinger had a thick bag strapped on tight. The manticore's quills and stinger were out of action; it had only its claws and teeth, neither of which could reach Travis through the bars.

He relaxed—then realized he had a similar bag over his own tail, covering the poison-tipped barb on the end. He brought the end of his tail closer and sniffed at the material.

Some kind of chainmail like what goblins wore under their armor. It refused to rip when he bit into it and tugged. And it stubbornly clung to his barb, the strap around the bag's neck pulled tight and impossible to undo with clumsy wings.

Still, at least he couldn't be stung by the manticore.

He turned to the cage on his left. Another figure stared at him in the gloom. This one stood tall, man-shaped and hairy, with a bull's head and oversized horns. Like the manticore, it glared balefully, snarling at him, puffing steam out of its flared nostrils, occasionally scraping one hoofed foot on the concrete as if it were about to charge him.

A manticore and a minotaur. It sounded almost poetic.

Travis eyed it warily, glad there were two barred walls between him and his bullish neighbor.

He squinted, trying to see beyond the huffing beast. Something lay in the next cage, but it was too dark to see. Looking out the front again, he could barely make out the shadowy figures in the cages opposite, but he knew they were all looking at him. Some were large and hulking, others small, one very long. Maybe he'd get a good look if and when the hunters turned the lights on . . .

The hunters!

Travis groaned as reality hit home. He'd been stupid enough to be captured by a couple of men who'd barely broken a sweat to bring him down. And he was supposed to be a wyvern shapeshifter starting a career of patrolling the borders, protecting the portals from attacks such as these! He was useless.

Where were they now? They'd brought him to this place, this warehouse, and dumped him in a cage with all the other prisoners. Now what?

He swallowed and steeled himself. "Where are we?" he called, his screeching voice echoing around the place.

A grunt came from the opposite side, and he heard the rattling hiss of a snakelike creature. He didn't understand a single word. There had to be *something* caged up in this place

51

that had some humanity in it. Was that a naga he'd heard? Could there be a centaur somewhere? An elf? Or were all these prisoners dumb beasts?

The manticore! He swung around to face it. It just so happened that his neighbor could speak in a normal human tongue if it chose to. "Where are we?" he barked again.

Then he realized how difficult communication was going to be while in wyvern form. Understanding the manticore would be easy if it ever spoke to him, but Travis had no way to form a sentence with his rudimentary vocal chords and rather stiff reptilian lips.

The manticore hunched lower, clearly tense.

Travis moved closer to the bars. "Wait—are you *scared* of me?"

The very idea startled him. A manticore wary of *him*? Travis Franklin, a mere twelve-year-old boy?

Only he wasn't just a boy. He was a shapeshifter now, and his wyvern presence had to be just as disconcerting to his neighbors as theirs was to him.

But scaring one another wouldn't get any of them very far. He had to know where he was, how far away from home, and why his dad hadn't caught up with the hunters' truck and saved him. If he had any hope of escaping now, he needed to communicate with some of the other prisoners. For that matter, maybe just talking to the hunters would help. Once they realized he was human, maybe they'd let him go.

I have to change back, he thought. *But how?*

Chapter 9
Cage With a View

Reverting to human form proved impossible.

Becoming a wyvern had been easy. It had happened almost instantly and without effort as he'd gone after Nitwit through the woods. Animal instinct had kicked in, and he'd followed the imp's scent as though she were prey.

Guilt weighed heavily on him. What had he been thinking, going after her like that? He must have terrified the poor thing! He'd been mean even *before* transforming into a wyvern, pushing her into meeting his parents even though she'd made it clear she wasn't interested.

Or had his mean streak been part of the wyvern's psyche taking hold? He held onto that notion. Maybe he wasn't *entirely* to blame for acting the way he had.

Travis gritted his teeth and shut his eyes, willing himself to revert to his human form. His mom and dad had always told him not to try too hard, to just imagine it being so and letting it happen almost in the background. *Huh! Easy to say!*

He was trying too hard now. He eased off, sitting calmly, staring into space as several fellow prisoners grunted and hissed and barked from all around. They'd been quiet when he'd woken, but now they seemed restless. Maybe they were *always* restless and had only fallen silent as he'd blinked awake.

Could he slip through the bars if he was human?

He pressed himself to the front of the cage, trying to be nonchalant, imagining he was human already. It was feasible he could squeeze out, wasn't it? He studied the bars, judging them to be about six inches apart . . .

No chance, he thought with dismay. *There's no way I can fit through those.*

He doubted anyone could, not even a naga, whose body was mostly serpentine. Maybe the water-dwelling variety could, because those types had no arms or shoulders, but the land-based naga had human upper torsos. Even so—a head fitting through six inches?

What about an elf? Were there any here? They were petite, surely small enough to fit through the bars and escape?

He mentally kicked himself. Any prisoners small enough to escape would have done so already! What was he thinking?

Travis reached for the bars, wondering how strong they were. But he had no useable fingers. His arms were incredibly long now, only they were wings! His finger bones were greatly extended, and the blood-red, leathery webbing stretched between each digit and then all the way back to his armpits. They were fabulous wings, but utterly useless in a small cage. He couldn't even grip the bars.

If he ever got a do-over with choosing what kind of shapeshifter to be, he would choose something with hands. Not being able to grip something between fingers and thumb was just plain inconvenient.

Speaking of shapeshifters . . .

It occurred to him that he'd lost his smart clothes. He thought back to when he'd first changed. His clothes had fluidly altered as he'd grown his wings, but after that—well, he had no idea. All he knew for certain was that he wasn't wearing them now. At least, he didn't *think* he was.

He checked himself over, looking for any sign of silky green material hanging off him, perhaps a cloak or reins. But there was nothing obvious. This would certainly make him think twice about reverting to his human form!

The cage door was located on the right-hand side and had an open slot at the bottom, easily tall enough to slide an arm through—if he had arms. *For trays of food*, he guessed. *So the prison guards don't have to open the doors at feeding time.*

Glancing to his left, he figured the minotaur would have rattled the bars a hundred times by now as well as butted them with its head. The cages were way too sturdy for a slender wyvern to escape from.

He sighed and slumped down. Why couldn't he have waited for his dad? Why had he rushed in and gotten himself captured so easily?

"Don't feel too bad," a shrill, fluty voice purred from the cage to his right. "They caught me, too, and I'm far smarter than you."

Travis whipped around and stared at the manticore. "Where are we?" he asked—but of course his voice was just as screechy as before.

The manticore tilted its head. "What a pity. Some decent conversation would have been nice, but no, I get stuck with a brainless dragon on one side and a grouchy troll on the other."

"Perfect company for a big old pussy cat!" a rasping female voice shouted from the other side.

The manticore gave a roar, then added, "Quiet, filth!"

"I'm a wyvern," Travis said nervously, knowing his words were unintelligible. "Not a dragon. And I'm not brainless."

He tried to see past the manticore's cage to the hulking shape beyond. So that was a troll? It had to be asleep judging by how still it was.

Frustrated, Travis looked around for something to write with. Maybe he could grip something in his jaws and scrawl a message on the concrete floor. But there was nothing. He let out a moan, somehow trying to convey that he wanted to say something and couldn't.

The manticore had already turned away, apparently bored. It lay down and crossed its front paws, then rested its chin and closed its eyes.

Travis let out a screech that echoed across the warehouse. Several animal noises replied—a frightened whinny, a serpentine hiss, a volley of deep barks, a few grumbling moans, and above them all a haughty man's voice that said, "Keep it down over there!"

"Yeah, you dragon-wannabe freak!" the woman squawked.

Travis looked for the source of the voices, but even though his eyes were becoming accustomed to the darkness, he still saw nothing but shadows within the cages opposite. The only source of illumination seemed to be from several small, round skylights high above.

All he could do was wait. But for what?

He lay on his belly, closed his eyes, and concentrated once more on reverting to human form. "I can do this," he muttered. "Just be human. It's easy, right? Look, I'm human already. I can just stand up on my two human feet and grip the bars with my human hands and stick my human nose out. Nothing to it."

He opened one eye, saw his reptilian wings stretched out before him, and closed it again.

"Okay, now I'm *really* ready to be human again. I'll just roll over onto my human back and stretch, then sit up and rub my human eyes with my human hands like I just woke up from a long sleep. Then I'll stand up and . . ."

Peeking through an eyelid, he groaned when he saw no change whatsoever. Still a wyvern.

A pang of worry came over him. What if he was stuck in this form forever? But no, according to Lady Simone, his immune system would kick in and work overtime to kill his shapeshifter ability, and he'd be human again eventually no matter what. At least until he started over and went through the program again.

"I'll be a faerie next time," he grumped. "Small enough to fit through the bars. Or an ogre, strong enough to break out."

His parents had told him about a prison just outside Carter known as the Prison of Despair. They'd been locked up in there once, and his mom had switched to her faerie form and snuck out. Uncle Robbie had bent the bars as well—but although they were easily able to escape, the consequences for doing so had been dire, and so they'd agreed to stay locked up until an opportunity arose. A group of shapeshifters could do anything. A faerie, a dragon, an ogre, a centaur, a manticore, a dryad, a harpy, a naga, and a weird lizard creature. Between them, with a bit of teamwork, they had the power to escape from any situation and deal with any foe.

And I'm all on my own, Travis thought morosely.

Except he wasn't. He had a whole warehouse full of potential teammates if he could make them understand. They couldn't escape the cages, but maybe together they could concoct some sort of plan . . .

He groaned again. Who was he kidding? He'd only just arrived. The rest of the prisoners in the warehouse, with the exception of the unicorn, had probably been here at least a day, a week, maybe a month—or much longer. They'd had plenty of time to chat.

"Do stop moaning," the manticore said from the next cage.

Travis gave a screech of anger and whacked his tail on the floor. Straw flew up and fluttered all around.

The manticore raised its head and peered at him. "My, that was like a temper tantrum. You'll be stamping your feet next."

With a bolt of inspiration, Travis leapt to his feet and began stamping, not caring how ridiculous he looked. The more ridiculous the better.

The manticore's eyes widened. After a pause, it said, "And flapping your wings while hopping on one leg?"

Travis happily complied, though he lost his balance and stumbled, falling flat on his face and causing another whirlwind of dry straw. He picked himself up and peered through the bars at the manticore.

The red-faced creature edged closer. "Raise your left wing."

"There you go," Travis said, doing as he was told.

"Wink three times."

Travis winked three times.

"Interesting," the manticore said. "You know left from right and can count. Far smarter than the average dragon."

"I'm not a dragon," Travis said.

The manticore seemed amused by the turn of events. "So you're semi-intelligent, able to understand me. Nod for yes, shake for no: Are you in fact what you appear to be?"

Travis shook his head vigorously.

"Ah! So you must be . . . a shapeshifter?"

Amazed and delighted, Travis nodded and grunted.

The manticore bowed. "Then allow me to introduce myself. I am Lightfoot, perhaps the stealthiest of my kind—though I grant you my skills leave much to be desired in light of my present incarceration. Alas, the human hunters proved they can be equally silent. It's my own fault. Not only am I light of foot but brave of heart—so brave that I frequently venture outside the comfort of my forest. And that was my downfall, for I would have been safer among the trees."

Travis listened, enthralled. It was the first time he'd spoken to a real manticore other than his mom and dad's friend Thomas. "I'm Travis," he said, again dismayed at the gruff squawk that emerged from his throat.

"Are you attempting to tell me your name?" Lightfoot said with a toothy grin. "I'll refrain from trying to repeat that awful sound you just emitted. I shall call you Tiny Dragon instead."

"I'm not a dragon!"

Lightfoot recoiled from Travis's indignant blast. "Well, until you can tell me your real name, Tiny Dragon it is."

Travis let out an irritated huff. Communication was so important, normally taken for granted in everyday life. He would never treat it so again. Being unable to hold a simple conversation with a cellmate was likely to drive him nuts in a very short space of time. He found it particularly annoying that a giant red-furred cat-monster from the forest could speak the human tongue so eloquently while he, *an actual human*, found it impossible to string two words together.

The manticore walked to the front of the cage and raised his voice. "It would appear we have something other than a simple dragon in our midst. A shapeshifter, I suspect."

A clamor of excited grunts and hisses filled the warehouse. Clearly a sizeable number of prisoners understood the human language just fine.

The somewhat haughty voice from earlier called out from the opposite side. "Then why won't he or she change back to human form and escape these bars?"

Lightfoot snorted. "Even a small human could not squeeze through these bars, Tallock. You know that. Though I do agree it is odd that this tiny dragon shapeshifter seems unable or unwilling to revert to his natural being."

"Don't trust it!" a female voice hissed, her voice reverberating. This was not the same woman as before. This one was altogether different, far more sinister. "*Na tu jem eh saduka. Ga sumb eh dalu.*"

Lightfoot sighed and shook his head, then turned to Travis with that perpetual smile on his eerie face. "Please excuse Varna. Her disposition is not exactly sunny." As if realizing something, he tapped his head and beamed, showing all three rows of needlelike teeth. "Forgive my poor manners. Tallock is a centaur, and Varna is a naga. Both reside in cages on the opposite side." He lowered his voice. "And between you and me, neither is equipped to deal very well with the present situation, being so short-tempered and hostile. I, on the other hand, have the utmost patience. And I firmly believe a solution to our dire circumstance is forthcoming."

The manticore's flowery words poured as easily from his mouth as water from a tap. Travis decided he was better off in wyvern form where he could listen intently instead of blurting out daft comments and making a fool of himself. Plus, he figured his twelve-year-old human self would appear puny and weak compared to the manticore in one cage and the minotaur in the other.

"I expect you're wondering exactly where we are," Lightfoot said, and Travis nodded eagerly, moving closer to the cage wall. "Well, unfortunately I don't know. All of us have been here awhile. Some have been here many months, others weeks, and a couple—you and the unicorn—just a matter of hours. We're all here for one purpose, though."

"Yes?" Travis grunted.

Annoyingly, the manticore changed the subject. "As for how you arrived here . . . well, I suspect you were transported in that enormous metal vehicle, yes?"

"How else, you fat, freaky, red-furred feline!" that annoying woman shrieked from the far side.

Lightfoot scowled and lowered his voice. "Ignore the harpy, Tiny Dragon. Answer me. You arrived in the metal vehicle?"

Travis nodded.

"And I expect you're wondering how those conniving humans managed to carry us so far without a few decent humans stopping them and asking questions?"

Close enough, Travis thought. *More specifically, why didn't my dad come after me? He couldn't have lost track of a huge truck driving on a lonely road away from the illegal portal!*

Lightfoot took the time to yawn, stretch, and smack his lips. "I believe great magic was involved. A cloaking spell of some sort. I believe Mr. Braxton has ties with a witch or two."

"Who's Mr. Braxton?" Travis asked.

Yet again, the manticore breezed onto another topic as if he enjoyed leaving his audience hanging. "These cages are impossible to escape from without a key, Tiny Dragon. If we have any hope of leaving this place, it has to be through careful manipulation and subtle persuasion. We have to *talk* our way out." He shrugged. "Either that or we escape during our usual afternoon stroll in the sunshine."

Afternoon stroll, Travis thought, his heart leaping. *In the sunshine!* That sounded perfect. No doubt he would be leashed or secured in some way, but anything had to be better than *this*, locked inside a metal cage.

"Just let me see the sky," he mumbled to himself. "Then I'll be away."

Chapter 10
Escape Plans

The manticore talked too much. After an hour of droning on about forests and how very few manticores could have survived the terrifying prospect of leaving the comfort of the trees, Travis tuned the creature out.

He was getting a better sense of his neighbors. A minotaur to his left, the manticore to his right, a troll beyond the manticore . . . and then, forty feet away on the other side of the warehouse, a centaur, a naga, a harpy, the hulking form of a one-eyed cyclops, and another catlike creature he couldn't quite make out. Also, he spotted the ghostly white shape of the unicorn he'd arrived with. It had finally calmed down and started sniffing at the cage bars.

Other sounds came to him, though. How many cages were there? He counted a dozen across the room from him and had to assume it was the same on both sides. Most, though, remained in darkness. Only those directly opposite afforded him a subdued view through the bars, and even then the occupants were mere smudges.

"Psst!"

He stiffened and slowly turned. Lightfoot the manticore seemed to be talking quietly to himself now, sitting by the front of his cage and staring out.

"Over here!"

That whispered voice again. Travis turned all the way around and squinted. The back of the cage stood close to the warehouse wall, but there was a three-foot gap. Enough for someone to hide back there. He shuffled deeper into the shadows, searching for whoever it was.

"Here," the voice whispered again, and this time he saw movement. A small figure crouched there, almost completely hidden in the darkness. If the lights came on, whoever it was would be clearly visible.

"Who's there?" Travis rumbled under his breath.

"It's *me*."

Though the voice was very low and hard to discern, Travis suddenly recognized it. "Nitwit? Is that you?"

The imp pressed her face between the bars. It looked like she might be able to squeeze all the way through if she tried. "Took me ages to find you. Are you all right?"

Travis nodded and went to lay down at the back of the cage where he could talk to his friend without alerting his fellow prisoners. "I'm fine. Can you understand me?"

"I'm an imp," she said as if that were all the answer he needed. When he looked at her blankly, she impatiently waved a hand. "Of *course* I understand you. You and I share a bond. I can hear you perfectly well."

"You can?"

She shrugged. "If I can track you over a distance, I'm sure I can figure out what you're saying."

Hope flared in Travis's heart. "So you brought help? You're here to rescue me?"

Now she frowned. "Rescue you? Um . . . well, no."

"What do you mean, no? My parents aren't outside? You didn't bring my dad?"

The manticore spoke then, his fluty voice sharp. "Hey, Tiny Dragon, what all this noise? Are you snoring?"

Travis made a few random noises that might sound a bit like a sleeping wyvern. After a while, Lightfoot turned away and continued mumbling to himself.

"We need a key," Travis urged the imp. "You need to go find a key. Can you do that? And—" He scowled. "I guess you'll have to unlock the door for me, because I can't do anything with these clumsy wings."

"Sorry, no can do," Nitwit said, chewing her lip.

"What?" Travis glanced around, then leaned closer to her, pressing his snout to the bars. "Find a key and get me out of here. You're small and fast. You can do it. You can probably vanish in a puff of smoke if you had to, right?"

In the darkness, her large eyes widened. "I wish I could help, but I really can't."

He blinked at her. "Why not? Why are you here if you can't help me?"

"I can't say," she said, looking miserable now. She shook her head. "And just so you know, I'm still mad at you for chasing me earlier."

Travis let out a sigh. "Yeah, I'm sorry about that. I kind of lost it, didn't I? I think the wyvern in my blood took over." He gritted his teeth. "But that's no excuse. I'm really sorry, Nitwit. I should respect your privacy. If you want to keep to yourself, then okay."

She reached through the bars and patted his wing. He barely felt a thing. "Just don't do it again. Look, I should go. Good luck, okay?"

"Wait. You're going to find a key for me, right? Look on the wall at the far end or something. Maybe there's a key rack."

She stared at him, then looked away. "You can't depend on me to help you."

He smiled, though he knew his snout probably twisted into a grimace. "Sure I can, Nitwit."

She shook her head and sank back into the darkness. He strained to spot her, puzzled. As dark as it was, he could quite plainly see the warehouse wall about three feet beyond the bars, and she definitely wasn't there anymore. Had she already slipped away? He hadn't heard the patter of tiny feet. She'd just *gone*.

It meant she'd go unnoticed, though, which was a good thing. He smiled to himself, hopeful that he'd be released from this place in the next few minutes.

And after that, he'd probably have to think about the manticore. Should he let Lightfoot out? He should, but manticores couldn't be trusted. When was the last time the ferocious beast ate? What about the minotaur? It seemed to be asleep right now, but if he opened its cage, would it charge out and stamp on him? Maybe his first port of call should be the cages opposite. Perhaps Tallock the centaur first. Tallock could then advise which others to let out.

No matter what, every living creature here would be released one way or another. Travis would see to it. He'd escape with a few cellmates, then fly home and fetch his dad. This warehouse would be shut down within hours.

Settling back, he waited by the front of the cage listening to the manticore's incessant droning.

* * *

Nitwit never returned.

It seemed like another hour passed. Travis couldn't understand what was taking her so long. It couldn't be *that* difficult to find a key!

In the meantime, several prisoners had woken from whatever deep slumber they'd been in and started making a lot of noise—grunts and roars and hisses, the clanging of bars, the stamping of hooves on concrete. The unicorn nickered over and over, turning in circles.

"What's going on?" Travis asked.

Lightfoot glanced toward him, his blue eyes standing out in the gloom. "You're hungry, too?"

"That's not what I said—but okay, I get it. Everybody's hungry. Is it feeding time?"

Now that he thought about it, Travis *was* hungry. Not that he'd be eating anything his captors gave him.

Excited hollers filled the warehouse, though it became apparent that the more intelligent prisoners such as Tallock and Varna refused to join in. Nor did Lightfoot, even though he licked his lips a few times. The rest hooted and yipped and rattled the bars, probably fifteen or so magical creatures that Travis hadn't fully identified, and a few that he had—including the minotaur to his left, which repeatedly rammed the cage door with its forehead while stomping and scraping with its hooves.

Just when Travis thought the noise couldn't get any louder, he heard the clang of a small door opening somewhere out of sight. Lights flickered on overhead, row upon row of long, bright-white fluorescents hanging between the round skylights in the vaulted ceiling. Just like that, all the darkness was gone, every shadow chased away, the cages opposite in full view.

Travis had time to run his gaze from one end of the warehouse to the other, seeing nearly a dozen prisoners either pressed to the bars or pacing about: a three-headed cerberus dog, a cloven-hoofed faun, a weird man-shaped creature with glowing red eyes and furry wings that had to be a mothman . . . and then the ones directly opposite, those he'd made out in the darkness earlier: the centaur known as Tallock, Varna the naga, a filthy harpy, the one-eyed cyclops, the catlike beast that he now recognized as a lamia, the frightened unicorn . . . and onward to the last three cages, one of which was empty, the next occupied by a very tall golem made of sticks and mud— and, in the final cell, one of those ugly, orange-skinned squonks.

Astounded, Travis turned his attention to the run of cages to his left and right. Beyond the minotaur, he saw a large winged creature with the head, shoulders, and front legs of a powerful bird and the body and hindquarters of a lion. A griffin! Its golden fur and feathers gleamed in the artificial light. To his right—

"Good afternoon, my friends!" a man's voice called.

Travis abruptly forgot about his fellow prisoners and shuffled to the front of the cage to peer out. An immaculately-dressed man came into view, his hair as black as his suit. Tall and gangly, he used a walking stick even though he couldn't be more than forty years old. He stood with his free hand behind his back, looking rather posh and aloof.

He was surrounded by a team of six men and women wearing dark-blue coveralls, one man pushing a cart loaded with slabs of meat and an array of covered dishes. The others began handing out the food, starting with huge raw steaks for the cerberus and a few others.

As Lightfoot eagerly reached through the bars to accept his steak, he grinned sideways at Travis. "I'm not too proud to accept sustenance when the alternative is to starve. You would be wise to do the same—but don't try to grab our host's arm, or it'll be the last meal you see in days. I learned that the hard way."

The man returned to his cart, grabbed another steak dripping with red juices, and approached Travis, who stared at it in disgust. He was supposed to eat *that*?

"Take it," the manticore urged, hunkering down so he could tear into his meal. "If not for yourself, then for me."

The man glanced at Lightfoot, clearly puzzled, no doubt wondering why a smart creature like a manticore would talk so openly to a dumb wyvern.

Travis tentatively pushed his snout through the bars until he could go no further. The man stepped forward and raised the meat, inching closer and closer until Travis was able to clamp his jaws on the prize. The man immediately stepped back, nodded, and moved on.

Repulsed, Travis pulled the steak in through the bars and threw it down behind him. It landed with a smack on the concrete, and watery blood seeped from it, soaking into the straw.

Raw meat wasn't for everyone, and the team knew it. They offered a variety of made-to-order plates to the centaur, naga, mothman, and faun; then a hefty leg of cooked meat to the cyclops; a cup of pure blood for the lamia, which she merely sniffed at; scraps of nasty leftovers thrown on the floor for the harpy; and a bowl of slop for the squonk, pushed carefully through the slot at the bottom of the cage door. The squonk ate for a while, then seemed to break down in tears as if struck by shame and guilt.

Nothing was passed to the golem. Travis understood that they had no appetites, being made of earthy materials such as rocks and sticks, all held together with mud.

It was a feeding frenzy in the warehouse, a terrible racket Travis wished he could shut out. He'd never heard so many smacking lips, noisy gulps, and crunching bones, mostly accompanied by hungry grunts and groans.

And all the while, the man in charge stood at the far end of the warehouse with his arms crossed and a smile on his face. "Eat up!" he shouted at last. "Eat—and then we shall take our afternoon stroll in the sunshine."

Lightfoot cleared his throat and looked meaningfully at Travis's discarded steak. "Forgive me, but if you're not going to eat that . . ."

Chapter 11
Mr. Braxton

Travis noticed that the catering team ignored the minotaur in the next cell, probably because it was a vegetarian and had plenty of fresh straw to chew on. Still, it remained at the front of the cage, gripping the bars and poking its horns out, excited by the mealtime ritual even if it didn't get anything special from it.

Feeling hungry but not *that* hungry, Travis flipped his raw steak over to the manticore's cage and concentrated on reverting to his human form. If he could only talk to this tall, skinny, suited man in charge, everything would be sorted out fairly quickly. These people wanted exotic, magical animals, not a human!

But no matter how hard he tried—or perhaps *because* he was trying so hard—he could not transform and become himself again. He was stuck in wyvern form.

"Wonderful, wonderful," the suited man said briskly from across the other side of the warehouse. Travis paused to watch him. "So we have a unicorn at last!"

"That's Mr. Braxton," Lightfoot murmured. "He's the leader of this rabble."

The tall man had stopped by the unicorn's cage. "A lovely specimen—but then, aren't they all? It's quite a bit larger than your average horse, too. I'll bet that horn could do some damage, eh?"

He laughed, tapping his cane on the floor. Then he grew serious, talking directly to the unicorn while all six of his team members continued handing out meals.

"I'll wager you're the most valuable specimen here, my beauty. I hear you have the power to heal. Is that true? I would very much like to see this happen. The question is, how do I convince you to show me? How do I even communicate with you?"

He stood there rubbing his chin for a while. The unicorn paced the cage, well back from the bars.

"How are your feet on this hard floor?" Mr. Braxton asked. "Don't worry, my darling, this cage is temporary. You'll be running around in your own paddock very soon. I intend to keep you no matter what you're worth. I have plans for you."

He turned away, his gaze flitting from cage to cage. Though forty feet away, he zeroed in on Travis and broke into a broad smile. He hobbled closer with his cane *click-clacking* on the floor.

"Wonderful, *wonderful*," he exclaimed. "Oh, what a glorious day! A unicorn *and* a small dragon. But wait—" He narrowed his eyes. "I do believe you're a wyvern, correct?"

Travis nodded vigorously, keen to show his understanding.

However, Mr. Braxton chose that moment to glance around at his team. "He's not eating his meal. Do we have any live chickens? A special treat for our newcomer? Perhaps a small goat?"

"I can get one, sir," one of the blue-coveralled women said.

"Do that, would you, my dear?" Mr. Braxton turned back to face Travis. "You're an unexpected treat. My men went looking for a unicorn and came back with a bonus. They said you attacked them out of the blue? Very unusual behavior, they said. Anyone would think that famous shapeshifter dragon had shown up again . . . but no, you're smaller and much more colorful. Yes, you're very pretty. Bright orange with blue markings and dark-red wings. How very *delightful*. What caused you to attack my men? What on earth got into you?"

Travis grunted and spread his wings, trying to think of a way to suggest that he wasn't exactly what he appeared to be, that he was just like his dad.

In the next cage, Lightfoot cleared his throat noisily. Mr. Braxton shot him a quick look before ignoring him and launching into a potted history about himself. But when Travis glanced over, the manticore quite firmly shook his head, obviously saying "No."

". . . decided to collect specimens of my own for the viewing pleasure of my very best friends and clients," Mr. Braxton said. "And, to my surprise, many offered to buy certain specimens for themselves. Well, how could I refuse? Of course, this practice is not entirely legal, so . . ."

Travis was distracted. Why would the manticore warn him not to reveal himself as a shapeshifter? Why would that be a bad thing?

Unless . . .

What if Mr. Braxton was the sort of person who would *do away* with loose ends? Was that it? If he discovered Travis was not, in fact, a valuable wyvern but instead a worthless human, would he *dispose* of him?

". . . fetch many thousands of dollars, so I'm happy to oblige. They could of course capture their own creatures, but the risk is tremendous—dangerous as well as highly illegal—and so I do the dirty work, so to speak, and reap the benefits . . ."

Logically, Mr. Braxton couldn't simply let Travis go. Not if he wanted to maintain his secrecy. These were hunters, used to brutal capture and murder. They wouldn't think twice about getting rid of Travis the moment they realized he had no value.

Heeding the manticore's warning, he slumped and kept very still, not wanting to give any sign that he understood everything the man was saying.

". . . but you, my wyvern friend, will be very well suited adorning the expansive grounds of a French chateau belonging to a dear colleague of mine. What a sight you would be! Visitors would roll up that long gravel driveway and through the archway to see you straddling the top, your wings spread wide and your tail hanging down!"

For a moment, Travis imagined himself doing just that and couldn't help feeling a swell of pride. But then he shook himself, dismissing the idea. Anger rose in him. How dare this man kidnap innocent creatures from their natural habitat and sell them off as pets, chained up and trapped forever?

Mr. Braxton chuckled and turned to the manticore. "I always hold out hope that there's some level of intelligence within every magical beast, even small dragons like this. What if we're wrong and they're every bit as smart as you and I? What if we just don't know it because they're unable to speak our language?" He sauntered closer to Lightfoot, his cane tapping. "As for you, my dear sir, I don't believe I can ever let you go. I enjoy our conversations too much."

Travis could well believe it. Both he and the manticore seemed to like the sound of their own voices. He imagined they could wile away the hours discussing everything under the sun, each with their own distinctive flair and posture.

Lightfoot stared back, his gaze unflinching. "I enjoy a good conversation too, Mr. Braxton. But make no mistake. If I ever get the chance, I will rip your throat out and devour every last morsel of you, leaving no trace that you ever existed."

Mr. Braxton's smile faded, and he visibly paled. His jaw tightened as he turned away. "Yes, well, that's why you're locked up. No afternoon stroll for you today." It looked like he was about to walk off then, but he paused and turned back to Travis. "I do wish you could talk, wyvern. I'd dearly love to know why you have silky strips of see-through material wrapped around your tail and midriff, and a curious waxy substance stuck to your feet. It's like you stood in a fire and things simply melted onto your skin."

Travis said nothing, though he was tempted to take a closer look. His smart clothes were still there? If so, they were well disguised.

Mr. Braxton nodded thoughtfully. "Yes, my people will need to take a closer look before we sell you. I do hope you weren't in a fire. Permanent burns and scarring will diminish your value."

The man headed off, and Travis breathed a sigh of relief.

He spent a moment quietly examining his smart clothes, which were indeed wrapped in thin, barely perceptible strips

71

around his midriff and the base of his tail, almost like a second skin. The silk had turned orange, blue, and red to match his vivid coloring. No wonder he hadn't noticed before! On the bottom of his feet, that strange waxy plastic clung on like he'd stepped in something sticky.

The team of men and women in blue coveralls spent the next five minutes finishing up with mealtime before making preparations for prisoners to step outside. Nobody had brought that live goat yet, and Travis was glad. Maybe they'd get to it after the afternoon stroll—but he wasn't planning to stick around for long.

With a noisy squeal, the giant roller door slid upward, letting in a flood of sunlight and revealing dry dirt and fields of green outside. Travis licked his lips as excitement welled.

The cerberus went first. Before they let it out of the cage, they reached through with a long pole ending in a loop of thick wire, and the cerberus sniffed at it suspiciously before allowing them to slide it over its middle head. It whined as if knowing what it was for. Once in place, they tightened the collar and then maneuvered the cerberus out of the cage. It struggled briefly but stopped when the wire crackled loudly. All three heads yelped.

After that, the cerberus—a huge canine by any standards— walked obediently alongside its master, the long pole acting like a leash. Travis watched with interest. What if the cerberus yanked free? With the pole dragging behind, could the three-headed dog run away without being zapped? Or was the collar operated remotely?

Some of the smarter prisoners understood the drill and complied with little fuss other than some sharp words. The centaur complained about the indignity of it all, and the naga hissed the whole time, but neither offered a physical challenge.

"Everyone values their outdoor time," Lightfoot said. "After several days and nights in your cage, you too will appreciate the need to comply. If you put aside the fact that you're a prisoner, the walk in the sunshine is actually rather pleasant."

One by one, the cages were emptied. Travis was surprised at how many Mr. Braxton let outside at once. More and more men arrived, all in blue coveralls. There had to be twenty or more, all working quietly and calmly, obviously practiced in dealing with potentially deadly monsters. Despite what Lightfoot had said, Travis could hardly believe none of them put up a fight.

The unicorn got its turn as well. "Make sure the collar is secure," Mr. Braxton warned.

Would an electrical charge really be enough to stop a frightened unicorn from galloping away? Travis began to think the collars gave out more than just an uncomfortable tingle. He suspected the charge could be ramped up high enough to incapacitate something as large as . . . well, an angry griffin or a crazed minotaur. High enough to be respected.

The harpy screeched and yelled obscenities, clearly enraged at having to wear the collar. She repeatedly knocked it away before they could get it over her head, so in the end Mr. Braxton calmly said, "Leave her. She can keep the manticore company this afternoon."

Cage after cage was emptied. Travis watched almost every prisoner on the opposite side of the warehouse head out through the roller door in no particular order—the weird mothman, the cyclops, the lamia, and the rest. Each wore the loop of wire on the end of a pole, led by a single handler. The harpy remained, sulking in a corner. The squonk seemed too upset to move, and it huddled in the straw, crying its eyes out. Mr. Braxton watched it for a while, then shrugged and moved on.

"Oh, for a chance to slip free of the dreadful shock-pole," Lightfoot said quietly. "It's humiliating, being controlled so easily by weak humans. And Mr. Braxton knows it." His voice took on a sarcastic tone. "He likes to spend some *quality time* with each and every one of his *delightful pets*, but he's a *very busy man* and can only spare a couple of hours in the late afternoon, hence we all go outside together." He sighed, his sarcasm evaporating. "I heard one of his handlers complain about this potentially dangerous routine a while back, and Mr. Braxton put him in a cage for a day and let him out for a walk on the end of the shock-pole. Now everybody just does as they're told. I ask you, who would work for a man like that out of choice? It seems a large paycheck wields considerable power in human culture."

Travis peered at the manticore with interest. It was said that these creatures ate their victims' brains and absorbed knowledge, and that was why they knew so much about human culture and thrived on meaningful conversation. It was easy to forget Lightfoot came from a forest.

It was time for the cages on Travis's side to be emptied one by one. He stared as something very quiet sidled by—a slender female figure covered in fine dark-brown bark with a head of hair that looked like jagged sticks. She fuzzed in and out, turning transparent, causing Travis to blink rapidly. Finally, he'd seen his first real, actual dryad up close.

A young ogre came next. It only stood ten feet tall, and its proportions were odd, its shaggy hair shorter than normal. It walked on unsteady feet, and Travis realized with horror that it couldn't be more than a young child. They grew to thirty feet tall, so anything much older than this probably wouldn't fit in the cage—and even if it did, it would break out very easily. Did Mr. Braxton *know* how young and innocent this ogre was? Did he care?

Travis felt his anger rising again.

A long-armed shaggy troll lumbered past. Ogres and trolls loved to scrap, but while ogres were dimwitted and good-natured, trolls tended to be conniving, greedy, and hostile. Still, this one shuffled obediently, the collar snug around its neck.

Apparently, some of the cages were empty, just a dryad, ogre, and troll before it was Lightfoot's turn. Except the men ignored the manticore and stepped up to Travis's cage instead. Mr. Braxton wandered over as they threaded the pole through the bars, the thick wire collar dangling like a noose. Both ends of the wire threaded into the pole so it could be tightened and loosened from the other end.

"Now, this is your first time, wyvern. Be good and stick your snout through, there's a good fellow. Then you'll get to enjoy a walk in the sunshine. I'll even give you a personal tour."

Travis was tempted to yank the pole out of their hands and break it into pieces. But what would that achieve? Besides, he had to see outside. Just to get out of the cage and into daylight—surely then he'd have a chance to escape, with or without an electrical charge thrumming through his body. Maybe he just needed to fly out of range.

He sniffed at the loop of wire. It hummed quietly.

"Do you have the dead man's switch on?" Mr. Braxton murmured.

The handler nodded. "And at full power."

The manticore called out from next door. "Wyvern, that means the gentleman has to keep the button pressed at all times to stop it from activating. It's a safety precaution. If he lets go—if you yank the pole from his hand and try to fly away—then the collar will shock you and *keep* shocking you until he gets hold of it again."

Both Mr. Braxton and the two handlers looked puzzled as they stared at the manticore for a long time. Lightfoot shrugged and yawned.

"That's a very accurate explanation," Mr. Braxton said at last. "I don't remember you advising the minotaur on his first day here, so why the wyvern?"

"I can be caring sometimes," Lightfoot said. "I felt it was my duty to help my neighbor understand."

"It'll understand quick enough if it tries to escape," one of the handlers muttered. With the pole still protruding through the bars, he eased the loop of wire over Travis's snout and head. Travis held still until he felt it tighten around his neck. Then he gently pulled at it, testing. It wasn't so tight it strangled him. The loop had locked in place with a few inches of breathing space—but not loose enough to slip his head out of.

75

Mr. Braxton opened the gate, and the second handler entered to take hold of the pole, careful to keep his hand over the dead man's switch the whole time. "This way," the man said.

Not now, Travis told himself. *Get outside before trying anything. Let them relax and think I'm being a good puppy. Then I'll act.*

And so he allowed himself to be led out of the cage. The manticore watched him go and quietly said, "When you get outside, just be yourself."

Though his words could be heard by Mr. Braxton and the handlers, they carried a double meaning for Travis.

He felt his heart pounding. *Be myself? He means be human. Easier said than done.*

But if he could do it, change back and be human just for a few seconds, maybe then he could escape this collar.

Chapter 12
Being Human

At the back of his mind, Travis remembered passing the minotaur and the griffin, then an empty cage, and then a small, blue-skinned elf on the far end . . . but he was too excited and nervous to give them much thought. Sunlight beckoned, and it felt warm on his reptilian skin as he stepped outside.

He obeyed the handler's gentle tugs, allowing himself to be led along a dry, well-worn surface of packed dirt that surrounded the warehouse. Just ahead, tall fences and hedges surrounded acres of grassy pasture. Like animals walking two by two onto Noah's ark, blue-coveralled handlers led their magical beasts through a twenty-foot-wide opening.

Travis began to imagine he was human again. *I have two feet*, he told himself, but frowned when he realized wyverns also had two feet. The reminder threw him off, and he started over. *I have two ordinary human legs, and I'm going for a walk wearing my smart clothes over my usual human body. No wings at all, no sirree! Just arms and legs like every other human . . .*

It wasn't working. His handler led him through the opening in the hedge, and suddenly there was long grass under his clawed, reptilian toes. He dragged his wings slightly, liking the feel of it. A breeze tugged at the webbing, and he wondered what would happen if he just took off, quickly and suddenly, and yanked the pole from the man's hands. The collar would activate, but how strong could the electrical charge really be?

He had no choice but to try.

With his heart thudding, he glanced around. Magical creatures were everywhere, spread out across the field, each with a handler whose blue clothing stood out clearly. A troll, small ogre, naga, centaur, cyclops, mothman, a bright-white unicorn, and more, all trotting calmly this way and that.

Behind him came the minotaur, huffing and snorting but obedient, and then the small, blue-skinned elf. The griffin emerged into the field at that moment, equally compliant. Another handler held his pole up with apparently nothing on the end—obviously the dryad had turned invisible.

Now or never, Travis thought.

He slowly lifted his wings . . . and beat them down *hard*, launching into the air and yanking the pole away—

—then crashed down in the worst all-over pain he'd ever felt, a violent crackling along every single nerve in his body, like he was on fire while a group of gremlins hammered nails into every square inch of his skin. "Argghh!!" he screeched, writhing on the ground and wishing he could claw his way out of his body and leave it behind—or better still, slip out of the collar and leave *it* behind! He was dimly aware of the handler rushing to grab the end of the pole . . .

The pain ended as quickly as it had begun, and he was left with a weird tingling sensation.

When his vision cleared, he glimpsed a number of his fellow prisoners staring at him from afar, and Travis swore they had sympathetic looks on their faces. *We've been there*, they seemed to say. *Hurts, doesn't it? Why do you think we're so obedient?*

But what really caught his eye was the expression on his handler's face. Rather than look annoyed or perhaps smug, he stood with his mouth open and his eyes wide. "Uh," he said after a while. He raised his voice. "Mr. Braxton? There's something you should see."

As Mr. Braxton came hobbling over, Travis finally realized what was going on. He glanced down and stared dumbly at his hands as he sat up. His *human* hands.

The handler held the end of his pole, but the wire loop had slipped off Travis's substantially slimmer human neck.

"Catch him, you idiot!" Mr. Braxton yelled, stumbling closer. "He's one of those shapeshifters! Get him!"

The handler broke out of his trance and gripped the pole with two hands, approaching Travis with a look of grim determination. But Travis had plans of his own. He jumped to his feet, noting his shimmering green smart clothes were neatly back in place around his body.

"Stay away from me!" he yelled, backing off.

Time to be a wyvern again.

"Now, sonny," Mr. Braxton shouted, still hobbling toward him. "Let's have a nice, friendly chat. Why didn't you tell us you were a shapeshifter? My heavens, I would have let you out of that cage in an instant!"

Travis dodged the wire loop as it was thrust at him. He glanced around, relieved that every other handler had their hands full. But five or six more were running in from the edge of the field where they'd apparently been on standby.

Rather than waste time talking, Travis frantically tried to shift again. He hadn't quite mastered that aspect yet. How had he done it before? He'd been chasing Nitwit through the trees, and it had just *happened*.

The wire loop came at him again, and Travis angrily snatched at it—then let go when he realized how stupid he was being. A split second after he let go, it crackled fiercely as the handler tried to zap him.

Travis turned and ran, heading for the biggest, most wide-open space he could find. He happened to race by the mothman, who stared impassively with weird red eyes. Though his furry insectoid face remained emotionless, his wings lifted, and it was clear he wanted to fly away with Travis. A word from his handler quickly changed his mind.

None of the handlers did a thing to grab him. They were probably trained to cling on to their prisoner to avoid panic and further escapees. Mr. Braxton, who had changed direction to limp after Travis, was hopelessly far behind. But other men sprinted after him, determined to catch him, and though they had no poles, they *did* have those stubby rifles loaded with darts . . .

"Come *on*," Travis muttered as he zigzagged between Varna the naga and Tallock the centaur. "Just *change!*"

The naga hissed, but Tallock said, "Go, boy! Get help—
arrghhh!"

His strangled cry almost caused Travis to stop. The
centaur's knees buckled as the loop of wire around his neck
crackled. The handler yanked on the pole, a scowl on his face as
he told the centaur to shut up.

Once past the cerberus, Travis found himself alone in a
huge expanse of grassy field. It sloped downhill, and in the
distance he saw a town scattered across the landscape. Behind
him stood the warehouse, its roof visible over the hedges, and
beyond that he spotted a gigantic mansion.

But he had no time to sightsee. The men sprinting after
him were *fast.*

Time to change.

He flapped his arms, hoping they'd turn into wings.

Nothing happened.

Come on, come on, I'm a wyvern!

He ran and ran, wishing the breeze would pick him up.

Far ahead, at the foot of the hill, he saw a fence and a
narrow lane. He wondered if a car would drive by, and if so,
maybe he could flag it down. But the lane was still an awful
long way off; the men would catch up to him first. He glanced
back, thinking they had to be close by now.

Then he gasped and stumbled to a halt, unable to
comprehend what he was seeing.

Or rather what he *wasn't* seeing.

The men were gone. Mr. Braxton and the twenty or so
handlers with their magical monsters were also gone. The
warehouse and the mansion—gone. Travis rubbed his eyes,
seeing nothing but an empty field.

He stood there awhile, confused. Listening hard, he
thought he heard shouts and the whinny of the unicorn, maybe
even the hiss of the naga. Yet he saw nothing.

The heavy panting of men rose in volume, and he rubbed
his eyes again, thinking he must be going blind. How could he
hear them but not *see* them?

And then they appeared. Five men exploded into being, one after the other in quick succession, running at full speed toward him and no more than thirty feet away.

Yelling with shock, Travis turned to run but knew it was already too late. Whatever spell of invisibility had made him pause with wonder, it had been all the delay the men needed. He tripped and stumbled, then fell on his hands and knees.

"Gotcha!" one of the men cried.

Travis spun around to see one of those dart guns pointing at him, and on impulse he lashed out—with a long, blood-red barbed tail. He'd transformed! It caught the man around the face, spinning him around and knocking him sideways. Whether the barb actually stuck into the man's skin or not was unclear, but the violent attack caused the other four men to skid to a stop and raise their own weapons.

Darts flew, and one hit Travis as he threw himself into the air. His wings instantly caught the wind, and he soared upward, glancing down to see if the men were firing again. But it seemed they each had to reload, and they didn't bother, probably realizing they'd lost their chance. They stood in a line, watching Travis in silence, diminishing in size as he rose higher and higher.

* * *

He felt woozy again. One dart had struck him in the belly, and he couldn't pluck the thing out while flying. It would be hard enough while on the ground, what with wings instead of hands; he'd have to use his mouth, or maybe reach up with a foot and scrape it loose. But right now he had to fly.

Fly where, though?

He tried to get his bearings. He had no idea where he was in the world, nor even where the mansion was. It had simply vanished. He spotted the five men, though, one still laid out on the grass and the others bending over him. He focused on them as he flew away.

Don't lose sight of this place, he thought over and over. *Gotta come back later with help.*

But he grew dizzier by the second and knew he wouldn't get too far. He flew as low as he dared and circled back. Maybe they would think he'd fled to safety, while in reality . . .

He came down hard and rolled, his wings flopping about as he tumbled to a stop. Lying on his back, he turned his head to see the fence and narrow lane he'd seen earlier, no more than twenty or thirty feet away. If the men assumed he'd gone for good, then he might be okay. But if they came looking, they'd easily spot him.

Trees lined the fence. Another stood nearby. It took all of his energy to drag himself over and slump down behind the thick trunk.

It wasn't a perfect hiding place by any means. His brightly colored reptilian skin probably stood out a mile against the green grass. But there was absolutely nothing he could do about it. Still, the overhanging branches might shield him if Mr. Braxton sent out a helicopter.

He fought the sleepiness, dipping in and out for a while. He became aware of a small figure leaning over him, and he squinted. "N-Nitwit?"

His imp friend smiled. "You did it. You escaped. I knew you would."

"No thanks to you," he grumbled. "Didn't you look for a key?"

"No," she said flatly. "Sorry. I would have, but . . ." She shook her head. "Anyway, that man in the suit showed up, so I had to leave. I had faith in you, though. I knew you'd escape somehow. And here you are."

"Thanks a bunch," he murmured, mystified by her refusal to help him. An idea popped into his head. "Do you even know where we are?" He struggled to wake properly, but the drug from the dart made his eyelids heavy. "You found me, so . . . so can you find your way home and get help? Can you . . . can . . ."

Nitwit drew back. "Just rest for now."

"You *have* to help me. I'm falling asleep, and . . . and I . . ."

Then everything fuzzed out.

* * *

When Travis woke, he stared up through overhanging branches at the half-moon wondering where on earth he was and why he was lying on cold grass.

Then it all came back.

He bolted upright, noting that he was in his natural human form. His silky smart clothes barely warmed him even though, being enchanted, they generated a little heat of their own.

He recalled snatches of what seemed like a dream: the rumble of a helicopter and distant voices, and thinking he'd be better off in human form if he wanted to avoid recapture. An orange-and-blue wyvern with vivid red wings would have stood out a mile. Perhaps being sleepy had helped him make the transformation. He hadn't thought too hard about it; it had just *happened.*

"That's the trick," he murmured. "Don't think about it. Just do it. Like riding a bicycle or swimming. Like *walking.* You don't think about it, you just *do* it."

Easier said than done, though.

He wondered what time it was. His stomach growled, and he realized he hadn't eaten anything since his early lunch in the lab. His parents would be worried about him—unless Nitwit had gone to find them. If she had, then they would be on their way by now. Or they'd be here already.

But what if the imp hadn't? What if she'd gotten lost on the way home? Or what if she just didn't care what happened to him? She'd proved completely unhelpful so far, and he had no idea why. He'd thought she was his friend.

"I'm on my own," he murmured. "It's up to me to break everyone out of those cages."

Chapter 13
Warehouse Break-In

The idea of such a risky mission filled Travis with dread. Not only would he have to avoid those blue-suited men with dart guns, he would have to be very careful letting the dangerous prisoners out. But he'd made up his mind.

He climbed to his feet and headed up the hill. He saw no sign of life in the darkness ahead, just empty fields. No tiny glowing windows, no street lamps, no flashlights, no cars, nothing. But he knew Mr. Braxton lived on top of the hill. He just had to get close enough to penetrate the wall of invisibility.

What a thing, he mused as he trudged up the slope. *An Old Earther using magic. I didn't even know magic worked in Old Earth.*

That wasn't strictly true, though. Magic worked fine in Old Earth; it just wasn't as plentiful. Invisibility spells and enchanted smart clothes needed very little to keep operating and were "self-charging" as his dad had put it; once kick-started, they just kept on going, even in Old Earth with only the faintest whiff of magic in the air. But it was different for living beings. He remembered his teacher saying once that so-called magical creatures—dragons, centaurs, naga, faeries, and the rest—were "unusual" to the natural evolution of the animal kingdom and required an abundance of magic to survive.

So Mr. Braxton's zoo was not only illegal but also a scam. He sold magical animals that, over time, would surely wither and die. How long would that take? Months? Years? Did the man even know? Had any of his customers complained? Maybe this was a relatively new venture for him.

Travis realized he'd been walking up the hill in plain sight of anyone on lookout. It was dark, yes, but Old Earthers had such things as night-vision binoculars. He darted to a stand of trees and waited there a while, looking for any sign of movement, perhaps a flashlight or two.

Yet all remained quiet. He saw nothing whatsoever.

Slapping his head, he groaned at his stupidity. The invisibility spell would mask everything, even beams of light. There could be a whole army waiting for him just inside its boundary, literally hundreds of searchlights pointing his way, and he wouldn't know it.

Or would he? If a beam of light pointed outside the spell, he would see that, right?

He shook his head. *Never mind. Just focus.*

If he wanted to get inside the grounds, he had no choice but to do it now under the cover of darkness in the middle of the night. If they were waiting for him . . . well, he'd just have to deal with it.

He continued walking, his heart thumping. What if he became a wyvern again? He could fly in, and then he'd be safe from the men with shock-poles. They could still shoot at him, but he'd be far safer high in the sky than walking across a field.

But that's only if I can transform, he thought glumly.

He tried as he plodded along, being casual about it, trying not to overthink the process. But even that was difficult. He became aware of trying hard not to think about it, which made him think about it all the more.

"Why is this so difficult?" he growled.

A light blinked on somewhere ahead. He stopped dead, looking around. He saw several lights, many of them coming from a square blackness standing on the the top of the hill. The mansion! Several windows were illuminated, along with a few external lights. Also, he saw a flashlight moving.

Not too far away stood another square building. The warehouse, shrouded in darkness except for another couple of flashlights bobbing about.

Travis backed up a few steps, and as he did so, all the lights vanished, along with the blackness of the silhouetted buildings. Moving forward again, everything reappeared.

85

So he stood just inside the perimeter of the invisibility spell. He assumed it was circular, probably cast from the mansion or the warehouse. It had to be dome-shaped, too, so that anyone flying overhead would see nothing but countryside. The whole place was a ghost.

And—he almost slapped his head at the realization—the truck that had brought him here must have had its own onboard spell! *That* was why his dad had been unable to locate the giant blue-colored trailer. From a distance, it was nothing but a phantom.

"Very clever," he muttered. "I'll bet you don't have many friends over for dinner, Mr. Braxton. They'd never find your house."

Feeling a little more confident, he hurried up the hill, using random bushes and trees for cover. The flashlights still bobbed about, but he could see them now, and he just had to keep to a safe distance while he . . .

While he what?

He hadn't quite figured this out yet. At the back of his mind, he knew he had to rescue the poor prisoners and shut this place down. It sounded like something his mom and dad would have done back when they were younger. Except of course they'd been part of a larger gang, nine shapeshifters in all.

Maybe I need a bunch of shapeshifter friends, he thought. But in fact, none of his friends wanted to be shapeshifters. His closest buddy Rezner, or Rez as he was commonly known, said shapeshifting was a dangerous game, and he didn't want magic altering his body and melting his brain. Travis smiled to himself. He was pretty sure his hotheaded friend would have failed the aptitude test anyway.

Maybe a visit to Uncle Robbie and Aunt Lauren was in order. He should hang out more with Mason and Melinda. Then again, Mason was only seven and couldn't be a shapeshifter for another five years. Melinda might be an option, though. At eleven, she was already prepping for approval. He kind of liked her, and it would be better to have a shapeshifter partner-in-crime rather than go it alone on dangerous missions.

But I'm on my own right now, so focus!

He found his way out of the field through the same opening in the hedge he'd passed through earlier that afternoon. Once on the dirt road, he slowed his pace and stuck close to the shadows, seeing the guards ahead. They were circling the warehouse in opposite directions, their flashlights jerking around. They happened to pass each other in front of the huge roller door, and as they vanished around the corners of the building, that door suddenly became unguarded. Travis figured he had a minute or two to find a way in before they reappeared.

He waited, though. The roller door had to be impenetrable, a steel wall that he had no hope of opening from the outside. He needed a smaller door. Better to go round back to where Mr. Braxton had entered.

So he ducked behind the hedges again and hurried around to the far side of the warehouse. There he squeezed through a gap and found what he needed—a human-sized door at the near corner.

The guards continued their marching. After they'd crossed paths at the back of the warehouse and moved on, Travis darted to the doorway and tried the handle, figuring he had time to hurry back to the shadows and rethink if it was locked. This was just a shot in the dark in case it happened to open.

It didn't.

The door was secured with an electronic keypad numbered zero to nine. The code could be anything! Dismayed, Travis skedaddled.

Hunkering in the bushes again, he watched and waited, knowing he would never force his way inside even in wyvern form. He just wasn't that strong.

But he *did* have wings. Maybe there was another way in. He vaguely remembered skylights from his afternoon in the cage. He chose his moment, then steeled himself and stood up. *Okay, time to change. No messing about this time. Just do it!*

He rushed out of the trees and into the open, expecting to see a guard at any second. He had to change right now or he'd be spotted. There was no question in his mind this time. He leapt into the air with his arms outspread . . .

And flew upward, his sleek wyvern wings catching the air and lifting him easily into the night sky.

Barely able to contain a whoop of delight, he soared upward as fast as he could. *Conviction,* he thought, remembering something his dad had said. *Telling yourself you can transform is not enough. You have to believe.*

It was true. Now that he'd done it several times, believing had been much easier.

He landed on the roof of the warehouse. Before he made too much noise with his scrabbling claws, he reverted to human form and windmilled his arms in an effort to stay balanced on the tin roof's gentle pitch. He moved to the apex and stood there looking triumphantly at one of seven evenly-spaced domed skylights, each about thirty inches in diameter.

He struggled with the one in the center, but it wouldn't budge. The next one was jammed shut as well, and the next. His hope had faded by the time he arrived at the end of the building, but to his delight—and maybe because he poured a little extra effort into it—the glass dome popped open at one side. He worked at it, yanking and fiddling, finding little catches inside to unclasp. The building wasn't designed to foil professional burglars, and now he proved that it couldn't even keep out a determined twelve-year-old kid with wings.

When he got it open, he looked down into darkness. After a while his eyes adjusted, and he realized he was right above some kind of shelving unit filled with boxes. He climbed inside the opening and eased himself down so he was hanging by his hands, then dropped.

He landed awkwardly, nearly rolling off a crumpled box. Climbing down the shelves, he arrived on a metal-floored platform, the upper level of a storage area. Steps led down to the concrete floor, and there he stood in front of the very door he'd been unable to enter earlier. He grinned at the thought of the guards passing by outside, unaware of his intrusion.

He wanted to switch the lights on, but that would probably create a sliver of light under the door. So he edged through the blackness, feeling his way, seeing soft light ahead. As he passed under the metal-floored gantry above and around more racks of shelving, he came to the main body of the warehouse, huge and open, where two dozen cages stood on opposite sides. The subdued lighting came from wall-mounted fixtures, just enough to see by, probably designed to emulate natural moonlight for the captives.

There were no keys on the key rack. It was a simple three-foot-square board with hooks, screwed to the wall and clearly labeled in cage order, twenty-four hooks in all. The keys *should* be there, but Mr. Braxton must have taken them away in case of intruders. Their absence would make it really difficult to get the cages open.

Travis walked between the barred cells, seeing shapes within. Some stirred as he approached, and finally a voice hissed from the right-hand side, "You're a fool for coming back."

Travis made a note to rescue Varna the naga last.

"Is that you, boy?" Tallock the centaur called loudly.

"Quiet, you blithering idiot!" the harpy snapped. "Are you trying to bring the guards running?" She stuck a scrawny arm through the bars, reaching for Travis. "Here, my handsome little friend, come and let me out first. Then I'll help you rescue everyone else."

"Don't listen to her," Varna whispered loudly. "She's a liar. If you let her out, she'll probably use you as a distraction to save her own sorry skin."

A few other noises rose in the gloom: grunts and moans and deep, rumbling growls. Also the sniffling of the squonk. Travis looked around. Now that his eyes had adjusted to the darkness, he saw that everyone was present as they had been before. Except for one.

"Where's the unicorn?" he asked.

A high, fluty voice came from the left-hand side. "Mr. Braxton took her away after your escape this afternoon. He was quite annoyed as he hobbled off the field."

Travis wandered toward the manticore. "Why just the unicorn?"

"She's his most treasured prize. He's been after one for some time, and now that he has one, he's not going to risk losing it just because of a young upstart like you."

The slur took Travis by surprise.

The manticore smiled. "His words, not mine. He's always boasted that nobody would ever find this secret hideaway, protected as it is behind an invisibility spell . . . but I saw anxiety in his face, a gnawing worry that an escapee, even a mere frightened boy such as yourself, might have the gumption to find his way back here if he made note of the surrounding area. And it turns out he was right. Here you are, and I assume your army of rescuers is waiting outside?"

Travis felt his stomach turn over. "Uh, well, not exactly. It's just me."

Lightfoot stared impassively at him through the bars, his blue eyes gleaming. "Just you?"

"I was shot!" he protested. "I spent the rest of the day asleep in a field and only woke up a while ago." He thought of Nitwit. "I sent a friend for help, though," he added, knowing that was probably unlikely.

"What friend?"

"An imp. She followed me here. She would have helped me escape, only she couldn't find a key."

Didn't even bother looking! Why am I lying for her?

Several prisoners murmured at this news. The minotaur next door made a questioning sound, suggesting it understood more than it appeared to.

The manticore looked puzzled. "I don't recall seeing an imp."

"She was quiet, and you were talking to yourself. Anyway, I escaped, and she went home to get help."

"And how long should we wait for this help?"

Travis shrugged.

Lightfoot pressed his face to the bars and lowered his voice. "What's your name, boy?"

"Travis."

"Well, Travis, I might suggest you let me out of here. We'll make our escape together. Tonight. This minute."

A silence fell across the warehouse. It seemed everyone and everything had heard the manticore's whispered words.

"I can't," Travis admitted. "There are no keys. Mr. Braxton must have taken them all."

After a pause, a very deep voice spoke from one of the cages on the other side. "He did. Or one of his men did, anyway."

The harpy let out a squawk. "Ooh, the creepy mothman speaks! First time for everything, I suppose."

Lightfoot sighed. "The mothman is right. I recall the sound of keys being dumped in a box sometime after my fellow prisoners were back in their cages this afternoon. I didn't sense much in the way of alarm; it was merely a precaution. These people rely heavily on their invisibility spell, and without keys, these cages are impregnable. And I doubt Mr. Braxton expects much trouble from a mere boy, even a shapeshifter." He winked at Travis. "You are, after all, a very *small* dragon."

Travis felt a sense of hopelessness settle in him. "So now what?"

"There's only one thing you can do, young Travis. You'll need to go find those keys."

"But where?"

The manticore shrugged. "Mr. Braxton has them somewhere. You'll have to investigate."

Full panic set in. "You want me to break into the *house?*"

Chapter 14
Home Invasion

The mission had gotten a whole lot more complicated. Travis peeked out the door and waited for the two pacing guards to vanish. He slipped outside and pulled the door shut. The keypad let out a tiny beep to indicate it was locked again. Travis sprinted for the hedges.

Since the cages simply could not be opened without explosives or perhaps a very clever lock-picking goblin, Travis hurried as quietly as he could along a dirt track, a full set of keys on his mind. He turned left onto a paved road. Not too far away, the house loomed in the night sky, easily the biggest home he'd ever laid eyes on. Why on earth would someone need so much space?

On his way up the hill earlier that night, he'd only seen one flashlight bobbing outside the house. In reality, there were a dozen or more. That made sense. Even Mr. Braxton wouldn't completely ignore the fact that a shapeshifter had escaped his cage.

He stuck to the shadows, wondering how to get past them all. It seemed impossible.

Why are they out in force like this when the warehouse is so poorly guarded?

Now that he thought about it, a man like Braxton would consider himself the primary target if an escapee happened to return with vengeful friends—especially a shapeshifter. Unicorns wouldn't be a threat; they'd simply gallop to safety. Manticores were smart enough to find their way back with others of their kind, but their quills and stingers were no match for men with guns. A shapeshifter, though—he would alert the authorities, perhaps bring a group of *other* shapeshifters ahead of the police and Portal Patrol. Right now, Mr. Braxton was more concerned with his personal safety than the prisoners being released.

Travis looked up. Could he fly to the roof as he'd done at the warehouse? Maybe climb in through a high window?

On impulse, he darted out into the open. He figured one guard or another would see him darting around and breaking in through a window, so being spotted now shouldn't make a difference. Sure enough, a shout went up as he ran, and flashlights trained on him.

He sprinted directly toward the nearest guard, seeing the man fumbling for a weapon at his side. Travis transformed and launched as a dart or bullet whizzed by.

Ignoring the shouts from below, he whipped around the mansion, counting at least ten windows on the third floor at the front of the house, then more around the side and back. He flew in close and reached for one, grappling with his claws on the frame, then slipping down to the windowsill, his wings bumping against the wall. He lost his balance and tumbled backward but quickly regained control and tried the next window along.

At the back of his mind, he couldn't help thinking this was futile. Even if he got inside, where would he go? He'd have to be human again, dashing from one room to another in the vain hope of chancing across a set of keys for the warehouse! It was a terrible plan. But what else could he do?

None of the windows he tried were open, and if they were unlatched, there was no way to slide them up with his clumsy wings. So he launched himself at the glass and crashed through with his claws. A shard cut into his leg, but he had no time to think about it; he tumbled inside, awkwardly twisting his wings against the frame, wrenching one backward and causing him to cry out.

When he hit the carpeted floor, he rolled and immediately climbed to his feet, thinking he needed to be human again in order to—

He blinked, staring at his hands. He *was* human.

"This is getting easier by the minute," he murmured.

Feeling pain in his leg, he glanced down and was horrified to see a gash on his right shin leaking blood into his pants. The material had actually cut open, which was unusual for smart clothes. But even as he watched, the silky fabric knitted together in one fluid moment and covered the gash. The bloodstain remained, but it faded slightly.

"Ow," he said, wincing as he hobbled around the room.

It was an empty bedroom with a four-poster bed, a chest of drawers, and other ornate furnishings. Maybe a guest room. It didn't matter. Travis knew the keys wouldn't be here.

He hurried into the hallway, amazed at the size of the house. The wide hall stretched sixty feet or more, solid hardwood floors underfoot, the walls adorned with heavily framed paintings, a few busts atop pedestals. Travis hurried along, pushing at doors as he went, ignoring any that seemed like bedrooms. Maybe an office would be best? But that would surely be on the lowest floor, so he headed for the stairs at the end of the hall.

The center of the house was breathtaking. He arrived at a balcony overlooking a gigantic foyer three floors high with a grand staircase circling down to the lobby. He paused as men poured in through the main entrance door and spilled out of side corridors, a few speaking urgently into walkie-talkies. Some wore the familiar blue coveralls, and others wore black suits, but all were intent on coming up the stairs after Travis.

This is hopeless! he thought in despair.

Abandoning his key-finding mission, he dashed back along the hallway only to find another suited man emerging from a door on the left. When the young, thin-faced guard spotted Travis, he stopped dead, his eyes widening.

As the sound of stampeding feet came up the spiral staircase, Travis fought a surge of adrenaline and tried to appear calm as he faced him. "I need the keys for the cages, and you're going to get them for me."

The man, who had to be in his early twenties, smiled. "Sure about that?" he said as he slowly reached inside his jacket. Travis glimpsed the butt of a handgun.

"The keys!" he snapped, and transformed.

It was getting easier each time. Once more a wyvern, he leapt on the young guard, knocked him to the floor, and pinned him down. He whipped his tail around and placed the barb against the man's cheek, digging in but not puncturing the skin. Behind him, the mob was just now arriving at the top of the stairs.

His prisoner gasped for breath. Travis had run out of time, but rather than let him go, he gripped the man's fine suit in his jaws and dragged him along the hall. The helpless man slid easily along the hardwood floor, yelling all the way.

Without letting go of his prey, he twisted his head just enough to glance backward. Guards crammed the top of the stairs. Weapons came up, but none fired—yet. One man shouted instructions, and the small army charged along the hall, their shoulders bumping against framed paintings.

Travis found the room he'd first arrived in and yanked his hostage inside. Since he couldn't lock the door, he put all his wyvern strength into shoving the heavy chest of drawers sideways until it blocked the doorway. Though not as powerful as an actual dragon, he judged he was at least as tough as two men. The chest would delay his pursuers a few seconds more.

"L-let me go!" the man on the floor cried, struggling to stand while absently smoothing down his suit. "Just get out of here while you can!"

He suddenly reached into a pocket, but Travis had been watching for this move. As a small handgun emerged, he spun and whacked at it with his tail-end. The gun flew across the room and hit the wall. The man yelled in pain, holding his hand as he doubled over.

Pounding on the door meant time was again running short. The handle jiggled, the door opened an inch or two, and then the heavy chest began sliding bit by bit as arms and faces pressed through the gap.

Travis snapped his head forward and grabbed his hostage's suit again, pinching it between his jaws in a vicelike grip. He yanked the man toward the window.

"Wait, what are you—LET ME GO!"

But Travis didn't let go. He tucked his wings in tight and hopped out backwards, pulling the man with him.

Despite the added weight, he beat his wings hard and flapped straight upward with ease. Hardly able to contain his excitement, he took off with his prisoner into the night, leaving the house behind. Shots fired, people shouted, and he heard engines revving up.

But when he next looked down, with his terrified prisoner still dangling from his jaws, the mansion had vanished. Despite the continuing noise below, now there was nothing but an empty field with trees and hedges. The long driveway leading up to the house had vanished as well, cut off about three hundred feet away. It just ended. Anyone searching for the house from above would certainly want to investigate, but casual pilots wouldn't notice.

My dad would never find this place, Travis thought as he circled around the nonexistent property. *I've almost lost track of it myself.*

He descended, angling toward the dark hills, listening for revving engines. After a few seconds, the house and warehouse came into view once more, along with a few other small buildings he hadn't paid much attention to earlier. The driveway was once more complete, and lights shone all over as men scrambled this way and that.

Travis flew as far away as he could without losing sight of the warehouse. He landed among some trees on the far side of the hill, well off the beaten track and safe for the moment.

Releasing his prisoner, he shifted to human form and began speaking even before his smart clothes had finished arranging themselves. "I need keys for the cages. Where are they?"

The man, who had stumbled and fallen to his knees in the grass, shook his head in obvious disgust. "Do you seriously think I'd tell you? If you get the keys, then you'll let the animals escape, and they'll overrun the place and kill everyone, and we'll all be out of jobs, and . . ."

He rambled on while anger rose in Travis's chest. His arms grew longer and developed blood-red webbing before he even realized what was happening, and his face lengthened into a reptilian snout. As he tried to yell at the man again, a screech erupted from his throat instead. Adrenaline surged, and he snapped his jaws a few times, knowing he could sink his teeth into this man and rip a limb off. Trembling with a frightening urgency, he stalked forward, ready to pounce.

"Whoa!" the suited guard shouted, putting up his hands in a placating gesture. "Don't hurt me! Look, I just do as I'm told. I'll tell you anything if you leave me alone and promise to let me go. I don't get paid enough for this! I'm just a house guard, not an animal handler."

Travis screeched again, then fought to reverse his slow transformation. When his snout flattened and something in his throat loosened up, he yelled "Keys!" in an oddly inhuman voice.

"Th-they're right there in the warehouse," the man said, his eyes wide.

"Not any more," Travis growled as his wings shrank with a creaking, leathery sound. "Your boss took them."

This gave the guard pause. "Well . . . they could be anywhere, then. Ask one of the guys in blue."

Travis tried to control his thumping heart beat. "There have to be some spares."

"Maybe." He eyed Travis for a moment, then sighed. "The boss has a master key. He carries it everywhere."

This puzzled Travis. "Why?"

"Why not? He owns everything—the house, the warehouse, the staff, the trucks. Why wouldn't he have a master key?"

"Then why have a rack full of keys in the warehouse?"

The guard shrugged and looked for a moment like he was done talking. But after a moment, he said, "It's easier for the handlers to have individual keys when they're letting animals out for a run. Does it matter? Electronic locks would be best, like on the warehouse doors, but Braxton doesn't trust them. He likes old-fashioned keys with *weight* and *substance*—like the cages, which are bolted through the concrete and impossible to break open without a truck or a bomb. And if you went that route, you'd kill the occupants. So yeah, he has a master key. Gives him a sense of power."

Exhausted, he hung his head and lapsed into silence.

"There must be another way to get the cages open," Travis insisted.

The man shrugged and murmured, "Wait until that ogre grows to full size? Then it *might* be strong enough to bend the bars."

Travis sighed. So he could either dig around in the house again for the complete set of individual cage keys, or . . .

Or he could go find Mr. Braxton.

Chapter 15
Cabin on the Lake

"Where's Mr. Braxton?" Travis asked the fresh-faced, black-suited guard. "Where's the unicorn?"

The man sighed. "Kid, I'm just a low-paid grunt. He took off in his limo right after all the animals were locked up. He had a convoy—his limo, a couple of Jeeps, and the semi-truck with the unicorn. They went west."

"Where?"

"I don't know."

"Then I'll have to transform and sting you with my poisonous tail."

The man screwed up his face. "To his cabin, I think. I heard someone mention it."

"Where's his cabin?"

"I don't know. Ask someone else."

Travis placed his hands on his hips. "I'm warning you. I can easily be a wyvern again and tear you to pieces."

"Be *what* again?"

"A wyvern." Seeing the man's blank expression, he rolled his eyes and added, "A *dragon*."

"Oh. Look, buddy, all I know is that the cabin is west of here, maybe an hour's drive. On a lake. Just follow the main road to Pullman's Lake. It's a straight shot. There's a bunch of cabins out there, but he owns the biggest plot of land."

Wow. This guy knows quite a lot when he puts his mind to it.

"Just let me go, okay? I'll take the night off. You busted my hand, so I'm not much use anyway." He held up his hand as if to prove his point, though nothing seemed out of place. He had a bruise developing, but that was all. Maybe it was broken, maybe it wasn't.

"I'm going now," Travis said, stepping back. "You're staying right here."

The man frowned. "Well, I figured I'd walk down the hill and call a cab to pick me up on the road. I'm done for the night. I'll just head home and—"

Travis transformed and swung his tail around before he could talk himself out of it. He winced as the side of his barb clobbered the man around the side of the head, and he took a moment to check on him afterward. The guard lay there holding his head for a moment, then let his hand flop to the ground. He was out of it, hopefully without a concussion or anything.

As Travis flew back to the warehouse, staying low, he couldn't help feeling bad about the man he'd terrified then knocked senseless. Truthfully, scaring him was fine. But the physical harm part? Not so much. What if the man had brain damage?

No more bashing people around the head, he told himself. *I'm supposed to be a responsible shapeshifter, and that means staying in control.*

His dad had mentioned this aspect of being a dragon, how animal rage often built up inside and needed suppressing. Or if not rage, then a simple callousness toward enemies. Travis vowed to watch for that.

He spotted a lot of men as he flew over the warehouse. They'd spilled out of the mansion and down the lane, and they seemed to have the whole place covered. Not just the warehouse, either. At least six of them had spread out around a smaller building not so far away. Travis eyed it curiously, wondering what was inside. On high alert like this, the guards had inadvertently drawn attention to what seemed to be a very special place worth guarding.

Clearly a rescue was out of the question now.

Travis sighed, knowing he'd screwed up by entering the house so brazenly. He had to let things cool off here. Besides, as long as he stayed away, no harm would come to the prisoners.

Mr. Braxton wanted them protected at all costs. It would be okay to leave them a while longer and come back when things were a little quieter.

The kidnapped unicorn was more important right now. Travis circled and tried to get a sense of direction. He remembered where the sun had been that afternoon, which would have been to the south, which meant west was *that* way. Or thereabouts.

He flew low, looking for the main road. Behind him, the pinpricks of light suddenly cut off as the invisibility spell kicked in, though the buzz of noise continued for a while before fading. Ahead, he found the road in the darkness and stuck to it, gliding easily just above the treetops. Yes, it headed roughly west. It had to be the road his hostage had mentioned earlier.

Traveling at a fast clip, he swooped out of sight every time he spotted a car coming toward him with headlights glaring. Who would be driving at this time of night? It had to be well past midnight by now. Old Earthers were a funny bunch.

He figured he would be at his destination in about half the time it would have taken the convoy—so about thirty minutes. As he flew, he wondered what his parents would do in this situation. Go fetch help? Yes, but what if Mr. Braxton was torturing that poor unicorn, trying to get at its magical powers? What exactly was he hoping to find, anyway?

It's my fault, he thought with dismay. Back when he'd first run into a group of hunters near the portal, Travis distinctly remembered telling them unicorns had the power to purify pond water and heal wounds. That was some pretty awesome power, and if anyone could harness it somehow, it was Mr. Braxton. Travis imagined the man at some factory or other, overseeing the production of tiny vials of healing potion with hefty price tags.

But what would he do to the unicorn to get at this magical power?

Travis watched the road carefully, wishing it were daytime so he could see better. Still, signs were illuminated, and he picked out the lettering on each as he flew by. He felt a jolt of surprise when he came across one that read PULLMAN'S LAKE. The sign indicated the entrance was next left.

He slowed when he came to that entrance, a narrow lane with a huge brown sign to one side. He'd arrived! But now he had to find Mr. Braxton's cabin. That might prove more difficult.

Rising into the air, he looked down on the trees and buzzed around until he came to the lake itself, a massive mirrorlike surface that perfectly reflected the half-moon. Mr. Braxton would almost certainly have a cabin on the shore, but it was a big lake with plenty of lakeside properties. Travis circled around, looking for a huge truck, two Jeeps, and a limousine. Surely they wouldn't be too hard to spot!

There was no sign of the convoy. Travis kicked himself and muttered, "Because it's invisible, doofus."

He flew around the lake again. If the truck had an onboard invisibility spell, then he wouldn't see the convoy or the cabin. The spell would surround the whole property. Which meant . . .

He searched again, this time looking for precisely *nothing*, the suspicious absence of a cabin where there should be one. They were fairly evenly spaced around the lake, about thirty of them in all, but there were a few gaps along the shoreline. Mr. Braxton might be located in one of those odd spaces.

Daring to fly lower over the trees, he made sure to pass over each of the empty spaces. The first was fairly small, the second about the same, but the third was huge—and suddenly he found exactly what he was looking for: a dark-blue truck and trailer, a black limousine, and two dark-green Jeeps, all parked outside a fair-sized log cabin a hundred feet from the water's edge.

And there was the unicorn! It was tied to a tree to one side of the cabin.

She, he corrected himself. *The poor girl.*

Even in the darkness, he could tell the nearby trickling stream offered lush grass along its banks. The animal stood absolutely still, one rear hoof lifted slightly. Travis guessed the unicorn was asleep. He knew equines could sleep standing as well as lying down, though they never laid down unless they felt safe—which she most likely didn't right now.

Fighting a surge of excitement, Travis found a safe place to land without getting snagged on any trees. This particular mission could end up being a little easier than he'd expected. All he had to do was untie the unicorn and make it run off. It didn't belong in Old Earth, but that problem could be dealt with another time, perhaps another job for Ellie the shapeshifter.

Travis reverted to his human form and took a moment to check his injured leg, having to squint in the darkness and twist around to find the faint moonlight. Though he'd caught himself on glass when he'd broken into the mansion, the wound seemed fine now. The silk material had repaired itself fully, the bloodstain had mostly faded, and the gash on his shin was but a faint mark. He suspected it would be gone after he'd transformed a couple more times. His shapeshifter healing power worked perfectly!

Feeling emboldened, he crept through the trees toward the cabin, guided by the soft white glow of the unicorn. The closer he got, the more awed he became. The animal was tied to a sturdy railing surrounding the porch. Unicorns stood quite a bit taller than horses, very powerful if attacked but mostly timid, easy to scare. Rescuing this one would mean getting close, and Travis knew he was in danger of getting stabbed by that long horn, especially if she woke suddenly and acted without thinking.

He paused. Lights shone from inside the cabin. A figure moved past the window, but otherwise all seemed quiet. The vehicles stood silent and dark in the driveway, the truck and trailer taking up way too much space.

Travis considered the possibility of loading the unicorn into the trailer and driving away. But wistful thinking wouldn't get him anywhere. He doubted he could lead the flighty animal onto that truck again, and he certainly couldn't drive something this size. *Just untie the rope and let the unicorn run away*, he told himself.

His mind made up, he crept forward again, stepping out of the trees and inching toward the unicorn. Her eyelids fluttered and snapped open.

"Shh," Travis whispered, holding up his hands. "I'm here to help."

The unicorn whinnied loudly and danced about, straining at the rope.

Stopping, Travis was uncertain how to proceed. With all this noise, the men would be out here any second, but he needed a bit of time to calm the unicorn before approaching.

"Shh," he said again.

And then he heard the scuffle of leaves and twigs behind him.

He swung around, realizing too late what the unicorn had gotten so upset about: not so much *his* presence as the two men sneaking up from behind with their dart guns raised.

"Don't move or we'll shoot," one man said.

Chapter 16
The Potion

Instead of transforming, Travis stood there and dithered. He could quickly shift and fly away, but he guessed the men would get a couple of darts in him first. Then they'd find his unconscious body not far away and lock him up.

Or he could do as they said and remain still. For now.

A door opened, and footfalls sounded on the cabin's wooden deck. Mr. Braxton emerged with three men behind him. But there was a woman, too, and she didn't fit in with this gang at all. She had a New Earth look about her, with somewhat straggly grey hair and a long moth-eaten robe. She looked as old as the hills but moved like someone in her twenties, which Travis found a little creepy.

"Good evening, shapeshifter," Mr. Braxton said cheerily. "I was wondering when you'd show up. Now we can secure you and get some rest at last. Madame?"

He hobbled aside and allowed the old woman to come down off the porch and approach. She grinned, showing blackened teeth. She was surprisingly tall, towering over Travis as she reached into her robe and pulled out a tiny bottle. Uncorking it, she held it out and said, "Drink this."

"Huh?" he said, backing up. "No way!"

"It's either drink this or be shot." The woman's voice was scratchy and coarse. "Which do you prefer, shapeshifter?"

Travis eyed the bottle. "What is it?"

"Something to soften your mood. I put drops in the water to calm some of the animals in the warehouse. The minotaur, for example. Makes it a little less angry. Take it."

Travis thought about the way the minotaur had constantly butted its head against the bars and stamped its hooves. *That was calm? A little less angry?*

She thrust it forward, and Travis caught a whiff of something repugnant.

"Do as she says," Mr. Braxton warned. "Come on, boy, drink—and then you can come in and have a bite to eat while the rest of us get some sleep."

The moment food was mentioned, Travis's stomach rumbled. He scowled, angry at himself for even thinking about accepting a meal from these monsters.

Still, he *was* hungry. And the alternative—getting shot with darts—was not so pleasant. Besides, maybe he'd have a better chance of escaping later when their guard was down.

Saying nothing, he took the bottle from the woman's outstretched hand and swallowed the contents. It tasted like something rotten, and he almost gagged. Throwing the bottle back to her, he faced Mr. Braxton and said, "There. Happy?"

"I will be in a moment or two," Mr. Braxton said. He turned and hobbled back inside the cabin, his cane banging on the deck. "Bring him in. Make him a sandwich."

Travis allowed himself to be pushed and shoved into the cabin, fighting the anger that rose in him. If he could only breathe fire like his dad, he'd roast the lot of them and burn the place down! Well, maybe not roast them, but he'd certainly give them something to remember him by. *Nobody messes with the Franklins*, he growled to himself.

As he was passing through the doorway, he suddenly felt strange. His anger evaporated, and a pleasant sense of calm descended on him. He knew in the back of his mind that this was the potion he'd drunk, but still, he felt pretty good about it now. Maybe these people weren't so bad. They could have killed him, and instead they were inviting him in and offering him a sandwich.

Before he knew it, he found himself seated on the sofa with a plate on his lap. He stared at it, wondering how it had gotten there. He didn't remember that part.

"Milk?" Mr. Braxton asked.

One of his men offered a full glass, and Travis took it.

Sipping the milk, he tried to focus on the details of the cabin. He got as far as three sofas, a rug, and a huge fireplace, but he kept getting distracted. He opened his mouth to say something to Mr. Braxton but found the man wasn't there anymore. Nor was the old witch. Only two men remained, and it seemed they kept moving around . . . only they never seemed to actually *walk* anywhere.

He went to take a bite of his sandwich, but to his surprise he found his empty plate on the coffee table before him and an equally empty glass by its side. Had he eaten already? He didn't remember.

He glanced toward the windows. It was totally black outside, only the sky was lightening before his very eyes, from purple to red, then streaks of blue. And as the sun peeked over the trees, he became aware of activity in the cabin, men emerging from rooms and Mr. Braxton hobbling into view.

"Good morning, shapeshifter," he said with a smile. "I trust you had a pleasant few hours? Now, wasn't that preferable to dart guns? At least now you've eaten, and all of us have gotten some rest. Perhaps staring into space all night isn't quite the same as sleep, but Madame Frost enjoyed questioning you."

Travis stared blankly at him. "Huh?"

The grey-haired woman appeared just then, her arms folded and a disgruntled look on her face.

Mr. Braxton laughed. "Well, 'questioning' is stretching it, but she did get a few responses from you after all her yelling."

Yelling? What yelling? Travis blinked, recalling vague snippets of a dream involving a woman screaming at the top of her lungs inches from his face . . .

"She asked you about your shapeshifting abilities," Mr. Braxton said, seating himself on the sofa opposite. He winced as he lowered himself down and stretched out his left leg. "You eventually said 'new.' How new?"

Anger rising again, Travis clamped his mouth shut.

"You gave your name as Travis. Is that correct? And we were able to glean that your father is the infamous Hal

Franklin, the man who unified the worlds two decades ago. The dragon shapeshifter who created portals all over the land, connecting Old Earth to New Earth and allowing everyone to roam freely between the two dimensions. The very same man who, today, wishes to close the portals down and separate the worlds again."

"He just wants to keep people like you out!" Travis snapped.

"Indeed. But people like me exist *because* of people like him. He unified our worlds twenty years ago, and in the last ten years has actively sought to restrict entry."

"Yes, because Old Earthers are ungrateful."

Mr. Braxton raised an eyebrow, looking amused. "I've heard this argument many times. Old Earthers spilled into your magical world to escape this virus-stricken planet all those years ago, and we were so grateful to be out of our bunkers and biosuits that we were more than willing to accept what we were given. I was just eleven years old when the virus hit. My family was wealthy enough to secure a place in a bunker, and there we stayed for thirteen years. Can you imagine that, young man? I was in my mid-twenties by the time your father unified the worlds, and I can't tell you how wonderful it was to leave that bunker behind. Just to breathe fresh air was enough. Trust me, your people had our endless gratitude."

"And then you turned bad," Travis said.

Mr. Braxton laughed. "Not exactly. We simply wanted more. Your people imposed so many rules on us: Don't enter this forest because of the manticores and naga, don't go near the ogres in the south, leave that lake alone because of the miengu, and so on. We listened at first, but after a few years we began to question your wisdom. Why shouldn't we just take the forest if we want to? Why not set up homes on the lake with the miengu? And those ogres could be put to great use! They love working and don't need a paycheck. Frankly, your people don't know how good you have it."

"But we *do*," Travis insisted. "That's why my mom and dad and Lady Simone and everyone else have closed so many portals. To keep greedy people out."

Mr. Braxton nodded. "Yes, it appears the honeymoon period is over. Your father did a great thing in unifying our worlds, but now that our world is virus-free, we should all go home and leave you alone. Is that it?"

"Pretty much," Travis muttered.

"Never mind that we've introduced so much of our technology into New Earth—"

"Nobody wants your technology!"

"Well, now, that's not quite true, is it? You can't deny that certain—"

Travis stood up suddenly, and three men immediately went for their weapons. He remained there, wanting to transform and smash his way out of the cabin but knowing he wouldn't get far.

Mr. Braxton remained seated, looking up at Travis. "Regardless of all that, the people of Old Earth—which by the way I consider the *truth* Earth—now find themselves ostracized. We're closely monitored, and just getting *into* New Earth these days is a chore. Portals are few and far between, usually too far away to bother with: all those checkpoints and questions, the feeling we're being spied on the whole time. Meanwhile, your people just wander back and forth between worlds without a care. It's like you own an enchanted nature reserve and have the right to impose rules on outsiders, while your people are free to come and go as you please."

"Sounds about right," Travis muttered, still standing there with his fists clenched.

Mr. Braxton climbed to his feet, wincing again and leaning heavily on his cane. "Well, forgive me for claiming a slice of your world and creating a nature reserve of my own. Come outside, young man."

He hobbled away, and a couple of armed men closed around Travis.

"Where are we going?" he asked loudly.

It was the grey-haired woman who answered. "To see the unicorn. Relax, boy. Nobody's getting hurt today. Quite the opposite, with any luck."

The morning sun felt good, but the air was chilly. Steam rose off the calm lake, and patches of mist drifted through the trees. The unicorn was no longer tied to the porch railing.

The group—Mr. Braxton shuffling along in front, followed by Madame Frost and Travis, then the two armed men behind—moved through the woods not far from the shore. Nobody said a word, and Travis sensed a need to keep quiet to avoid startling the unicorn.

This made him wonder. What if he made a lot of noise as they got close? Would that cause her to gallop off? It wouldn't help if she was tethered, though, and he'd probably end up with a few bruises after the men pounded him into the ground.

The group stopped. Madame Frost pushed Travis forward to where Mr. Braxton stood. There, the three had a good view of the unicorn.

She lay in the grass among the trees, looking quite content even though three more armed men stood just beyond, looming in the mist. "Is she hurt?" Travis whispered.

"She's fine," Madame Frost murmured. "Just enjoying the moment the same way you enjoyed sitting on the sofa for four hours straight."

Travis groaned. The unicorn had tasted that awful potion?

"We're studying her," Mr. Braxton said, turning to Travis. "She's much better off calm and relaxed, don't you think? This is the best we can do to emulate her natural state in the wild. We're hoping she'll show us something."

"Show you what?"

"Something. Her magic. Her healing power." Mr. Braxton tapped his left thigh. "Car crash injury. It hurts to this day. Muscles and ligaments all torn up, never healed correctly, just a big old mess that makes me limp and causes me grief. But your world has such marvels, Travis. Dryads that work wonders with medicine, magical beasts than can heal . . . Am I wrong to want some of this magic for myself?"

"By stealing a unicorn?" Travis said.

"It was either that or doing a deal with one of the miengu. I hear they can heal sickness?"

"Yes, but just sickness, not injuries." Travis caught himself and ground his teeth together.

"Ah. So a unicorn is my best bet, just as I thought. Easier to catch, believe it or not. We tried to fetch one of those slippery miengu creatures, but they're far more agile underwater than we humans will ever be."

Travis thought about mentioning Jolie, a shapeshifter who lived on the banks of the very lake Mr. Braxton was talking about. She spent her days in a wheelchair, her entire lower half missing thanks to an accident with a portal; its magic had shut off when she was partway through, and her severed fishtail had stayed behind. But unlike being cut in two by a sharp blade, this was a *magical* dissection, and her life-threatening injury had been remedied so it seemed she'd been born that way, like it was a product of nature gone awry.

He bit his lip. The less he said the better.

"Perhaps *you* know something of these wondrous animals, young Travis?" Mr. Braxton purred. "How does one become *healed* by a unicorn?"

Travis crossed his arms. "I have no idea."

The man sighed. "Then I have no use for you or the unicorn, in which case . . . " He snapped his fingers. "Let's wrap this up. Kill them both."

Chapter 17
String of Lies

Travis felt a surge of panic. Would Mr. Braxton really murder him and a unicorn? It had to be a bluff. Yet . . .

As Mr. Braxton turned and started hobbling away, the two armed men drew their weapons. They had bullets that could kill. Travis swallowed and held up his hands. "Seriously? You wouldn't. You *can't.*"

One of the three hunters on the far side of the unicorn emerged from the mist and picked his way through the long grass. He drew a knife, ready to do something horrible to the hapless equine. Travis was on the cusp of transforming and taking his chances, zipping straight upward and hoping none of those bullets found him. But the unicorn would have no chance. Even if she were fully alert, she would never get away from these people alive.

Travis was certain Mr. Braxton was bluffing. But he wasn't *absolutely positive.*

"All right," he said loudly. "Fine. I'll help you."

All eyes darted to Mr. Braxton, who paused and stood very still, facing away. The witch stood by his side, looking at Travis with a look of amusement on her face.

Mr. Braxton turned. "Well, that's good to hear, boy. It would be a terrible shame to waste such a fine specimen and a young lad with a promising shapeshifting career." He struggled back to where Travis stood. "Now, what can you tell us?"

Oops.

He thought hard for something to say, some plausible hint that he actually knew something about unicorns. If only Ellie were here. She knew everything. "I can tell you one thing for sure," he said carefully, nodding toward the unicorn. "She's not gonna do a thing while drugged up to her eyeballs. I sat on the sofa for hours, right? It felt like minutes. The idea of transforming and escaping never even popped into my mind. She's in a daydream at the moment. We'll have to wait for her to wake up."

Mr. Braxton frowned. "But then she'll bolt."

"Not if you're there when she wakes, sitting calmly by her side," Travis lied. "She'll be wary of you, but she won't bolt. And she'll see your injury and want to fix it."

A silence followed. Travis maintained a poker face, his heart thumping. The lies had flowed smoothly from his lips, and it had all sounded pretty believable. More than anything, it bought him time. Now Mr. Braxton would have to wait an hour or two.

That is, if he believed the lie.

The man cleared his throat. "And how, exactly, does the unicorn perform the, uh . . . the healing?"

Travis waved his hand about as if it were obvious. "Oh, she'll touch the injury with the end of her horn. That's where the magic comes from. It'll shoot out in waves, and you'll see a faint glowing."

Again with the fibs! Was it right to feel proud of himself for lying so convincingly?

Mr. Braxton rubbed his chin. "And you know all this how?"

"I know a shapeshifter unicorn." This much was true at least. "Her name's Ellie. Friend of my mom and dad's."

The man looked at the grey-haired woman. "Madame Frost? Do you think the boy is telling the truth?"

"Possibly."

"How about we use the calming drug again? You used it on the boy this morning, and he readily answered your questions."

She grimaced. "Readily? Yelling in his face over and over just to elicit a sleepy response isn't the easiest way to question a prisoner. He was practically comatose—as the unicorn is now."

Mr. Braxton sighed. "Well, don't you have a spell just for detecting lies? What do I pay you for, my dear woman?"

"You *haven't* paid me," she said icily. "You promised to trap dragons for me."

"I'm leading up to it!"

"I'm here for one thing only," she went on, jabbing a finger at him, "and that's a dragon's fire gland. When are you going to deliver?"

He shook his head and scowled. "Let's discuss this later. Can you make a lie detector or not?"

She shrugged. "There's a spell I know. It's not the most trustworthy of truth serums, but—"

"Do it."

Travis's heart sank. *A magical lie detector?*

He was doomed.

* * *

The men locked Travis in a bedroom on the main floor. The first thing he did was check the window, but it had shutters on the outside. He slid the window up and tested them for strength. They might give if he were an angry, determined wyvern, but how long would it take to break through? The men could burst in at any moment.

Sitting on the bed in the glow of a bedside lamp, he thought long and hard about all the mistakes he'd made. Going after the hunters on his own, taking too long figuring out how to shift back and forth at will, entering the mansion to find the cage keys, coming after Mr. Braxton without a backup plan . . . If he was to be a hero like his dad, he needed to *think* first.

He smelled something weird brewing in the kitchen. He imagined the witch stirring a cauldron of bubbling, steaming potion and shook his head in disgust at the silly vision. She was old and grey-haired and wore a long robe, but she didn't have a pointed hat and broomstick, nor did she have warts and cackle like a harpy. She wasn't a picture-book witch with a green face and hooked nose, just a regular if eccentric woman who probably lived alone in the woods somewhere.

"Psst!"

He spun around. Seeing nothing, he narrowed his eyes and searched every nook and cranny—behind the bedside table, under the bed, inside the closet . . .

"Psst!"

"Nitwit?" he whispered, astonished. "Are you here?"

Sure enough, his impish friend emerged from a large trunk against the wall. He'd assumed it was full of clothes or bedding, but it was completely empty—except for Nitwit.

"What are you doing here?" he cried. "How—?"

She climbed out, shooting anxious glances toward the door. "Just checking on you."

He tried to gather his thoughts. "Why are you *here*, in this room?"

"I had to hide somewhere. It was just coincidence that you ended up locked in here."

"Rotten luck, you mean. We're locked in together."

She wrung her hands. "I wish I could help you. I just—" She sighed. "I'll explain some day. But for now, you have to help yourself."

Nitwit looked on the verge of tears. Travis sighed and put a hand on her tiny shoulder. "Hey, it's okay. I don't understand what's going on with you, but you're here, and that means a lot to me. I just hope you don't get caught."

Suddenly worried for his friend, he spun the imp around and pushed her back toward the trunk.

"Get inside," he ordered. "Stay quiet, okay? There's nothing you can do for me while we're locked in the same room together, but once I leave here, then the door will be open. Just stay out of sight, all right? Escape when you can. Don't take any risks for me. I can take care of myself—sort of."

She climbed inside and huddled low as he stood over the trunk and held the lid open.

"Did you go home?" he asked her. "Did you speak to anyone? Bring help?"

As she opened her mouth to speak, a key rattled in the door, and Travis quickly closed the trunk lid and sat on it.

The door opened, and the witch stood there. "Come on out. The truth potion is ready."

"Great," Travis said. "I'm *so* excited."

The witch led the way to the living room, and he sat once more on the sofa he'd spent so long on that morning. Mr. Braxton sat opposite, his expression serious. As usual, men stood all around, two in black suits, three in hunting gear. Was the truck driver somewhere, too? Some of the men had mean faces, but one or two seemed like ordinary, everyday people. What drew them to a life like this? Working for someone like Mr. Braxton? Just money?

"Drink this," Madame Frost said, handing Travis a glass of what looked like murky water.

Knowing he had no choice, he drank the liquid and grimaced at the taste. His mind raced as he swallowed it down. What would Mr. Braxton do when he uncovered the lies?

"What's your name?" the man asked.

"Travis Franklin."

How old are you?"

"Twelve."

"What kind of shapeshifter is your mother?"

"A two-hundred-foot pink sea monster with purple spots."

The moment he lied, something happened to his face. He felt numb on one side, and when he touched his cheek, he was shocked to find it had swelled outward.

Mr. Braxton's eyebrows shot up. "My, my, that's really quite effective, Madame Frost. Puffy-faced and blue-skinned."

Travis lifted his trembling hands, which had turned a weird shade of blue. The coloring faded immediately, and the swelling on his face subsided. Still, it left him shaken and dismayed.

"I'll ask again," Mr. Braxton said. "What kind of shapeshifter is your mother?"

"A faerie."

"Ah, look, no puffy face or discolored skin. It looks like the lie detector works just fine, Madame."

She said nothing, but Travis suspected she still wasn't convinced her potion was reliable. Maybe he could wriggle out of this after all . . .

"I have a friend here," he said defiantly. "She's going to rescue me."

Mr. Braxton smiled. "The unicorn? She's going to rescue you?"

"No, not the unicorn. I mean a *friend*. She followed me all the way to the warehouse, and then she followed me here to this cabin."

He lifted his hands to look at them. No blue skin, no puffiness. "Oops. Did the lie detector stop working?"

A silence followed. Mr. Braxton looked puzzled. "Let's be clear about this. Do you have a friend here or not?"

"Yes."

"Here in the cabin?"

Travis steeled himself. "Yes."

All the men in the room glanced around, and Mr. Braxton looked from Travis to Madame Frost. "Is the potion working or not?"

She leaned down to study Travis's face. "I'm not sure. I told you it was unreliable."

"But it worked just now!"

Madame Frost said nothing but reached out to pinch Travis's cheek. "Who is this friend of yours?"

Travis had been waiting for this. "She's a tiny little imp!" he cried happily. "Big ears, big eyes, cute little thing, very pretty. Her name's Nitwit. She follows me everywhere. I saw her just a moment ago."

Mr. Braxton rolled his eyes and sighed heavily. "Clearly the lie detector doesn't work after all. This is a waste of time."

"No, wait," the witch said, looking all around with a frown on her face. "That might actually be the truth. Ask him something else. Ask him about the unicorn—"

But Travis interrupted her, choosing his words carefully but putting on a manic voice as if he were telling the biggest whoppers of his life. "You want to know about unicorns? I plan to be a unicorn myself one day." He counted off on his fingers. "And a minotaur, and a mothman, and just about everything else you have in those cages. I can be anything I want, because I'm a special kind of shapeshifter that nobody's ever seen before."

"Get him out of here!" Mr. Braxton snapped, struggling to his feet. "Take him to the unicorn and secure him. We'll soon find out if he's telling us lies. I'll be there shortly."

Madame Frost looked like she wanted to protest, but Mr. Braxton was already hobbling away with a look of disgust on his face. So she looked at Travis with narrowed eyes instead.

As he was yanked to his feet by guards, Travis mentally punched the air. *Fooled them with the truth this time!*

He found it marvellously ironic that Nitwit had saved him just by being here, and his short-lived, rebootable shapeshifting ability had actually allowed him to boast quite truthfully. Sometimes, the truth really was stranger than fiction.

Then again, all he'd really done was delay the inevitable. Now that he was once more being frogmarched through the woods to where the unicorn lay, he wondered what would happen when she woke to find Mr. Braxton sitting by her side. Travis had no delusions that she would take kindly to his presence and heal his leg wound. More likely, she would leap up and stab him through the heart.

And then guns would fire, and everything would get really messy.

Chapter 18
The Unicorn Wakes

Travis wished he knew more about unicorns. He suspected his knowledge was only marginally less vague than Mr. Braxton's, and that didn't bode well.

He'd heard they could purify poisoned water. Throughout history, people had been known to dip a unicorn's horn into a pool to clean it. But if the water was badly contaminated, the horn would become hot and start smoking.

Of course, this suggested the poor creature had been butchered first, its horn cut off and stolen. Travis would never let that happen here.

He'd also heard unicorns could heal sickness, rather like the miengu water spirits could. As far as he knew, neither could heal physical injuries. That was a lie on his part, an embellishment to feed into Mr. Braxton's personal desire to have his leg fixed. So even if Travis could find a way to persuade the unicorn to perform some magic, it would never be enough for the man.

He pondered all this as he loitered behind some bushes with Madame Frost and a squad of five armed guards. Thirty feet away, Mr. Braxton sat next to the unicorn. He'd used a knife to cut open his left pant leg to expose a scarred lump on his thin white thigh.

The unicorn was showing signs of returning to the present. She had lain quite peacefully for hours now thanks to the trough filled with drugged water. Travis couldn't help wondering why she'd been affected at all. If she was able to purify poisoned water, why didn't her magic work on Madame Frost's potion? Wouldn't that be classed as a form of poison?

This made him worry that everything he'd heard about unicorns was a myth. What if they were nothing more than just pretty white horses with single horns projecting from their foreheads? Sure, they were unusually large, and they seemed to glow with energy, and they galloped at an incredible pace when they weren't hemmed in by Jeeps . . . but what if they had no actual powers?

"I'm surprised *you* don't know everything about unicorns," he whispered to Madame Frost. "You're from New Earth, and you mess around with magic potions and stuff."

Kneeling in the dirt next to him, she remained still and replied in a low voice. "Hunters have been catching unicorns for thousands of years and cutting pieces off. The horn is the most valuable. If ground down into powder, it can be applied directly to wounds or added to potions to cure all manner of injuries and illnesses."

Travis looked at her in surprise. So they *could* heal injuries? "But that's in powder form," he said. "Which means cutting it off."

"And that's exactly what Mr. Braxton will do if you're wrong about this," she warned.

Swallowing, Travis looked again at the unicorn, lying so peacefully in the grass. Mr. Braxton was a frail man for someone in his forties, but his words carried a lot of power. If he wanted the unicorn dead and her horn cut off and ground into powder, Travis had no doubt he could make it happen.

"Have you actually seen unicorns heal people?" the witch asked, now looking at him with a distinctly suspicious glare.

"Not with my own eyes, no," Travis answered truthfully. "My dad knows a unicorn shapeshifter, a friend of Lady Simone's. Her name's Ellie. I bet *she* could heal Mr. Braxton—if she wanted to."

And if she could heal people, she'd be in pretty hot demand, he thought to himself. *Instead, she ran off with a herd and was never seen again.*

In fact, she'd shown up a few years ago, a woman aged fifty-something who'd spent decades hidden away in a distant village with unicorns roaming nearby. She'd come home for some reason, but had never opened up about her past life, at least not publicly. Why had she run away? If anybody knew, that person was Lady Simone. These days, Ellie came to help whenever unicorns were involved, which wasn't very often.

"Well, not long now," Madame Frost murmured.

Growing more and more anxious by the second, Travis ran through escape plans in his mind. He wasn't too worried about himself. He figured he could transform and shoot straight upward before anyone had a chance to react. But the unicorn would almost certainly be killed and butchered when it turned out she couldn't—or wouldn't—heal Mr. Braxton's injury.

Scare her off, he thought. *Make her jump up in fright and bolt. Maybe she'll get away.*

That would only work if these five armed men were hesitant to shoot. Travis let the thought percolate in his mind before slowly letting out a long breath. It was risky, but . . .

The pure-white equine blinked and started as if waking from a dream. She snorted and nickered, then shook her head and jerked, looking around as if mystified. She hadn't spotted Mr. Braxton yet.

Travis made a show of looking worried. "No, no, no!"

"What's wrong?" Madame Frost hissed.

"He's in the wrong position. He's going to get himself killed."

He climbed to his feet, and immediately five men reached for their weapons.

Travis held up his hands and looked straight at the witch. "Don't let them shoot me. If they shoot me, Mr. Braxton will most likely die."

"What are you—?" she started, climbing to her feet.

But Travis darted out from behind the bushes and hurried toward Mr. Braxton, ignoring the frenzy of whispers behind him. He imagined half a dozen guns pointed at his back, but nobody fired. At least not yet.

He tapped the man on the shoulder and spoke loudly. "You're sitting in the wrong place. You have to move."

Both Mr. Braxton and the unicorn jumped at the sound of his voice. The unicorn whinnied and struggled to her feet.

"What are you *doing*, boy?" the man roared, his face darkening.

"You're too close. Get up and sit over *there*. She's waking up too fast, and she'll stab you through the heart if she sees you right on top of her like that."

Mr. Braxton grabbed his cane and tried to stand, grumbling something that Travis couldn't quite hear. He didn't care. All he wanted was a bit of confusion and enough doubt that nobody would start shooting. Plus, now he was helping Mr. Braxton to his feet and using the man as a shield. The men wouldn't fire even if they wanted to—and hopefully they wouldn't shoot the unicorn unless ordered to.

"Come over here," Travis said, urging Mr. Braxton along. He guided the man toward the bushes where Madame Frost and the men hid—though they didn't seem to be trying to conceal themselves anymore. "See, she's awake now and pretty scared."

"Well, why the devil did you tell me to sit *next* to her, then?"

"Because I thought she'd wake up a bit slower."

Travis glanced behind him. The unicorn was fully awake now, clambering to her feet and swishing her tail. He made sure to keep himself and Mr. Braxton between her and the armed men, reducing their chances of a clear shot.

"This is a trick!" Madame Frost yelled suddenly. "Look at that boy's face! I see treachery written all over it!"

Mr. Braxton stiffened and looked at Travis, then tried to pull away. "Let go of me," he demanded. He raised his voice. "Kill him! And kill the unicorn!"

Still no shots—because they had no clear target.

Time to go, Travis thought. *If I haven't forgotten how to shapeshift.*

But he transformed easily, spread his wings, and screeched over his shoulder as loudly as possible. If the unicorn wasn't fully alert already, she was now—and she bolted away, leaves flying as she tore through bushes without a care. Shots fired, and bullets struck tree trunks, but the fast-moving equine was gone within seconds, a flash of white through the woods.

"Shoot the boy!" Madame Frost screamed.

Another shot fired, but only one. It zinged through one of Travis's wings as he started flapping them. The rest of the wide-eyed men dithered because Travis had Mr. Braxton's neck locked in his jaws from behind. The only safe target they had was a pair of six-foot blood-red wings, and they were a blur.

In one smooth motion, Travis locked his clawed feet around Mr. Braxton's waist, digging into his expensive suit, shirt, and flesh. The man yelled out, but then Travis was away, shooting upward through the trees with his prize.

He glanced down in time to see Madame Frost, the armed men, the cabin, the truck, the limousine, and two Jeeps vanish from sight, replaced with untouched forestland. But although the invisibility spell had kicked in, they could still see *him*, so he shot away as fast as possible in the direction the unicorn had fled.

He hated that the poor unicorn was running scared, but at least she was running. Ellie would have to come looking for her another time. Right now, Travis had work to do.

"Put . . . me . . . down!" Mr. Braxton gurgled, obviously in a lot of discomfort.

Travis didn't try to answer. He loosened his jaws a little, hoping his grip around the man's waist was secure. He flew over the trees a while, trying to spot the unicorn, but then gave up and circled around, making a wide arc. He'd gone after her deliberately, not so much to catch her but to give Madame Frost the *idea* that he was trying to catch her.

"What are you doing?" Mr. Braxton shouted. "Are you going after her or not? Put me down! You'll never get away with this! I have a lot of highly paid bodyguards and hunters, *and* a helicopter. They'll be after you any second now!"

Let them come, Travis thought. *Let them fly out here to the cabin while I'm heading back to the warehouse.*

He flew low, following the main road east, keeping his eyes open for a mansion that he expected to appear out of thin air sometime in the next thirty minutes. Mr. Braxton complained the whole time, his pant leg flapping, his tie flicking up and tickling Travis's snout. When a dark speck rose from a hilltop and Travis heard the steady *chop-chop* of rotors, he made a note of the position on the horizon then swooped down to hide among a stand of trees in a field.

The helicopter would be flying over shortly. In the meantime, Travis planned to lie low. He landed and let go of Mr. Braxton, who stumbled and fell into a patch of mud. The man was a sorry mess as he sat up and tried to smooth his ripped and crumpled suit with trembling hands.

"You'll be sorry for this," he warned.

Travis reverted to his human form, suffering a momentary bout of dizziness as he did so. To avoid looking weak in front of his enemy, he held still for a moment until the feeling passed, then answered, "Better to be sorry than dead."

"You'll be both before long," Mr. Braxton snapped.

Travis kept his distance. The disheveled man wasn't the toughest of villains, but he was angry and desperate.

The dizziness was gone now. Was that normal? He guessed it was. He *hoped* it was. Or it could be that he was shifting too many times in succession. It must take a toll on his body each time, especially as it was a new experience for him.

The sound of the helicopter increased, and Mr. Braxton looked skyward. There was no way to see it from beneath the trees, so he started hobbling—a difficult task without his cane.

"Stay where you are," Travis said calmly, his heart thumping. He'd never had confrontations like this before. The man could physically attack him. "Or I'll transform again and sting you with my barb."

He hoped he wouldn't have to for several reasons.

Mr. Braxton scowled but halted. "You don't have it in you."

Travis ignored him. "I want the key."

"What key?"

"The master key in your pocket."

He said it so boldly that Mr. Braxton looked surprised for a moment. Then his lip curled. "Who told you? I'll fire the idiot."

"Give me the key, or I'll rip your nice suit apart until I find it."

"Go ahead. This suit's ruined anyway."

Travis shrugged. "Fine. Don't blame me if I rip out a few chunks of flesh at the same time."

Now was not the time to worry about shifting too often. He transformed again, spreading his wings to make himself look bigger. When he advanced on Mr. Braxton with his tail swinging around, the man's eyes opened wide. Then, scowling and cursing, he fumbled in his pocket and withdrew the key.

As Travis reached for it, Mr. Braxton flung it away.

Sucking in a breath, Travis watched it arc through the air and fall into the grass. Trying to keep an eye on its location, he waited patiently while the helicopter flew by overhead. Its tail end came into sight as it headed west toward the cabin. Mr. Braxton shouted for all he was worth, to no avail.

Then Travis stamped out into the open to find the key. As he was searching, Mr. Braxton hobbled away through the trees, wincing and complaining as he went. Travis let him go.

It took a few minutes to locate the key. When he did, it took even longer to pick it up. He could have reverted to human form and slid it into a pocket in his smart clothes, but he couldn't help wondering again how many transformations were considered safe and normal. What if he wore down his ability before it had time to settle in? What if his immune system was already working to prevent further shifts? He had no idea how long he had with this wyvern form.

He eventually picked up the six-inch key in his jaws and gripped it tight, terrified of dropping it. Then he took off and flew at top speed toward the spot on the horizon where the helicopter had risen into the sky.

Now to release the prisoners, he thought.

Chapter 19
Risky Diversion

The mansion and warehouse popped into view just ahead. Travis stayed low and veered right, unwilling to be spotted. He brushed the treetops and swooped in for a landing as close as he dared. He'd have to walk the rest of the way on human feet.

Shifting was as easy as ever, and this time with no dizziness. Maybe pacing himself was the answer. He wished he'd kept count of all his transformations back and forth, though. *Let's see: First outside the laboratory, then later back to human when I escaped Mr. Braxton's afternoon stroll, then wyvern again straight afterward—*

Noise distracted him. The place was swarming with people. One way or another, the guards and handlers were on high alert. There had to be fifty or more black-suited guards, men and women in blue coveralls, and a few casually dressed hunters. They were spread out between the mansion and the warehouse, some guarding the smaller outbuildings he'd noticed earlier.

The huge roller door to the warehouse remained firmly shut. It couldn't be later than mid-morning right now, and Travis doubted the prisoners would be taking their afternoon strolls today even if he was patient enough to wait around. And he knew the back door was secured with an electronic keypad.

The skylights again, then. But with this many guards around, he'd be seen for sure, and armed men would surround the building before he unlocked the first cage. He needed a distraction. What about the smaller building he'd spotted from the air? It had guards, but maybe not as many. If he could release whatever was inside, maybe it would keep them busy for a while. It couldn't hurt to try since he planned to release all the captives anyway.

So he spent some more time creeping around, careful not to be spotted. When he came across the small building, he waited patiently to see how many guards were circling it. It looked like seven in total, three in black suits and four in blue coveralls, all crunching on the gravel. The black-suited men carried rifles and pistols while the handlers toted their weird-looking dart guns.

Seven guards was still too many. *I need a distraction for my distraction,* he concluded.

From his vantage point among the trees, he could just about read the sign posted on the building's roller door: WARNING! DEADLY ANIMALS.

Aren't they all?

The manticore, the griffin, the minotaur, the cerberus . . . All could be considered deadly animals, but they were housed in the much bigger warehouse, which had no such signs.

So what's in here?

The building was large enough to contain a fire-breathing dragon, but the sign indicated more than one creature lurked inside.

Travis looked up at the roof, hoping to spot a few skylights. No such luck, though. No windows, either. Just one giant roller door at the front, and a single small door at the back, most likely secured with one of those keypad locks.

A man in blue coveralls wandered past, scanning the woods. Travis ducked down, holding his breath, listening to the crunch of gravel.

He had a crazy idea. Before he could stop himself, he deliberately made some noise, wriggling around and cracking a twig or two. He stopped to listen.

The handler had stopped also.

Silence.

Then soft, approaching footfalls. Travis remained still while those light, crunching noises turned into clumsy shuffling as the man stepped into the woods to investigate.

Still Travis waited.

The handler sighed and muttered, "Chasing squirrels now? Get a grip."

He sounded close. Travis poked his head around the tree trunk and saw the man just fifteen feet away, pushing through a thorny bush.

Now or never, Travis thought—and transformed.

He leapt as far as he could, raising his wings and flapping them just once to aid in his jump. The man started to turn and just had time to open his mouth before Travis came down hard on his back, pushing him flat on his belly, then pinning him underfoot and squeezing a muffled "Umph!" out of him. The dart gun went flying.

Realizing this was no time to be weak, Travis applied all his weight and brought his tail around, the barb long and vicious-looking. He still couldn't sting him, though. As far as he knew, that would be fatal. So he angled his tail and whacked the handler, wondering if there was a trick to judging what was hard enough to render someone unconscious but light enough not to cause permanent injury.

In this case, he opened up a gash on the man's temple but failed to knock him out. He seemed dazed, though.

Travis reverted to human form and climbed off, then grabbed the fallen dart gun and pointed it. *Just pull the trigger*, he thought. Only dart guns didn't seem so straightforward. He fiddled with a dial on the backend, some sort of pressure setting, looked for a safety catch, released it, and aimed. When he pulled the trigger, it let out a soft *phut!* sound, and a dart hit the man in the back of his left thigh.

"Ow!" he said, jerking and reaching for the dart. "What— what did you—?"

"Shh," Travis warned, "or I'll have to transform again and sting you with my stinger. That will kill you. I just need you to be quiet. Go to sleep, okay?"

The man rolled onto his back, already looking groggy. He was balding and middle-aged, average build and not too tall. He would do.

Travis leaned in close. "I need the door code."

"Forget it."

"If you don't tell me," Travis warned, "I'll make sure those dangerous animals find you when I let them out. You'll be sound asleep while they're chewing on your legs."

The handler blinked rapidly, obviously fighting the sleepiness. "W-what?"

"And if you give me the wrong code, I'll drag you out into the open and make sure you're the very first person they come across."

"You can't let . . . let the animals out," he said, slurring his words. "Too . . . too dangerous. They'll kill *everyone* . . ."

"So stay here. Just lie still and fall asleep. Give me the code, and you'll be safe. If you don't give me the code, I'll find another way in and come back to get you later."

The handler's eyelids drooped. "9-5-2-1-6," he mumbled. "But don't let them . . . don't . . ."

He tried to say something else, but then he went limp and still.

Now let's hope his uniform fits me, Travis thought as he memorized the code.

* * *

Five minutes later, wearing blue coveralls that were too big for him, Travis crept through the woods toward the small building. Before he stepped out onto the gravel, he folded up his sleeves a couple of times and then did the same around his ankles. It helped, but he still looked like a kid in adult's clothing.

It'll have to do, he told himself.

There was no perfect moment to step out into view, so he did so boldly and casually, the spent dart gun tucked into the holster at his side. The belt with the holster had a compartment with a few more darts, but he had no interest in figuring out how to load them.

He strolled with his head low, taking what he thought was a non-suspicious route to the building's back entrance, a kind of nonchalant amble rather than a deliberate stride. One of the black-suited guards glanced at him from afar, and his gaze lingered, but Travis kept his face down.

No shouts of alarm came. Not yet, anyway.

He made it to the door, timing his arrival to coincide with the least amount of guards and handlers in the vicinity. One was directly in front, facing the other way. Another paused at the corner, looking out toward the trees.

Travis reached for the keypad and punched in the code: 9-5-2-1-6. A soft click sounded. He grasped the door handle and turned it, and the door opened inward. With a sigh of relief, Travis slipped inside without a backward glance and quietly closed the door again.

Someone outside shouted.

He sucked in a breath and fumbled with a deadbolt. It was just a small one, and he guessed he'd have very little time before someone broke the door down.

Travis left the lights off and sprinted through the gloomy building, taking everything in at a glance. Four cages, the same type as the ones in the bigger warehouse. Inside—

Trembling, he dug out Mr. Braxton's master key and approached the nearest cage. Inside, a terrifying tan-colored creature rose up on four legs, a huge lion head swinging to face him. But this was no lion. Atop its back, something moved about beneath a loose-fitting chainmail sack.

A goat's head, Travis guessed after studying the rest of the creature. *And a snake's head on the end of its tail.*

In fact, the entire tail looked serpentine, shiny and scaly as it writhed.

People began pounding on the door he'd locked behind him. They obviously had the electronic keypad disabled and were throwing all their weight at the door, trying to force the deadbolt.

"Chimera," Travis said loudly, standing near the bars as the monster edged closer. "I'm going to let you out. I'm here to help—so don't attack me, all right? You can go free. But there are people outside, and they're going to try and catch you again. You'll have to fight your way out. Do you understand?"

He had no idea if the chimera monster was smart enough to comprehend what he was saying, but just in case, he quickly stripped off his blue coveralls to reveal his silky smart clothes. Maybe it would help get the message across that he wasn't one of the handlers.

He put the key in the lock and turned it, and the bolt slid back with a thunk. He withdrew the key and reached for the latch.

Behind him, the feeble deadbolt gave out, and the door flew open. "Kid!" a voice shouted. "No! Don't do that!"

The chimera roared, and Travis flinched, momentarily distracted. He saw men spilling in through the doorway.

This either works—or I die horribly.

He threw back the latch and yanked the gate open. The chimera leapt out and stood there, roaring at the group of men who had stopped in the doorway. They all started backing up.

Since he hadn't been attacked yet, Travis took that as a good sign. Mindful of the monster's baleful glare, he reached for the metallic sack that covered the goat-head growing directly out of the lion's broad shoulders. The chainmail bag was secured with a sturdy belt, which he undid with twitchy fingers while the snake-head coiled around and hissed at him. When he pulled the sack off, he stared in wonder at the head and neck of a goat, and it stared back with wide eyes. It bleated rudely at him as he stumbled back.

The building's back door slammed shut, and Travis smiled at his temporary victory. All the men had abandoned the chase now that the chimera was loose, but they would be gathering outside very quickly.

As the chimera swung to face him with the three heads growling, bleating, and hissing in unison, Travis held up his hands and said, "Steady, now. I'll open the big door for you. Get ready to fight. They're going to be waiting."

The chimera stood its ground, unmoving, while Travis hurried to the huge roller door. He flipped a switch, and the massive metal wall slid upward with a noisy rattle.

Daylight poured in beneath, and the boots of half a dozen guards came into view, then their blue pant legs or black suits. Next came their weapons, held at the ready.

The moment the roller door had risen above the height of the people standing outside, the goat-head—which had been bleating like crazy for the past half-minute—opened its mouth and spat out a sizzling fireball the size of a human head. Men threw themselves aside as the flaming ball hit the ground and exploded, sending gravel in all directions.

Travis was already running—back into the building, dashing past the chimera to the other three cages, his master key at the ready. He'd already glimpsed what was inside a couple of them but hadn't been ready to handle the information. Now he was.

As the goat-head bleated and coughed up more fireballs, and men outside shouted and let off what seemed like random shots into the darkness of the building, Travis quickly unlocked the other three cages and swung them open.

Then he backed into the shadows and watched the chaos unfold.

Chapter 20
Deadly Creatures

Roaring savagely, the chimera ran outside into the scattering crowd. Travis heard the bleating of the goat's head and another fireball launching, but then the creature was gone, no doubt chasing its prey in all directions. Briefly, he thought about the unconscious handler whose coveralls he'd stolen. He wished there was some way he could keep to his promise and ensure the man's safety, but he doubted rampaging monsters would be interested in a sleeping body among the trees when there were plenty more targets running about in a panic.

A woman sprang from the second cage Travis had opened, her shoulder-length dark-brown hair suddenly erupting into flames. Over a knee-length white frock, she wore dull metal armor that covered her shoulders and torso. Though she stood on two legs, they were grey-furred and hoofed like those of a giant goat. Travis almost expected her to teeter awkwardly as if on stilts, yet she moved fast, clip-clopping across the concrete floor.

She hissed and bared her fangs at Travis where he cowered in the shadows, the flames on her head leaping higher. Then she looked toward the open roller door, and her eyes blazed with excitement.

"I'm free," she murmured. "But the daylight hurts my eyes."

Travis had never seen an empusa vampire before and ordinarily wouldn't want to. She was probably thirsty for blood. The sun wouldn't kill her, but she squinted and snarled at the brightness outside.

He was distracted by movement from the third cage. There, a hulking form rose to its feet, and as it did so, the dull red glow throughout its rocklike body brightened to a vivid orange, and smoke began to rise. The bars of its cage were blackened from where it had gripped them multiple times, and some of the metal had warped. This beast was easily eight or nine feet tall and probably twice as broad as the average man. When it stamped out of the cage, it left smoldering footprints in its wake. The cage floor was badly charred.

Travis squeezed himself farther back into his corner, fearful of what he had released. He struggled to remember what this beast was called. Part of being a shapeshifter was the endless researching of all the magical creatures of New Earth, and this one eluded him for now.

Unlike the empusa, it calmly stomped over to the roller door and outside, setting off a new volley of shouts and gunfire. Neither darts nor bullets bothered this hulking creature, because it was formed from molten rock that cooled and heated depending on its mood. Right now it was excited, and it glowed like lava.

Cherufe!

The name of the rock monster popped into Travis's head, and he let out a sigh.

The empusa vampire woman seemed unable or unwilling to step outside, and she stood there flinching with one hand shielding her face, her hair still on fire. She watched the cherufe stomp away, then spun around to face Travis. "The man, *Mr. Braxton*," she said, her voice dripping with hatred. "Tell me where he is."

He licked his dry lips. "I . . . I dropped him off about half an hour's walk from here, to the west."

She considered for a moment. "It's too bright outside. I will wait until nightfall."

With that, she retreated from the daylight and clip-clopped past where Travis hid, shooting him a glare as she went.

"You can come out. I won't drain the blood of the person who released me from this hell. Are Braxton's people conquered?"

"Huh?"

She hissed with impatience. "Do you have the situation under control? Am I safe here?"

"Well, kind of. I mean, maybe. It's safe-ish, I guess."

Without another word, she bent her goatlike legs and sprang upward—and kept on going. Travis gasped, staggering backward as she soared all the way to the underside of the pitched roof some twenty feet up. Clinging to a metal beam, she scrambled into a sitting position and seemed to shut down. She was almost completely lost in the darkness, though she wouldn't be if someone switched the lights on.

Travis looked toward the fourth and last cage. Nothing emerged from that one. He couldn't be sure he'd seen anything in there, but since nobody would lock an empty cage, he waited nervously for whatever it was to wake up.

He saw and heard nothing, so in the end he got up and wandered over. Outside, he heard the continuous yelling of guards and handlers in the distance, plus muffled explosions and thumps. The chimera and cherufe seemed to be having a blast, and the noise came from the direction of the mansion. If Mr. Braxton returned, it would be to a big old mess.

"Oh," he said, spotting a tiny sign fixed to the bars of the cage door. Under the sign hung a pair of complex-looking goggles like binoculars attached to a head strap. He peered into the darkness of the cage. In the center, reverently placed on a simple table, stood a rectangular metal box about three feet long. It had dozens of holes punched into the top and sides. "Okay, I'm not releasing *that*."

He looked again at the tiny sign. BASILISK: DO NOT OPEN WITHOUT GLOVES AND GOGGLES.

He shuddered and eased backward. On second thought, he closed the cage door and locked it, pocketing the key. Why on earth had Mr. Braxton acquired something so deadly? More to the point, *how*? Basilisks were extremely rare, small six-legged lizard creatures no longer than his forearm. If spewing the nastiest venom in the world wasn't enough, they could kill with one glance of their tiny eyes.

Best leave that alone for now, he thought, and turned away.

He strode over to the great roller door and into the sunshine. To his delight, he saw nobody at all. He heard plenty of yells, though, coming from the direction of the mansion. Either people were running for their lives or they were staying to fight off the fiery monsters. A chimera shooting fireballs and the cherufe burning everything it touched—a hot twosome indeed!

Travis hurried away, heading for the giant warehouse, eager now to finish his mission and release everyone.

As he arrived at the huge building, he wondered briefly why the empusa vampire had been separated out and caged alongside the chimera, cherufe, and basilisk. Could it be because she had a fiery hairstyle? Maybe she lobbed fireballs of her own just by flinging her head from side to side. He couldn't recall learning anything of that sort. Maybe she just had a rotten attitude and couldn't be trusted.

Funny how such dangerous beasts as the manticore, cerberus, minotaur, and griffin were allowed to go for walks in the sunshine, though.

He clicked his tongue. Maybe that was the answer. She couldn't go out in the sunshine, so maybe she was allowed out at night, and housing her here avoided disturbing all the others. Or maybe she really could lob fireballs. It didn't matter. Mr. Braxton probably had a reason for everything.

Pleased that nobody was about—at least not here outside the warehouse—he entered the five-digit code into the keypad and crossed his fingers it would work. It did; the door unlocked, and he threw it open and marched inside, flicking on lights as he entered. Then he stopped dead as six or seven handlers launched themselves at him from all around.

"Argh!" he yelled, going down under a mass of heavy bodies and limbs.

"Stick him!" one man shouted. "Quick, before he—"

Travis transformed and thrust his wings out, shoving the men off. He sprang to his feet and whipped his tail around in a circle, mostly out of instinct. He connected with at least three bodies, and the rest jumped back as fast as those who had been hit.

Travis swung again and let out a savage roar. His barb tore through the clothing of the nearest handler and sliced across his chest. The man yelled, clutched at his wound, and staggered away.

Seeing a dart gun coming up to point in his direction, Travis leapt forward and snapped at the weapon with his jaws, his sharp teeth catching the man's arm in the process. He yelled even louder, his gun dropping to the floor.

After another swing with his tail and leaping about in a rage, Travis suddenly found himself alone. The men scurried to safety, fighting over each other to squeeze through the exit.

It was only after they'd gone and a silence had fallen that he realized what he'd done. He'd acted so fast and ferociously that he'd barely been in control, and now he'd sliced into the flesh of at least one man with his barb—meaning that man was poisoned. Whether he deserved it or not hardly mattered. If he died from the injury . . .

Travis began to shake. He reverted to human form and knelt on the floor by a rack of shelves, feeling sick. He'd also bitten down pretty hard on another man's arm, and whacked three more around the head. Was he justified? It didn't matter. He'd never hurt a soul in his life, and now it was possible he'd *killed* someone.

He swallowed and fought back tears. Maybe he wasn't cut out for this line of work. What would his dad have done? As a full-grown dragon, how many people had he hurt really badly? He wasn't sure he liked how that made him feel.

"Boy!" a voice called, echoing through the warehouse. It sounded like Tallock the centaur. "Are you there?"

Travis rubbed his eyes and climbed to his feet. "Yeah."

"Then come free us!"

When he walked between the silent cages, it seemed all eyes were on him. Suddenly, he was struck by indecision. Who could he trust to let out? He considered himself lucky he hadn't been fireballed by the chimera, or melted by the touch of the cherufe, or had his blood sucked out by the empusa vampire. Would he be so lucky with some of the prisoners here? The minotaur, for instance. They were known for their unrelenting, bullheaded anger. Griffins were normally passive unless provoked, in which case they could get nasty. Even Lightfoot the manticore—or *especially* him—might turn and kill him once freed.

"Travis," Lightfoot said then, his fluty voice soft and calming. "What are you waiting for? I hear commotion in the distance, so I gather you released our fellow captives from the neighboring building. Is the vampire still lurking in the dark? You should consider yourself fortunate the empusa is not picky about the blood she feasts on; anyone's will do, and no doubt she's looking forward to a feast tonight when she emerges. However . . ." He raised a foot and pointed a clawed finger to a cage on the opposite side. "I suspect that her cousin, the lamia over there, has her gaze fixated on *you,* and you alone. She will drink nothing *but* the blood of a young child."

Travis turned to find the dark-grey, scaly, catlike lamia staring at him through the bars. Her human face reddened, and she turned away, her serpentine tail curling around.

He shuddered. That was the problem. Releasing all these creatures seemed the right thing to do, but he had to be sensible about it. He couldn't let them all run around the Old Earth countryside! They needed to be led into New Earth, and he had to make sure they didn't kill him in the process.

He tried to imagine such a variety of species, some of them deadly, escaping the warehouse without squabbling. Sure, they had a common enemy and might band together, form a truce of some kind . . . but he couldn't be sure they were all smart or even restrained enough.

He'd made the chimera understand, though. Facing one of those in the wild certainly would have been fatal. Yet it had recognized him as a friend even though he'd first appeared wearing those hated blue coveralls. Maybe *all* these beasts, frightening or otherwise, were smarter than they looked.

Lightfoot raised his voice. "I can see your dilemma, boy. Release me now, and I'll ensure your safety and offer sound advice."

"Let *me* out first," Varna the naga hissed from the other side. "You cannot trust a manticore. He'll eat you the moment you open the cage door."

"I have to agree," Tallock the centaur said. "Let either myself or the naga out first. We'll ensure the safety of the rest."

Lightfoot sighed. "It's just like those two to form an alliance and pit themselves against me. But ask yourself, Travis: Who was it that gave you valuable advice at a crucial time? Remember, it was I who discouraged you from showing Mr. Braxton that you were more than just a wyvern. If you had alerted him to your shapeshifting nature while still caged, you might be dead right now. With a simple shake of my head, I saved your life."

Travis stared into the manticore's gaze, torn with indecision. He definitely needed help with this rescue and had to let *someone* out first.

But who?

Chapter 21
Releasing the Prisoners

Travis fingered the master key, undecided.

In the distance, he heard another explosion and wondered just how much damage the escapees were doing to the house. The fact that the noise continued unabated was a good sign, indicating that the armed guards were incapable of stopping the chimera and cherufe.

"You need to choose, boy," Varna warned, unable to still her thick, serpentine coils. She gripped the bars and stuck her face between them, baring her fangs. "But let me tell you this: My imprisonment is not just an attack on me but an insult to my people." Hatred blazed in her eyes. "Humans are a scourge. We naga have tried to keep to ourselves despite the invasion of mankind, but this—this is *intolerable*. When I get out of here, there will be a reckoning, and it will certainly help your cause if you show me you're not like Mr. Braxton and his thugs." She raised her voice. "*Let me out!*"

"Hear, hear," Tallock said.

"You're one to talk, centaur!" a small voice cried out. Travis looked to find the small, blue-skinned elf speaking up for the first time from the opposite side. Her English was good; the majority of elves had picked up the dialect in recent decades. "Centaurs created the virus that tainted this world in the first place. It was because of centaurs that the two Earths ended up unified. It's *your* fault these humans invaded our homes."

"Yes, you two-armed, four-legged half-breed!" the harpy yelled.

"Now, that's hardly fair," Tallock protested. "That episode was a long, long time ago, and it was merely a handful of centaurs, not our entire species. Why, there are always rotten eggs in every—"

"Oh, do be quiet," the mothman grumbled, rising to his feet and turning his glowing red eyes to the centaur. Then he looked at Travis. "Make up your mind, child. But do it now."

Travis looked at the hatred written across the naga's face and decided she might actually be more dangerous than the manticore right now. Maybe he should let the mothman out first, since he seemed so calm and collected.

On the other hand, he felt that Lightfoot might be the most likely to take offense if he 'chose' another over him. And he needed the manticore's protection. *Better to keep your friends close but your enemies closer*, he thought, remembering a saying he'd learnt from his dad.

He'd made his decision.

"You know what I am," Travis told Lightfoot. "I'm going to let you out first—but *don't try anything*, or I'll shift and whack you with my barbed tail. It has as much venom as yours."

Lightfoot tilted his red-furred head. "Don't *try* anything? I can assure you, my friend, that I will leave you well alone. We share a camaraderie, you and I, and once you release me from this cage, I will owe you my life."

Aware of several protests from all around, Travis moved toward the cage door and inserted the key. It turned easily, and the door swung open.

Lightfoot padded out, suddenly much bigger than Travis remembered. If the manticore struck, there would be no time for shifting into wyvern form and retaliating. Travis would simply be on the floor, flopping about helplessly with poison-tipped quills sticking out and waiting for the final death-blow of that scorpion-tail stinger.

Except it was still covered with a metal mesh bag. He relaxed a little.

"I'm much obliged," Lightfoot said with a wink. "Now, let's see about releasing the others."

"I'll start with Varna," Travis said shakily, hurrying across to the naga's cage. *Keep your enemies closer*, he told himself again. Maybe she wouldn't see being released second as a huge slur.

When he unlocked the cage, she shoved the barred door open before he had a chance to open it for her. She slithered past, glaring at him as she went.

"You're welcome," Travis muttered.

Aware that the manticore and naga now faced each other in the middle of the floor like two gladiators preparing for battle, he quickly released the centaur. Tallock clip-clopped out with a sigh of relief.

Travis moved on to the mothman. The red-eyed man with the creepy, insectoid face and long, soft-grey wings stepped out with poise and stood there with his arms folded across his chest. His legs and feet were distinctly buglike, and Travis decided the mothman was easily the creepiest thing he'd ever seen.

Glancing around, he figured the elf was no threat to anyone, and neither were the dryad nor the faun, who had remained silent the entire time. What about the golem? It had no emotions at all, being made of sticks and mud and animated by magic. And then there was the ogre and the troll, and the harpy, and—

The manticore trotted up to him. "Since you have the key to these cages, I suggest you be the one to unlock them. But let's carry out the task in a certain way. First, we'll release those who are of no threat to us or each other."

Travis was impressed that the manticore seemed unconcerned with his scorpion tail being covered. Fretting over it before releasing the other prisoners would have been selfish.

Under his guidance, Travis opened the cages belonging to the dryad, the elf, and the faun. The three timid prisoners barely made a sound as they scuttled over to the huge roller door. The elf flipped the switch, and the door rattled upward. As soon as there was enough clearance, the three of them ducked under and vanished into the flood of daylight.

The harpy squawked for attention, and the minotaur pounded his horns on the bars. But Lightfoot pointed to the golem next. "That creature is harmless. Let it go."

As the eight-foot man-shaped figure strode from the cage, Travis and the others parted and watched it stamp outside without a word.

"A lonely soul," the mothman said quietly. "No home, no family. Only a maker."

Travis warmed to the mothman. Anyone who cared about the well-being of a stick-and-mud creature couldn't be all bad. Meanwhile, the harpy scoffed and mocked from her cage. "You're letting that big bag of dirt go before *me*? It's not even alive! Yank its finger and it'll crumble into a shower of wet soil full of worms. It's useless!"

"Now release the young ogre," Lightfoot said. "And after him, the troll—but not until the ogre is clear, otherwise they'll start brawling."

Both monsters emerged from their cages with a mixture of grunts and growls, the first looking eager and happy to be out, the second pounding its fists like it wanted some payback. Rather than make a dash for freedom, Travis suspected the troll would charge toward the house and bash some heads together. And the ogre probably would, too, if it had the wit to think of it.

"And now the minotaur," the manticore said.

At this, Tallock, Varna, and the mothman sidled away, distancing themselves from the minotaur's cage. Even Lightfoot backed up, and Travis paused with key in hand.

"Hey," he complained. "Don't leave me all alone!"

"You'll be fine," Lightfoot assured him. "Just stand clear as you open the door."

Trembling, Travis unlocked the cage while trying to avoid the minotaur's hostile glare. It huffed and puffed, blowing steam from its nostrils and stamping its foot as it gripped the bars. When Travis pulled the cage door open, it let out a bellow and came thundering out, thrashing its horns from side to side.

Travis hid behind the wide-open cage door as the minotaur came at him. It pressed its deeply lined face to the bars, glaring balefully at him where he cowered, the door squeezing him into a narrow wedge-shaped gap. One hefty shove and Travis would be crushed. Sweat broke out on his forehead, and he held his breath—not entirely by choice—as the bullish monster breathed putrid fumes on him.

Then it swung its head to the side, one of the thick horns *clacking* on the bars. The minotaur stared at Lightfoot and Tallock and the others, and the group retreated a little farther.

A fresh wave of shouts came from outside. The timing couldn't have been better. The mighty bullheaded monster bellowed, swung around, and made a dash for the roller door. Seconds later it was gone.

"Well," Lightfoot said as he padded closer, "he's a mighty fellow, isn't he? I wouldn't like to be on the receiving end of *his* ire."

Only a handful of prisoners remained. When Travis released the griffin, it acted in a similar way to the minotaur, charging out of the cage and looking like it wanted to mow everyone down just to vent some of its frustration and anger. It was enormous; it must have had a rough time confined in such a relatively small cage.

Any other time, Travis would have marveled at the splendor of the griffin's golden coat of fur and feathers, but right now all he could think about was its massive eaglelike beak as it snapped shut several times. He could easily imagine a person swiftly mangled and turned to pulp—assuming they weren't first clawed to pieces by giant talons or claws.

Unlike the minotaur, though, its eyes radiated intelligence. It tilted his head, then let out a rumbling growl and left. Once outside in the sunshine, it spread its huge feathery wings, flapped them a few times as if to shake out some kinks, then launched into the air and was gone.

"Where's it going?" Travis said. Worry gnawed at him again. "I'm not sure this is such a good idea. I mean, the people of Old Earth aren't used to seeing big monsters like that roaming about."

"The people of Old Earth," Lightfoot purred, "have been sighting such creatures for thousands of years. That's how their legends began—a dragon here, a mermaid there, creatures of our land ending up in this one either by accident or with purpose, crossing through portals and scaring the local villages. I believe they can handle themselves."

"Though blood might be shed," Varna said with a faint smile on her face.

That worried Travis further. "We should have—"

"Should have what?" Lightfoot interrupted. "Asked them to form an orderly line so you may lead them back to our world? Or leave them locked up a while longer and risk Mr. Braxton regaining control of his petting zoo?"

Put like that, Travis chewed his lip and reconsidered.

"My turn!" the harpy demanded, sticking her face between the bars, her yellow eyes manic. "Let me out! I won't be any trouble to anyone. I'll just fly away."

Lightfoot nodded to Travis, looking amused. "Let the grimy wretch go. I can no longer stand her stench."

Once released, the harpy almost tumbled from the cage in her hurry to get out. She gave a triumphant screech and said, "Do you need my help with anything? Well, too bad! So long, you miserable bunch!"

And with that, she flapped away, leaving a nasty odor in the air.

The lamia was next. Travis worried about this one. As he opened her cage, she had such a hungry look in her eye that he backed up and prepared to transform. The reptilian cat with the human head circled him, licking her lips, her gaze fixated on him alone.

"Leave," Varna suggested, slithering in front of the lamia. "This is neither the time nor the place for us to turn on each other."

She snarled, then said, "Just a tiny amount of his blood would be sufficient." She licked her lips, still gazing at Travis. "You're so very pure . . ."

"Leave," Varna said again, rearing up high.

Travis wondered who would last longest in an all-out battle—the catlike lamia or the powerful serpentine naga. Both had human heads with fangs, so it would be razor-sharp claws versus bone-crushing coils.

The lamia backed down. She slunk away, looking over her shoulder at Travis as she went. She didn't flinch at the sunlight like the empusa had. Both were vampiric in nature, but they couldn't be more different.

Just a few remained. Travis released the cyclops next. This hulking monster, mostly human in form but twice the height, had to duck as it emerged. It wore rags made out of animal skins and had a humanlike skull for a belt buckle. Barefoot, the cyclops straightened up with a great sigh, stretching and moaning, standing a little taller than the cage itself.

Travis felt anger stirring again. How barbaric, keeping these creatures locked up in cages too small to stand up in! The griffin had been cramped lengthways, its wings unable to spread, but the cyclops hadn't even been able to pace around.

"Go," he said boldly, pointing to the roller door. "You're free. Go stretch your legs."

The cyclops looked down at him with a huge, single eye in the middle of its forehead. There was nothing but smooth skin where its two humans eyes would normally be. Why this species had developed this way was a mystery. It blinked a couple of times, then grinned, showing uneven, blackened teeth.

"Me go," it boomed.

Then it jogged out of the warehouse, reaching up and slamming its fist on the hanging roller door above its head. The punch made a tremendous clang, and the door buckled out of shape.

"Just the cerberus left," Lightfoot said. "Though I'm not certain we should allow it freedom. Those animals are untameable and incapable of reason."

Travis frowned. "Actually, my dad met someone once who had a cerberus for a pet. It's just a three-headed dog."

"Then by all means let it out," the manticore said with an exaggerated bow.

"And anyway, he's not the only one left," Travis added, suddenly nervous about releasing the hound. "The squonk is still here with us."

He pointed, and the ugly critter cowered as everyone turned to look. It burst into tears, letting out a pitiful moaning as it trembled in its corner. Travis wandered closer. It was about the same size and shape as a pig but had orange hair and great folds of fat. With wide-set eyes rather like a pug dog, and enormous ears like a hyena from Old Earth, it couldn't be much uglier. But on top of all that, it was riddled with warts.

"Hey, why are you crying?" he asked softly.

"It's crying because we're all looking at it," Tallock the centaur said. "There are a number of squonks around my shelter in the forest, and they're best left alone."

Alarmed, Travis noticed a puddle spreading slowly from beneath the squonk as tears streamed down its face. It didn't seem possible that anything could cry that much, and although it looked like it had peed itself, he knew that wasn't the case. The squonk was simply dissolving.

He looked away, horrified. "Did I just kill it?"

"I believe we all did by looking at it together," Varna murmured. "We shamed it to death."

"Look away!" Travis demanded. "Maybe it'll be all right."

Trying not to look, Travis fumbled with the key in the lock and opened the cage door. Then he whispered, "You're free, squonk," and led everyone away.

The group moved on to the last cage at the end of the warehouse next to the damaged roller door. The cerberus lay on the floor, but it perked up when they all peered in at it. Three normal-looking dog heads faced their way with ears pricked. The creature was grey-haired and larger than most dogs, its shoulders much broader.

"I suggest we gather in a line and show strength in numbers," Lightfoot said. "Perhaps it won't attack us if we stand our ground together."

And so, with the naga, centaur, mothman, and manticore standing side by side, Travis unlocked the cage and pulled the door open. The cerberus, growling, came out with all its ears flattened and tail down.

Without warning, it leapt toward the manticore, barking its heads off—but Lightfoot's clawed paw swept around and batted the cerberus on one of its noses. The creature yelped and backed off. Every muscle in its body was taut, and it looked like it might pounce again . . . only now it kept glancing toward the sunlight, and Travis knew it was more interested in escape than a savage battle.

Or maybe it was just thinking about going after the humans.

It suddenly darted outside, for a moment looking like an ordinary dog trotting off for a walk—except this one was much bigger, and it had three pairs of ears sticking up. *And three sets of jaws to chew with*, Travis thought with a shudder.

"And now we need to find Mr. Braxton," the manticore growled.

"H-he's not here," Travis said quickly.

The naga hissed and said, "Then we'll kill every last human on the grounds of this hateful place."

Travis swallowed, a terrible feeling rising in his gut.

Chapter 22
Burn, Burn, Burn!

Though eager to escape, some of the prisoners couldn't resist charging up to the mansion to see what was going on. Travis found himself at the rear of the group, no longer in control. Despite their obvious dislike of each other, they had formed a temporary alliance for their short trek up the hill. When the mansion came into sight, the group stopped dead. Travis gasped and backed away.

The fearsome chimera had started fires everywhere and was still busy shooting fireballs through windows. Meanwhile, the cherufe stomped around on the gravel driveway going after any humans foolish enough to stick around and mount a defense. A handler in blue ran away with a blackened, smoking shoulder. A guard fired round after round into the cherufe's back, which it ignored. One of the hunters' Jeeps, which had been burning for a while, exploded with a deafening bang and threw molten projectiles everywhere.

The cerberus dashed past, barking like a pack of dogs. Travis spun around to see another handler yelling in terror and dropping his pole. The man reached for his dart gun but fumbled with the holster, and the cerberus pounced and brought him down.

"Stop!" Travis shouted in desperation.

But his attention was diverted to something worse. Inside the burning house, two women tried to escape the minotaur's wrath by climbing out of a window. They managed to get the window open, and one red-haired woman dropped into the shrubs outside, but then the minotaur stamped into view and fell upon the second woman with his deadly horns.

The redhead in the shrubs sprinted away—and the griffin swooped down out of the sky and snatched her up.

The troll and the ogre appeared around the corner of the house, busy fighting each other, punching and kicking as they tumbled about in the grass. They completely ignored what else was going on and had no interest in a dazed man in blue who staggered past just five feet away.

"We have to stop this!" Travis said to Lightfoot, gripping the manticore's red-furred shoulder.

A pair of blue eyes gazed at him. "This is exactly what these people deserve. They *imprisoned* us. Now we have escaped, and we are here for our vengeance."

"You were just supposed to go home!" Travis yelled. "Not *kill* everyone!"

"Oh, nonsense. I'm sure most of them fled to safety. Only the most foolish remained loyal to their precious Mr. Braxton and stayed behind to fight. And now they're paying the price."

The one-eyed cyclops appeared in an upstairs window. The powerful monster dangled a screaming black-suited man over the sill and grinned happily.

Travis brushed past Lightfoot and approached Varna. "Please help me stop this! You're a naga. Your people live near ours. We're *neighbors*. I know putting you all in cages was wrong, but killing these men and women isn't going to help."

"I disagree," Varna hissed. "It'll help me regain some of my dignity. Meanwhile, the political fallout between humans and everyone else is inevitable now—because humans crossed the line and locked us up in cages like animals!" She leaned forward and bared her fangs. "*Su da falleh.* We're *not* animals."

Travis didn't dare to mention that the squonk actually *was* just an animal. Now was not the time to split hairs. "I get all that, but if you kill these people instead of just running away, then the people who run Old Earth, the Government and all those important people—they'll turn on you and send armies through the portals to hunt you down!"

The cyclops yanked his dangling captive back inside, and further yells came from the room. The guard might have been better off dropped into the shrubs below.

Varna raised an eyebrow at Travis, then looked at Lightfoot. "Have you coached this boy in political matters?"

"I have not," the manticore said with a half-smile. He turned slightly and offered his bagged tail to the centaur. "Tallock, would you mind?"

The centaur looked a little doubtful as he reached out to fiddle with the clasp on the tightly drawn belt holding the chainmail sack in place.

Lightfoot turned his attention back to Varna. "I suspect Tiny Dragon is right to some degree. The humans may feel that our attack here is . . . unjustified."

"Unjustified?" the naga cried incredulously.

Tallock spoke up. "If I were in charge here, I would capture these humans and put them on trial before executing them."

"How tedious," Lightfoot said with a yawn. "What say you, Mothman?"

The mothman had stood unmoving the whole time. Now he lifted his wings. "It's time to leave. The enemy is dealt with. There's nothing more to say on the matter." Instead of leaving, though, he remained where he was and looked around with his glowing red eyes. "Would anyone care to point me in the direction of the nearest portal?"

Another explosion made Travis jump. Smoke billowed from an upstairs window of the mansion. A direct hit. The chimera's goat-head had already started bleating again, readying itself for another fireball while the lion-head roared and the snake-head hissed and spat.

The cherufe, whose trail of blackened footprints crisscrossed the entire driveway and much of the grass on either side, headed toward the front door. It had already been smashed from its hinges, and flames licked at the door frame from within. The cherufe calmly stomped inside, apparently looking for trouble and uncaring of raging fires.

More black smoke poured out of several windows, and a small part of the roof collapsed with a crash. There wouldn't be much left of the mansion if this attack continued.

A cackling from above caused them all to look up. The harpy fluttered by in an ungainly way, screeching, "Yah, *die*, all of you! Burn, burn, burn! Miserable human scum! Where's your boss-man now, eh? Not so rich and powerful anymore, is he?"

"I must be elsewhere," the manticore said suddenly. His scorpion stinger, now freed from the bag, rose and bristled. "Thank you, Tallock."

"Where are you going?" the centaur asked.

"I have unfinished business. I can't say it's been a pleasure meeting all of you, but at least it's been interesting."

With that, the manticore sauntered off.

"Unfinished business?" Varna repeated, frowning. "What does he—Oh. He means to find Mr. Braxton. Well, in that case, his unfinished business is also *my* unfinished business."

With that, she slithered off after Lightfoot, who looked at her with annoyance but said nothing. The odd twosome headed west, which happened to be the right direction, though how they expected to find the elusive Mr. Braxton was a mystery.

Tallock and the mothman didn't seem to share the need for personal revenge on Mr. Braxton. But Travis needed their help. "I have an idea," he said, gears turning in his head. "You wanted to find a portal to get back home to New Earth? So do I. And I know who can help us with that."

Both the centaur and the mothman stared blankly at him. "Who?" Tallock asked.

Travis spread his hand. "Mr. Braxton, obviously. He has the power to open portals, right? That's how he brought a unicorn back. So if we find him, he can open a new portal for us to return to New Earth."

A dozen flaws in his idea sprang to mind, but he pressed on. All the escaped prisoners would eventually find their way back to New Earth, separately or otherwise. What worried him was how much damage some of these irate creatures would do in the meantime. Perhaps if he could open a portal right here near the house and gather all the escapees . . .

"I need you to bring everyone together," he said. "The chimera, the minotaur, the ogre and troll, the cherufe—all of them. And then go find the others—the elf, faun, dryad, cyclops, and the rest. Can you do that? I'll go with Lightfoot and Varna and bring Mr. Braxton back."

He started to head off but found the two of them still staring at him.

"What?" he demanded, knowing he was just a twelve-year-old trying to give orders to a respected centaur and creepy mothman, both of whom were adults. "Look, who rescued you? It was *me*, remember? Now do something for me in return!"

* * *

He had to admit he felt quite good about himself after he'd issued orders to Tallock and the mothman. Of course, they might choose to completely ignore him. Time would tell.

Travis caught up to the manticore and naga shortly after and asked Lightfoot how he intended to find Mr. Braxton.

The manticore looked surprised. "You can't smell him on the wind?"

"What? *Smell* him? No, of course not."

"I pity you humans with your feeble olfactory senses."

Travis sniffed the air, then shook his head. He had to trot to keep pace with the others. "Seriously, you can smell him? From far away? Where is he?"

"His unique odor is wafting quite strongly on an easterly breeze, emanating from a line of trees at the far edge of the meadow. Do you see the small barn that stands near the road on the other side of the fence?"

"Uh, yeah," Travis said, squinting. The barn looked like an old ruin. It might have been part of a farm once; a cluster of small buildings stood farther up the hill beyond the road. "Are you saying you can smell Mr. Braxton from there? He's *inside*?"

Lightfoot nodded sagely. Then he chuckled and said, "It helps that I also saw him in the distance earlier, staggering down the road, right around the time the harpy was cackling from above. He was just a tiny figure, but I kept my eye on him, and he slipped inside the barn."

Travis rolled his eyes. "So you *saw* him, meaning your sense of smell isn't as great as you made out."

"Oh, I can assure you—"

"Enough of this pointless banter!" Varna snapped. *"El tussa de farak.* We are not friends." She glared sideways at the manticore as she slithered along. "I aim to take Mr. Braxton back to my tribe, where we shall make him pay for what he has done to me. And then we'll present what's left of him to the human council and demand recompense for this outrage."

Lightfoot's scorpion tail rose stiffly as he walked, the stinger protruding from the ball of quills. "I think you'll find I intend to devour him, after which there will be nothing left. Ah, look, trees ahead. I must admit, my nerves are on edge after being out in the open for so long."

Now Travis had to break into a jog to keep up. "Before you do *anything*, we need him to do something for us. For all of us, so we can get home without hunting all over the place. He can open a portal like he did near Carter. He must have the know-how and gear to do it."

The manticore suddenly started running, shooting ahead and calling back over his shoulder, "My apologies, Tiny Dragon. I have waited for this moment. Mr. Braxton is mine."

His red-furred feline body crashed through some low hedges and into the next field, and Varna gave an angry hiss and tore after him, her powerful coils thrashing from side to side as she dipped her head and leaned forward. Travis halted, knowing he would never keep up.

At least not in this form.

He transformed and sprang into the air, pumping his wings and soaring over their heads in a matter of seconds. He gave a soft roar and headed for the barn. If he wanted Mr. Braxton's help, he had maybe a couple of minutes at best.

He glanced behind as he glided across the fields. The manticore remained in the lead, but the naga wasn't about to give up. Beyond them, higher on the hill, the mansion stood with black smoke drifting from several windows. Two specks in the sky circled around and around: the harpy and the griffin. Below, dots moved about, mostly escaped prisoners but probably a few handlers and guards as well.

All at once, the entire property—and everyone around it—vanished as the invisibility spell kicked in. But then it flickered. The house and nearby buildings fuzzed in and out of existence.

Maybe the spell is wearing off, Travis thought. *Or maybe it was damaged in the fire.*

He imagined a smoking potion or an enchanted talisman or something equally eccentric set in place by the witch. Perhaps it stood on a table in Mr. Braxton's office, or maybe she had a private room of her own. Either way, something had gone wrong.

He smiled to himself. *Good.*

The barn stood right below, a muddy patch out front revealing a line of sloppy footprints leading inside. He landed by the huge double doors. A smaller door stood open, and he scampered toward it, reverting to human form as he did so. When his clawed wyvern feet shrank, he couldn't help grimacing at the feel of cold mud splashing up onto his ankles.

"Mr. Braxton," he called softly, unwilling to go inside. "You need to come out here. I'm going to fly you away from this place."

After a silence, a faint voice echoed out. "Why should I?"

"Because if you don't, the manticore will be here any second to eat you alive. That's unless the naga gets here first to torture you."

Chapter 23
Bag of Tricks

Mr. Braxton poked his head out of the small, rickety door. He looked around, then scowled. "You're lying."

"Okay, bye then."

Travis turned away and started toward the road.

"Wait," Mr. Braxton said. He limped slowly from the barn, his pant leg flapping open and showing the old car-crash injury. "For all I know, you're here to *take* me to the manticore. Or to something worse. How do I know I'll be safe with you?"

"You don't," Travis said shortly. "But listen."

They both stood in silence, looking through the trees toward the east. The field was just visible beyond, and faint sounds could be heard—the patter of feet, and a continuous scuffling noise, both accompanied by panting. A second later, something moved in the distance, a flash of red.

Mr. Braxton sucked in a breath and took a step backward. "All right, fine, take me away from here."

Travis pursed his lips. "Are you sure? I wouldn't want to—"

"Take me away at once!"

"Before I do, I need to know where to go. Where's the nearest portal? Or can you make us a new one?" Seeing Mr. Braxton's blank expression, he added, "The quicker we all get home, the quicker you get your house back—what's left of it."

The crashing in the woods grew louder, and now *two* figures bobbed about.

Mr. Braxton limped closer to Travis. "My resident witch can make a portal. She has magic rocks in her possession."

Well, duh! Of course she'd be the one to ask about a portal.

"Head for the cabin," Mr. Braxton said urgently. "Madame Frost is on her way to collect me right now, so we'll probably meet halfway if we stick to the road."

"How do you know that?" Travis demanded.

"Because I spoke to one of my men just now."

"Spoke to him how?"

He patted his pocket. "By phone, you idiot!"

Oh.

Travis was tempted to leave Mr. Braxton right here and go off without him, but when he heard the snarl of an approaching manticore and a savage hiss close behind, he knew he couldn't just leave the man to his death.

He transformed, noting with satisfaction how Mr. Braxton's eyes widened in awe. Snatching him up in his claws, Travis lifted off just before Lightfoot came racing through the trees.

"No!" the manticore roared. "Bring him back, Tiny Dragon!"

But Travis flew away, following the main road west.

Unlike the last occasion he'd carried Mr. Braxton in his claws, this time the man seemed unruffled—no complaining or hurling insults, just calm acceptance. After a while, he raised his voice above the rushing wind. "It would appear you saved my life just then. For that, my young friend, I am grateful."

Travis couldn't reply. If he could, he would have said, *I'm not your friend.*

Mr. Braxton hung limply, looking all around with interest. "This really is a remarkable way to travel. I was too frightened earlier, but now things are different. You and I could strike up a spectacular friendship if you'd allow it. What do you say?"

Travis let out a screech, causing the man to flinch.

"Ah, well, should I take that as a no? Look, I understand, really I do. I imprisoned all these wonderful creatures and must be some kind of monster. But you've made me see the error of my ways, and I vow to you now, dangling a hundred feet off the ground, that I shall abandon my hobby and never trap an animal—I mean a *magical creature*—again."

The temptation to drop the smooth-talking rich man was strong.

"But you and I, young man, could be allies in this topsy-turvy world. I'm very wealthy, you know, and I wouldn't hesitate to share that wealth with you, my new shapeshifting friend, if I could engage you in conversation every day and learn more about your divine world—"

He gasped as Travis deliberately loosened his grip for a split-second.

"What are you—My heavens, you nearly dropped me!"

So stop talking, Travis wanted to yell. Instead, he let out a snarl and swooped low as if to drag the man on the road. Now *that* would hurt. He listened with glee as Mr. Braxton began yelling in terror and lifting his feet high to escape a nasty scraping on the concrete.

Chuckling to himself, Travis slowly rose just a little. He remained at that altitude, enjoying how the road sped by below. It gave him a surge of adrenaline to see how fast he could push himself, especially when he tore around bends instead of cutting across them. The double yellow lines in the middle of the road were almost hypnotic.

A horn blared out of nowhere, and he heard the sound of a roaring engine. Puzzled, he scoured the road ahead, seeing nothing. Yet the noise grew louder and louder—

He screeched as a giant blue truck and trailer appeared out of thin air and thundered toward him. One second it wasn't there, the next it was, and he soared upward in a panic. The truck shot past below as Mr. Braxton yelled in terror.

Right behind it came the black limousine and two Jeeps, the convoy on its way back to the house from the cabin. They must have delayed returning for a while, otherwise they would have been home already. As Travis turned and paused in mid-air to watch, the vehicles promptly vanished again, their sounds dwindling.

Travis flapped after them. When he came within a hundred feet or so, the convoy re-appeared, no longer protected by the invisibility spell.

He shot past the vehicles and found a place much farther ahead where he could land in the middle of the road. Once Mr.

Braxton's feet touched the concrete, Travis let go and thumped down next to him.

Again the approaching roars of engines and nothing to see.

Then the truck materialized and came to a juddering halt, its brakes hissing. The limo stayed out of sight, but the Jeeps screeched around the stationary truck and stopped in the grass to one side of the road. The drivers jumped out, guns raised.

Mr. Braxton staggered away from Travis, his pant leg flapping comically. "Don't shoot!" he yelled. "Just—just slow down, everybody."

Madame Frost appeared with two black-suited guards, probably from the limousine at the rear. "Are you all right, Mr. Braxton?" she asked, eyeing Travis warily.

"I'm rattled but alive. Believe it or not, this boy saved my life from an escaped manticore and deranged naga. However, there's a price. He wants to open a portal so my prized exhibits can easily return to their world."

The witch, with two guards close by her side and three hunters nearby, approached with caution. "That would mean all your hard work was for nothing," she said. "Give the word, and we'll bring the wyvern down."

Mr. Braxton sighed and pointed to the horizon. "You can't see my house from here, but it's on fire. Smoke is billowing into the sky."

Travis couldn't help squinting over his shoulder. Sure enough, a faint blackness hung high in the air over the hill where the invisibility spell couldn't reach.

"I suspect this shapeshifter released every last one of the monsters," Mr. Braxton went on, sounding bitter now. "Is that true, boy?"

Travis gave a nod.

Madame Frost threw up her hands in exasperation. "Then it's over. We can't round them up like they're sheep. The chimera alone—and the cherufe—and—" Her eyes widened. "Oh dear. Please tell me you didn't release the basilisk? If you did—"

159

Now Travis shook his head.

"And I'm supposed to open a portal just because this boy said so?" she demanded, glaring at Mr. Braxton. "He let all those dangerous creatures out of their cages, so he can deal with the hazard himself. Let them roam wild in Old Earth. There's a town nearby, lots of rich pickings! Before long, the authorities of this world will be called out, and they'll have no choice but to shoot all the monsters dead."

Travis reverted to human form, unable to bite his tongue any longer. With weapons raised and pointing at him from all around, he stepped between Mr. Braxton and Madame Frost and pointed east. "And then I'll make sure to bring an army of dragons to burn the rest of the house to the ground. My dad's a dragon shapeshifter, you know. He can make that happen—and he will." He turned to Mr. Braxton. "The invisibility spell won't help you anymore."

"The cloak? Ah, yes, it has its limitations."

Madame Frost strode forward, looking like she wanted to use her fists on Travis's face. "You have other houses, Mr. Braxton. We can abandon this one."

"What?" He looked aghast. "That house costs more than you could possibly imagine, my dear. Besides, determined shapeshifters could track me down. Even with cloaks over all of my properties, there's still a paper trail and plenty of people who know me. It would be a matter of time. No, I think it would be best to . . . Hmm."

Mr. Braxton rubbed his chin, looking thoughtful.

Then he snapped his fingers. "Dart guns—bring the boy down—*now!*"

At his command, several weapons made a *phut!* sound, and Travis staggered back with three darts sticking out of his chest.

"Not this again," he moaned, clutching at one and yanking it free.

"And before you grow wings and take off," Madame Frost shouted, "just imagine how poorly you'll fly while unconscious. I suspect you'll come down with a sickening thud."

Travis transformed anyway, and the two black-suited bodyguards rushed to grab Mr. Braxton and hurry him to safety. The rest scattered, and Madame Frost stood there laughing as Travis stumbled away with outspread wings

Fighting a wave of giddiness, he leapt into the air and flapped to the roof of the truck. It took mere seconds to reach the rear end, and then he crashed down on the hood of the limousine. Without hesitation, knowing he had only a short time before he fell unconscious, he whacked the windshield with his barbed tail. It hurt, but the glass shattered. He leaned inside, looking around with slightly blurred vision.

Where is it? Where is it?

Seeing nothing of interest, he jumped down on one side of the long car, staggered unsteadily, and used his tail again to smash the side window. He barely felt anything this time, perhaps because the drug was numbing him, dulling his pain.

Madame Frost yelled at him, and he heard her stamping alongside the truck with hunters at her heels.

Where is it? Where—

He sucked in a breath. There! He grabbed a partly open leather bag that lay on the seat. Something glowed within, bright and orange, exactly what he was looking for. This was Madame Frost's bag of tricks, and he wanted it.

His muscles felt leaden. Groaning, he snatched up the bag in his jaws, backed away from the vehicle, and launched into the air with every last ounce of strength—just as the witch and a bunch of men came running up. They let off round after round of real bullets, and he felt a couple zing through his wings and one strike his tail. Grimacing, he tore away into the sky, ignoring Madame Frost's screams of outrage.

A few hundred feet up, dizziness swept through him again. He stopped climbing into the sky and dove instead, trying to get low as quickly as possible while he was still conscious.

With the bag gripped in his jaws, two of the three darts still sticking out of his chest, small holes through his wings, and a bullet lodged in the flesh of his wyvern tail, Travis figured he'd probably earned his right to tell his friends he'd been on his first real shapeshifter mission. Of course, first he had to make it through alive.

He glanced behind, half expecting there to be no sign of the truck, limo, or Jeeps. They'd probably blinked out of existence by now. But to his surprise, they were still parked by the roadside in plain sight. He was far away by now, and Madame Frost's invisibility spell should have kicked in . . . only it hadn't.

Tumbling through the air, he crash-landed through some trees and broke a multitude of branches on his way down. He hit the ground and flattened bushes, sending leaves and twigs and clumps of soil scattering in all directions. When he skidded to a halt, he let go of the precious bag and stared at it without moving. His wings felt like they were bent out of shape, and his right leg hurt. And so did his ribs. In fact, pretty much everything throbbed.

But he had the bag of tricks. Four egg-shaped geo-rocks spilled out, each small enough to fit in the palm of a human hand, the magic within glowing strongly. When he woke from his latest drug-induced slumber, he would use one to create a portal and send everyone home.

He focused on other things that had fallen from the bag: a selection of small bottles filled with liquids, a well-thumbed journal stuffed with notes and held shut with a band of elastic, and a small ragdoll with pins stuck in the eyes.

The ragdoll mesmerized him. As he drifted off to sleep, disjointed thoughts fluttered through his mind. One of them made sense, and he smiled to himself.

The ragdoll. The pins in the eyes.

He had Madame Frost's invisibility spell.

Chapter 24
Beacon of Light

He woke to darkness. Or near-darkness, anyway.

He groaned and sat up. He was in human form, and his right leg still hurt. He touched his chest, thinking his ribs felt tender and bruised. The darts had fallen out when he'd reverted back, and he picked them up with disgust.

One good thing about being shot through the webbing of his wings and a bullet lodging in his tail was that none of those injuries lasted long. In human form, he had neither the webbing nor the tail, so those wounds were simply gone.

Or were they? He rubbed the base of his back, just off center, and winced. It seemed the flesh of his tail had somehow migrated to his torso as he'd changed back. It made some kind of twisted sense; after all, every ounce of his transformed body had to come from somewhere, and return there afterward. And he had a similar pain under the bicep of his right arm. He'd been shot at least three times through the webbing, but one must have nicked his flesh, and that wound remained.

Another transformation or two would fix the injuries. He'd have to suffer through until then.

The geo-rocks glowed stronger than ever in the subdued light. He stuffed them back into the bag and piled the small bottles on top, then carefully placed the ragdoll in there, too. The pins were still intact. He figured they needed to be there for the spell to continue working.

He gingerly climbed to his feet and, with the bag held tightly in one hand, headed out of the woods, noting that the sun was descending on the horizon.

Dusk was good. Dusk was better than midnight or the early hours of the next morning. He'd been asleep the whole day, but he'd expected to be out for longer. Where was everybody now?

Had they gotten impatient and dispersed across Old Earth, seeking their own way home?

As he trudged into the open to get his bearings, he thought about his mom and dad. They had to be worried sick, knowing he'd been snared by hunters and taken off to some unknown place. His dad must have gone nuts after losing the truck in broad daylight. Even if he'd figured out it was protected by an invisibility spell, it would have been too late to do anything about it. The hunters had escaped and could be anywhere.

Travis planned to finish this mission in the next hour or so. He would find his fellow prisoners, set off a geo-rock to create a portal, send everyone through it, and then go find the witch's other ragdoll invisibility spell at the house to make sure it was destroyed. With the house revealed for his dad to find—

Well, he didn't know what would happen to Mr. Braxton and Madame Frost. That was up to the adults.

He realized that the mansion was already perfectly visible on the hilltop, along with the warehouses and other small buildings. The invisibility spell had been flickering the last time he'd been here. The ragdoll must have burned in the fire, taking the spell with it.

One less thing to do, then.

All was quiet. A little *too* quiet. Had the staff abandoned the place and left it to the monsters? Or had Mr. Braxton and the witch taken it back?

Travis almost hid the bag under a bush. It would be foolish to walk around with it until he knew who was waiting for him. But he really didn't feel like coming back for it, either. He was tired and wanted to get this done. Besides, the invisibility spell contained within would work to his advantage for a while. *Not much good at close range, though.*

He gripped the bag tightly. Just let anyone try to take it from him.

As the sky darkened to purple, Travis arrived at the warehouse and peered in through the massive roller door. Nobody was around.

He headed over to the smaller building where he'd released the chimera and others. It was silent and dark.

The house, then, he thought as he started to leave.

Just then, a woman pounced on him and threw him down. She leapt onto his aching, bruised chest, her hair suddenly igniting and shooting flames into the darkness. "What kind of demon appears out of nowhere like that?" she snarled.

"Stop!" Travis yelled. "It's me!"

The empusa vampire paused with her fangs bared, inches from his throat. Then she eased back and tilted her head, her flames dying. "Oh."

"Invisibility spell in the bag," he explained, gritting his teeth. "Please get off me. I think my ribs are broken."

Actually, he was pretty sure they weren't, but if he won her sympathy, then all the better.

She patted his chest gently. "I can fix that. I can give you some of my blood and heal your wounds. Would you like that?"

"I'm a shapeshifter. I can heal myself, thanks."

She scowled. "Then get up and stop complaining." With that, she sprang at least eight feet in the air and landed neatly. "I've had a nap, and now it's time to leave this place. I'm hungry. Who can I eat around here?"

Travis climbed to his feet and picked up the bag. "Where are the others? Have you seen anyone? Or have you been here the whole time?"

"The last one," she said flippantly, looking at the bag he held. "What do you have in there?"

"Our ticket home. Want to help me? I could do with your fiery hair. Come with me up to the house."

He walked past her and headed outside. Behind him, she said, "Oh, aren't we the bossy one? Just a wee lad, too."

She came after him, though. Travis grinned. This was the second time he'd ordered adults around and gotten away with it. Did that make him a natural leader? Or a little brat?

He led the way to the mansion. It stood as silent as the warehouses, a distinct burnt smell lingering in the air. Almost all the windows had been smashed, there were severe black streaks up the exterior walls, and part of the roof had collapsed. Despite all that, the place remained mostly intact, so somebody must have put the flames out. The fire department?

"Where is everyone?" he wondered aloud.

The empusa vampire eased up behind him. "I smell people. *Things.*"

"Things?"

She stood there with tiny flames flickering in her hair.

Travis dropped the bag and stepped aside. "I'm going to transform. I'm just going to be a wyvern for a minute and make a lot of noise, okay? Don't go away. Just stand there and make your fire as bright as possible, like a beacon."

Without waiting for an answer, he transformed and spread his wings. As she recoiled in obvious shock, her hair brightened considerably, flames licking high.

Yeah, just like that, he thought.

He screeched for all he was worth, his wyvern vocals echoing off the mansion walls and escaping into the evening sky. If he didn't get a response from this, then maybe he'd move the beacon to the roof.

Where *was* everyone? Why was nobody—?

Then he realized he was being a fool. He snatched the witch's ragdoll out of the bag and shook it in his hand. No wonder nobody was coming; an invisibility spell surrounded him! He pulled out the pins, threw the doll away, and resumed his screeching.

Shortly after, a figure appeared in the mansion's grand doorway. It was the cherufe, a hulking rock figure who stomped out onto the lawn. And then another figure appeared, a shaggy troll looking a little beaten up, limping badly and holding one of its shoulders. Travis wondered how the ogre had fared.

To his delight, more and more of his fellow prisoners arrived—the chimera, thankfully calm and silent, the minotaur grunting and huffing, the cyclops, the lamia . . . and from the far end of the massive lawn where neatly trimmed hedges grew, the faun, elf, and dryad.

Just when Travis thought that was all of them, the ogre shoved its head out of a second-story window and groaned. It then climbed over the sill and half fell into the shrubbery below. The troll scowled and emitted a long, low growl.

Suddenly, overhead, the griffin flew in, followed by a cackling harpy. The first landed on the torn-up gravel driveway, but the harpy stayed airborne and yelled, "About time you showed up, you sad little excuse for a dragon!"

"Nice to see you, too!" Travis shouted back, his voice coming out as a curious bark.

And finally, one last group appeared out of the shadows: the manticore, the naga, the centaur, the mothman, and— standing very tall in the background—the golem.

They were all here. All except two.

He reverted to human form. "No unicorn?" he shouted.

"Unfortunately not," Lightfoot said in his fluty voice as he trotted up.

"And the squonk?"

Everybody who understood looked at one another. It was the naga who replied. "Do we care?"

"Of course we do! That poor thing is one of us!"

The mothman's red eyes were crazy-bright in the darkness. "Perhaps it's still in its cage. If indeed it hasn't dissolved into tears."

Travis clicked his tongue. He hadn't seen nor heard it, but he hadn't checked the cage either. What if it had been there the whole time, cowering from him? Or what if it was in fact dead? "Would someone please go fetch it?"

At first nobody offered, but then the ogre started shuffling toward the warehouse.

Surprised, Travis smiled and said, "Thank you, ogre."

Lightfoot padded closer. "We have unfinished business, Tiny Dragon. You stole my meal from me. Where is Mr. Braxton?"

"He's . . ." Travis stopped, thinking hard. Where would he be right now? Somewhere far away if he had any sense. But he didn't want to antagonize the manticore. "He's around. Let's deal with him later. First, we need to create a portal."

"And then I get to eat some humans," the empusa vampire said, licking her lips.

The lamia smiled. "And I get to eat dragon-boy here."

Travis glared at her. "Really? Are you still going on about that? I'm not your dinner, so get over it."

Trying to ignore the sense of dread he felt at so many hungry eyes pointing his way, he reached for the bag and took out a geo-rock. *I'm surrounded by killers*, he thought. *I can't imagine this many different species have been this close before, walking around free without trying to attack each other.*

In fact, it had to be the first such grouping in the history of New Earth. Of *both* Earths. Tonight, and tonight only, there was a sense of camaraderie, a truce that would surely never be repeated. These creatures hadn't just come together as freed prisoners, they were here on the lawn to return home. Or most were. Some had other things on their mind—like a certain Mr. Braxton and his staff for dinner.

"Haven't you all eaten plenty already?" he asked nervously, wondering just how many had been killed here tonight.

Tallock clicked his tongue noisily and swished his tail. "These savages have enjoyed chasing the humans around while I put out all the fires."

"*You* put out the fires?"

The centaur drew himself up. "If I hadn't, then I suspect the smoke would have drawn the rescue services—those red vehicles with water hoses and so on."

"Fire trucks," Travis confirmed. "So nobody's been here? No police?"

He had to assume the invisibility spell had worked intermittently all afternoon. *Maybe* passers-by had seen plumes of smoke in the air, but they would have been unable to pinpoint its source. And certainly none of Mr. Braxton's employees would have called the fire department and given away the secret poaching operation.

"We can't stick around here long," Travis said, holding up a geo-rock. "We need to leave."

The glowing energy rocks were literally as old as the hills. For thousands of years, ancient tribes had cracked them open and caused explosions for one reason or another—sacrificial ceremonies, absorbing the released power, letting evil spirits out, and such. The explosion was small but powerful, and usually the person cracking it open with a hammer or rock died for their cause.

The opening of a portal was purely a side effect, and a random one at that. In fact, it had taken a very long time to find a connection between portals and geo-rocks.

"We need to break this rock open," Travis said, holding the thing high above his head. "But it will explode, so we need to do it safely. Maybe . . . maybe I'll drop it."

"And then?" Varna the naga said, looking puzzled. "How does the portal open?"

"It just does," Tallock the centaur said. "Trust me, I know everything there is to know about—"

"Quiet," Lightfoot snarled. He turned to Travis. "Do it. Send everyone home."

"Let *me* do it!" the harpy screeched, swooping in out of nowhere. She must have been circling in the darkness above, listening intently.

She snatched the geo-rock from Travis's outstretched hand and made off with it. As everybody roared at her, the harpy cackled and halted in mid-air, flapping her wings to hover in one place.

"You'd better stand back," she called. "Here it comes!"

Everybody scooted away as the geo-rock came hurtling down from the sky. It smacked the gravel driveway—and exploded.

Along with the deafening boom that echoed through the evening sky came a crackling static charge and a display of blue sparks that lit up the entire driveway and front of the house. Travis felt his hair stand on end, and goose bumps rose on his forearms.

It faded slowly, leaving nothing but a smoldering, black-streaked crater in the gravel.

Chapter 25
The Portal

Travis would never get over how much explosive energy geo-rocks contained. Now it had escaped. In theory, it had created a smoky portal.

"So where is it?" Varna hissed, breaking the dead silence.

"When the energy escapes from the rock," Travis said, repeating what his parents had told him, "it forms into a portal, but not always close by. It might be a ways off."

"How far off?" Lightfoot demanded.

"Up to a quarter-mile," Travis said.

Tallock cleared his throat. "He's right. Cracked open like this, the energy is not focused and takes a second or two to coalesce. In that short amount of time, the planet rotates a little to the east and moves on through space while the energy remains at a fixed point in space. It's rather interesting if you take the time—"

"Where's the portal?" the manticore said stiffly.

"Well, you see, it's almost impossible to figure out unless you're a scientist of the highest order, and unfortunately I'm just a simple architect . . ."

"Simple is correct," Lightfoot muttered.

". . . But it will be close, in one direction or another."

Though everybody present looked left and right, turning to see if the portal was floating a couple of feet above the ground some distance away, Travis knew that "one direction or another" could also mean up and down. The centaur clearly knew it, but there was no sense in riling everyone up.

It could be a hundred feet in the air, Travis thought. *Or a hundred feet underground.*

It didn't help that portals were a smoky black substance, like inky clouds pulsing in and out. With the evening sky already pretty dark, it was going to be hard to find the way home.

"Spread out!" Travis called. "It's gotta be around somewhere. Make sure to look up as well. It might be, uh, high off the ground."

Varna let out a huff of irritation. "Then how will I pass through this portal? I don't have the luxury of wings."

Lightfoot chuckled, his mood inexplicably improved now. "I'm sure the harpy would be delighted to give you a lift into the sky."

"I'll take my chances with the griffin," Varna muttered as she slithered away.

The search was on. Most of the group knew what a portal looked like—how could they not?—but a few weren't sure and had to be informed. But it wasn't long before everyone had split up to look, wandering off in different directions, plunging through trees and heading out into the nearest fields.

Travis went to check the warehouses and smaller outbuildings. It would be almost comical, with a strong sense of irony, if the portal had popped up inside one of the cages. It wasn't there, though. He came across the one remaining unopened cage containing the basilisk and stopped to think about how to handle it.

He could probably carry the box. As long as the deadly reptile stayed inside, everything should be all right. But he'd deal with it later once everyone had stepped through the portal into New Earth. He alone would come back to fetch the box.

He returned to the mansion, which seemed deserted now. He heard the beating of wings overhead and spotted the griffin's golden form shooting past. Inside the house, he saw a glow of light and fixated on it until he saw the empusa vampire move past a window with her hair on fire. The giggle of a female—either the elf or dryad—indicated that not all were taking the search seriously. And a sudden scuffling and growling noise from the far side of the lawn sounded like the ogre and troll had resumed their endless wrestling.

Finally, someone let out a screech. Then the harpy tore around in the night sky screaming with triumph. "I found it! It's here! I saw it first!"

"Where?" Travis shouted.

"Hanging over the house!" The harpy squealed with laughter. "Oh, it's going to be fun watching all you wingless wonders scramble about on the roof trying to get to it!"

Travis sighed and went to take a look for himself. The harpy was right; it hung there several feet above the apex at one end of the mansion's roof, silent and black, barely visible. It would be a very difficult and dangerous task for most of the group to reach it—and then there was the other side to consider. It probably hung at the same height in New Earth, only there wouldn't be a mansion under it.

Lots of ferrying around, Travis thought as he studied the portal suspended in the night sky. It breathed in and out, about fifteen feet wide. Quite a big one, though by no means the biggest. "So it's above the roof," he said when the news had spread and everyone was back together. "But that's okay. Some of us have wings and can give the others a ride."

The griffin and mothman obligingly spread their wings. The harpy shrank down, clearly not interested in helping anybody. Travis looked at the empusa vampire. She could certainly jump, but she couldn't fly.

"Let's start with someone small, like the elf," Travis suggested. "Then move on to the bigger ones like the cherufe and chimera."

The harpy changed her mind. "I'm not taking—All right, I'll take the elf. Gotta do my bit, right?"

The elf looked nervous. She shuffled her feet and glancing around like she wanted to run off and find her own way home.

The harpy spread her wings and launched, flapping about in a rather ungainly fashion .with her talons flexing. She clamped down on the blue-skinned elf's shoulders and shot into the air. Everyone watched as they plunged through the portal and vanished.

173

About half a minute later, the harpy returned empty-handed. She cackled as she came down to land. "I dumped her from a great height on the jagged rocks below. Who's next?"

A concerned murmur started up. Lightfoot padded up to Travis and nudged him with his red-furred shoulder. "Go take a look, Tiny Dragon. Nobody trusts the word of a harpy."

Feeling a little proud that he, apparently, was someone people could trust, Travis transformed again and sprang into the air. Any wounds he'd suffered had vanished with all these shifts back and forth, but he also felt a little drained. Was he simply tired? Or was his shapeshifting power wearing thin?

He flew through the portal, thinking he should have done this earlier. After a moment of blacker-than-black darkness, he shot out the other side and found himself in the same geographical landscape, the top of a hillside below and fields for miles around. The moon was unchanged, though there were fewer clouds about, and the stars seemed brighter.

Below, the elf was already skedaddling. She looked perfectly fine, not a jagged rock in sight. No doubt she had a long journey home, and if she wanted to get away from the manticore and others before the truce ended, then Travis wasn't about to stop her.

He swooped back through the portal and descended on the driveway. He didn't bother changing back again, just nodded at the manticore as he flapped around over the bizarre group of New Earthers. *Who's next?* he wanted to say. He picked on the minotaur, moving slowly but purposefully toward it, his claws outstretched.

The minotaur bellowed and swiped at him, and he backed off. Even though Varna tried to calm the minotaur and tell it what Travis was doing, he decided to try someone else. How about the lamia? The quicker she was through the portal the better.

Unlike the minotaur, she seemed eager for his assistance and turned to face him with a beckoning look on her face. But as he came in low to grab her, her expression turned to one of hunger and malice, and she leapt at him with her fangs bared. She packed a lot of power in that lithe feline body, and she caught him off balance and knocked him to the ground, pinning his wings so he couldn't fly away. He caught a glimpse of her wild eyes right before she bit into his neck.

She only had a human mouth, but the bite was sharp and painful even through his tough reptilian skin. Panicked, he rolled and thrashed, and she rolled with him, clinging with her fangs in his neck, her claws latched tight, and her serpentine tail coiled around both ankles. He felt a dreadful draining sensation, and he screeched and flailed in a desperate attempt to get loose.

It took all his effort to get his clawed feet free of her tail and into a good enough position to shove her off. Even then, it seemed those fangs remained attached until the very end.

Abruptly, she let go, rolled sideways, and pounced again. But this time Travis brought his tail around and clubbed her on the side of the head. She stumbled sideways and fell, then got back up, staggered, and fell again. She shook her head and blinked rapidly.

Her lower jaw was covered in Travis's blood. Appalled, he wished he could reach up to check his neck wound. Was it still bleeding? He backed off, huffing and panting, flexing his wings to check them over.

To his disgust, he realized nobody had come to his aid. Lightfoot, Tallock, Varna, the mothman—all of them stood watching. It looked like they'd at least taken a few steps forward, but now they seemed rooted to the spot.

The lamia sighed and wiped her chin with one paw. "Delicious," she purred. "It doesn't matter that you're in wyvern form at the moment. There's a young, innocent boy underneath, and he tastes wonderful."

Travis growled.

"You've broken the truce," the manticore snarled then, trotting forward. "You attacked our rescuer. You should leave. You're on your own."

With a smile, the lamia slunk away into the darkness.

Climbing to his feet and spreading his wings, Travis glared around at everyone. He wanted to scream, "Why didn't you help me?" Instead, he let out a furious screech, and everyone present recoiled, even the massive griffin.

Lightfoot sat and curled his tail around. "You fought well, Tiny Dragon. However, I'm surprised you didn't use your poison-tipped stinger."

"We were afraid to get close," Tallock explained, shifting on his hooves. "One scratch from your tail would be fatal. I'm sure you understand."

Travis turned away, still angry. Whether they made a good point or not, some help would have been appreciated. Even a shout of protest might have made a difference. *I'm done with them all*, he thought. *So much for trying to help. They can find their own way through the portal now.*

The group seemed to pick up on his sulky behavior and left him alone. Travis watched, annoyed, as the griffin was enlisted to carry the heavy minotaur through the portal. The bullheaded giant struggled ineffectually as the golden-winged creature hoisted it up to the roof and through the smoky cloud.

"I expect *you'd* like to be on your way now, yes?" Lightfoot said to Varna. "I'm sure the mothman would be delighted to carry—"

She interrupted with a scornful tone. "And leave you to claim Mr. Braxton as your prize? I think not. He's mine. Rather than simply devour him, he will serve a much greater purpose—as a powerful message to humankind that we naga are done with their overbearing presence in our world. I believe I will set the basilisk loose on the grounds of this property, ready to greet any who return here. And then I'll present Mr. Braxton's head on a post to the human councils—"

"I thought you wanted to torture him," Tallock said. "Now you want his head on a post?"

"We will torture him first. Then his head on a post."

"What an amusing image," Lightfoot said with a chuckle. "It would look rather like a cold, dead naga after rigor mortis has set in. But what you say is impossible, because there will be nothing left of Mr. Braxton before this night is out."

"Here comes the griffin already," the mothman rumbled. "Who's next? Tallock?"

The centaur looked horrified. "I will find my own way, thank you. There are other portals. I'm certain the authorities will be more than happy to let me through." He smiled. "I shall consider my journey home a pilgrimage of sorts. It will be enlightening to travel among Old Earthers."

When the griffin had chosen its next doubtful cargo, the cherufe, Travis watched with interest. The molten-rock creature had to calm down so it was cool enough to be clutched by talons and claws. Even so, clearly it was a colossal weight, and the griffin struggled to lift off.

Travis sighed and shook his wings open. It was time to go.

Lightfoot fixed his blue eyes on him. "Are you leaving us, Tiny Dragon? Then I'll say goodbye. And thank you. You released us from this prison, and for that we are all grateful. I assume you are heading home?"

Travis shook his head.

After a moment, the manticore's puzzled expression cleared. "Ah. You're going after the unicorn."

Now Travis nodded. *But before I go,* he thought, *I need to grab the basilisk before Varna lets it loose.*

Without another glance back, he flew straight to the smaller of the two warehouses and landed by the door. He reverted to human form, hurried inside, and flipped on the lights. Half a minute later, he left with a metal box under his arm. The box itself was light, but the basilisk felt like a brick at one end.

Keeping his eyes ahead rather than look down at any of the breathing holes drilled into the sides, he switched back to his wyvern form and gripped the box in his claws. He took off toward the mansion. Only a few of the group remained on the gravel driveway now, including the cyclops, golem, mothman, and centaur. The manticore and naga were busy arguing, and Travis huffed with impatience. *Just get along*, he thought as he shot through the portal too fast for them to spot him clutching his prize. He doubted Varna would be very happy to know he'd stolen her weapon.

Once in New Earth, he spotted the griffin dropping the cyclops nearby. Travis flew on, knowing he needed to get far away from all the escapees. He passed over the chimera and shuddered. Yes, *far* away.

When he eventually landed in some ferns, he put the box down and stepped back.

His clumsy wing-claws wouldn't be able to unlock it; he needed his human fingers, which again meant shifting. How many transformations did he have left? He still worried it was possible to wear out his talent. Luckily his neck wound had healed already, but what if he suddenly found he couldn't change anymore? His shapeshifting ability could desert him at the worst possible time.

He reverted to human form and, with trembling fingers, unlocked the box at arm's length. The moment the little door fell open, he leapt away to what he considered a safe distance. But *was* it safe? He had no idea how far-reaching a basilisk's deadly glare could be. If he'd thought to bring the goggles and gloves along with the box, maybe he would have been safer, assuming those things actually worked.

Despite his cold terror of the small creature, he couldn't help glancing back over his shoulder to see what a basilisk looked like. When he saw something—a tiny shape, perhaps a foot—emerge from the box, he gave a shudder, quickly transformed, and shot away into the sky.

As he flew back to the smoky-black portal, he wondered how many people or creatures in New Earth would run across that basilisk in the days and weeks to come. They would most likely die . . . and it would be his fault, because *he* returned the deadly lizard to the wild when he could have—

Could have what? Killed it? Left it locked in the box for someone else to open? Allowed Varna the naga to use it?

It was a wild creature, and as deadly as it was, it had a right to live.

He spotted the weird golem creature standing perfectly still while the griffin flew away. The last passenger?

Travis tore through the portal. Back on the grounds of the mansion, only the mothman and centaur remained, talking quietly. The manticore and naga had probably dashed off in a race to find Mr. Braxton. Travis doubted Varna could track the man down, but he wasn't so sure about Lightfoot. And where the manticore went, she would follow. Mr. Braxton's days were numbered.

Travis put it aside. *Find the unicorn*, he thought. *That's my job now. Find her and bring her home.*

Chapter 26
Sweet and Innocent

He flew around all night. First he headed back to the cabin, then followed the direction the unicorn had bolted when it had escaped Mr. Braxton's grasp. He circled around for ages, trying to spot a flighty equine in the dark woods.

He rested his wings and napped a while, then expanded his search, flying low over open fields and occasional cottages until he reached a built-up community, at which point he turned around. She wouldn't have gone anywhere near such a busy area.

He found a small group of horses in a paddock near a house, but the unicorn was not with them. She would have stood out next to the greys and browns of the other equines, especially being so big. Disappointed, he flew on, trying to figure out how far she could have galloped since her escape. The truth was, she could literally be anywhere by now.

Exhausted, he returned to the lake and landed on the shore not too far from Mr. Braxton's cabin. The eastern sky had an orange tint to it. He'd been searching all night! It was dawn already, exactly twenty-four hours since he'd last seen the unicorn. Why was he still here? He had to concede defeat and head home. This was a job for Ellie the shapeshifter.

Except first he had to figure out where home was. That alone was a challenge. He would have to fly back through the portal into New Earth, then head for miles in one direction or another trying to spot something recognizable.

Right now, though, he needed to rest his wings again.

"Hello," a whispered voice said.

Travis jumped in surprise. When he looked to his left, he spotted Nitwit crouching under his wing.

"How did you find me?" he said, realizing this was probably his most oft-asked question where his impish friend was concerned.

She didn't answer, though he knew she could understand him despite his wyvern form. Instead, she pointed toward Mr. Braxton's cabin farther along the shore. A light now shone from a window when it had been dark just moments ago.

Travis sucked in a breath. "Someone's there!" he exclaimed.

Nitwit put a finger to her lips. "Keep your voice down. It's so quiet on the lake, they might hear you. And you should be human again. You stand out like a bright orange-and-blue thing in the dark."

He shuffled backward until the trees shielded him, then reverted to his human form. Shivering in the cool morning air, he rubbed his arms and stamped a few times, envious of his tiny friend's thick clothing and leather boots. "So is that Mr. Braxton at the cabin?"

She frowned. "Don't know. But the unicorn . . ." She clawed at her throat, looking like she was about to choke.

"Are you okay?"

After a moment she gasped, "But the unicorn's here, too!"

"What?" He blinked and looked around. "Where?"

"Just through the trees," she croaked. Rubbing her throat, she added, "Sorry. It's getting easier, but . . ."

"What *are* you talking about?" he murmured, distracted. He saw no sign of the unicorn. Or did he? He squinted, seeing a smudge of white through the gloom. His heart started beating fast. His search was over, but now he had to figure out a way to get the unicorn home before Mr. Braxton emerged from his cabin. "Wait—is she tied up? Did he catch her again?"

"Why don't you go find out?"

Muttering to himself, he crept through the trees as quietly as possible. His impish friend followed close behind.

Travis looked back at her. "Seriously," he whispered, "how *do* you keep finding me? I'm hidden away out here in the woods, and you just show up?"

"I told you, we have a connection. I can read your thoughts and sense where you are."

She seemed out of sorts. Or perhaps worried. "What's wrong?"

She shook her head.

Clearly she had no intention of opening up right now. "How many of Mr. Braxton's men are in there? What about the witch?"

Nitwit flicked her long, black hair and sighed. "I have no idea. It was hard enough telling you about the unicorn." She gingerly rubbed her throat.

He frowned. "*What* was hard enough? Look, you must have seen *something* useful before you found me."

"I can try to guess, if you like."

He let out a grumpy huff. "You're a waste of space."

"It's not my fault," she muttered.

Her comment irked him. Not her fault? Was it also not her fault she'd failed to grab a key off the rack in the warehouse when she'd had the chance? And that she hadn't gone for help?

Before he could respond, he glimpsed movement ahead and froze. "She's right there," he hissed.

"That's what I said," she replied. "And now you just need to tame her and ride out of here."

He swung around and gaped. She looked deadly serious.

The unicorn grazed peacefully on the lakefront where the grass was lush, just thirty or forty feet through the trees. The rising sun's rays caused misty vapors to rise from the calm water. Mr. Braxton's cabin stood out in the early-morning light, a dark square in the mist. She'd returned to the very spot she'd escaped from a day earlier. Whereas before she'd been in a drugged stupor, now she was fully alert and ready to bolt at the slightest noise.

"She's lost," Nitwit said softly. "She can't find her herd, so she's back where she started, hoping the others will find her."

"But it's *dangerous* here."

"Not at the moment. It's quiet. Now's your chance."

Travis almost laughed aloud at the idea of taming a unicorn and riding her away. Nobody *ever* got close to unicorns, not even the gentlest of people—nobody except little boys and girls, whose sweet innocence was said to calm the beasts. Travis was twelve. Did he count as a sweet and innocent boy?

He scoffed and drew himself up. *Innocent, maybe. But sweet? Yeah, right.*

What was it he'd read? That the flighty equines had a sixth sense and somehow knew when a heart was pure? Only then would they let anyone approach. This was probably true of most animals to some extent, but unicorns didn't just have a vague *feeling* about a person's intentions, they actually *knew*.

"Nitwit," Travis whispered, not taking his eyes off the unicorn. "I think maybe *you* should approach her."

"Me? Not a chance."

"You're younger than me, right?" Actually, he had no idea if that was true, but she seemed at least a year or two younger. "You're much nicer than me, anyway. More innocent and sweet-natured. You have a better chance of taming her than I do."

"No," she said. "I'm not as innocent as you think."

"Just walk up very slowly and talk in a soothing voice."

"How about *you* walk up very slowly and talk in a soothing voice?"

Travis licked his lips. "I don't think I can."

"Then just go home. You don't have to be here."

Travis was torn. Mr. Braxton could step outside of his cabin any moment and go for a quick stroll. What if he or his men got off a lucky shot and brought the unicorn down?

He sighed. *This is nuts*, he thought as he edged forward out of the trees. *She'll stab me through the heart if I'm not careful.*

He moved softly toward the unicorn, his hands at his sides, feeling tiny against the massive equine. "Hello," he called in a low, soothing voice. "You're so pretty. Can I come talk to you?"

The magical animal jerked and swung her head around. Spotting him, she snorted and stamped a couple of times, her eyes widening and nostrils flaring.

Please don't bolt, Travis thought.

To his surprise, she held her ground and watched as he edged nearer. "You're so tall," he murmured, not caring what he said as long as he kept his voice calm and soothing. "Much bigger than horses, and much faster as well, I'll bet." He closed the gap to twenty feet, and still the unicorn waited, her gaze fixed on him, her tail swishing from side to side.

I'm really doing it, he thought in surprise. *I'm taming the unicorn.*

Taming was probably a stretch. Certainly befriending her, though.

Then, as Travis came within six feet, the unicorn spooked. She reared up with a frantic whinny and kicked her forelegs in the air, causing him to stumble backward and land in a patch of mud. The frightened equine came down hard and thrust her horn forward.

Travis sucked in a breath, and he heard Nitwit scream from the trees behind.

The horn jabbed at him—but stopped just as it touched his chest. For a second, it seemed like time itself had frozen. The unicorn waited, her long, spiral horn poised. One simple thrust and he would be skewered. He held his breath, hands planted in the mud behind, sweat dribbling down his forehead.

Then the unicorn eased backward and tossed her head, letting out a gentle nicker as if to reassure him that everything was okay.

Hardly able to believe he was still alive, Travis slowly climbed to his feet and rubbed his chest. His silky shirt was unscathed, but it certainly would have been pierced if the unicorn had wanted to dispatch him. Instead, it seemed he'd passed some kind of test. Or perhaps the unicorn had seen him as no threat whatsoever and shown mercy.

He began talking again, as softly as before. The unicorn simply watched without reacting.

Gradually, the tension ebbed. He edged close enough to stand under the huge equine's chin, then reached up and offered his hand. The unicorn sniffed and pushed her nose against his outstretched fingers. He almost fell over with the force of the contact, but he stood his ground and stroked her long nose, noting that his muddy hands left streaks on her gleaming white hair.

After that, the unicorn seemed utterly relaxed around him, even going back to some grazing. Travis turned and called to Nitwit. "Come on out."

But she remained in the bushes, partially hidden.

He moved about in a more assured way as if he and the unicorn were old friends, talking excitedly about crossing through a portal and finding a way home. *Easier said than done,* he thought. *It's one thing being around a unicorn, but leading her somewhere like a docile horse is something else.*

He didn't have a lot of experience with horses of any kind. He knew this one was easily more than twenty hands tall, which was usually about as big as horses got, except this unicorn was fairly petite and slender compared to others of her kind. He'd never ridden a horse, so that idea was out. He needed to figure out how to persuade her to *follow* him . . .

"I can't believe this," he said, patting her on the side of her neck. "I don't know *anyone* that's gotten this close to a real unicorn before."

There came a shout from the trees, and a man's voice said, "There, look! The unicorn! I *told* you I heard something!"

Travis swung around.

Mr. Braxton came hobbling into view with the witch at his side and an entourage of armed guards behind. Travis groaned inwardly. All the amazing progress he'd made was now going to be wasted. "You'd better go," he called to Nitwit, glancing over his shoulder.

But she'd already disappeared.

The unicorn began to get agitated, and he wanted to tell her to stay still and calm, except that he didn't want Mr. Braxton getting hold of her . . . so he murmured, "You need to go as well. Go on, get away from here."

She stamped around as Mr. Braxton's five armed men spread out, raising their handguns.

"Go!" Travis urged.

Still she waited, her gaze darting this way and that.

"What are you waiting for?" he yelled in her face.

Instead of bolting, the unicorn pushed past and sent him sprawling. He righted himself just in time to see her thundering from one armed man to the next, tossing her head as she galloped in a tight circle, letting out snort after snort. The only other sounds were gasps and cries from the men, and these were accompanied by crimson droplets in the air as the unicorn's horn darkened with blood.

A few seconds later, the unicorn came trotting back. She stamped past Travis where he knelt in the long grass and turned to face the only remaining adults—Mr. Braxton and the witch, both of whom stood absolutely still with shock.

Travis slowly climbed to his feet, stunned at the sight of five men lying dead on the ground with blood-soaked chests. He tore his gaze away and, fighting the urge to throw up, faced Mr. Braxton. "It's a *really* bad idea to pull a gun on a unicorn."

Mr. Braxton shook himself from his paralysis. His face darkened. "You trained her to murder my staff—not to mention that you destroyed my home and released a small fortune back into the wild. You've ruined *everything*, boy. But you won't leave these woods. Do you understand me? You're done." He glanced sideways at the startled witch. "Do it, Madame Frost."

The old but surprisingly spry woman whipped her hand out of a pocket in her robe, and a shower of pale dust flew toward Travis and the unicorn. It sprinkled across the grass and dissolved. Some of it got into his smart shoes. She reached for another handful and flung it all around her and Mr. Braxton.

Travis waited, his heart thumping, ready to transform and fly away if anything weird happened. But nothing did. Instead, he and the unicorn stood there facing Mr. Braxton and the witch, just thirty feet apart, in absolute silence.

Mr. Braxton smiled. "Now the doll, Madame Frost."

She smiled also, pulling a ragdoll from another pocket. It was very similar to the one he'd seen earlier, perhaps even the same one rescued from the house. Either way, all he could think about was the invisibility spell. What possible use could that be right now?

"What are you doing?" he finally asked, perplexed. "What's the dust for? Why are you—?"

A vicious pain jabbed into his shoulder and lanced down his arm and chest. He yelled out and threw himself backward, certain he'd been shot. Lying in the grass and writhing in agony, he was dimly aware of the unicorn rearing up and stamping around him—and then she launched herself toward Mr. Braxton and the witch with her head down and horn jutting.

But she didn't get far. She jerked and reeled backward, whinnying and dancing as though her hooves were on fire. She dashed off into the trees, circled around, and came back from another direction, her head once more lowered as if to skewer Mr. Braxton and Madame Frost from behind.

Again, she halted and reeled backward, dancing about and crashing through shrubs. She almost staggered into the lake in her effort to retreat from whatever burned her hooves.

Travis sat up, the pain in his shoulder suddenly gone. He rubbed it vigorously, still expecting to see blood pour out any second now. But he saw nothing, not even a tear in his silky clothing.

"Hit him again," Mr. Braxton said.

The two of them stood there unconcerned that a unicorn danced around behind them. Madame Frost raised the ragdoll in one hand and a long pin in the other. With a manic grin, she jabbed the pin into the doll.

Travis screamed.

Chapter 27
Death in the Woods

The excruciating pain in his thigh hurt so bad that Travis thought his leg had been lopped off above the knee. He felt for it just to confirm it was still there, his eyes too watery to see anything more than a blur.

"Stop, stop," Mr. Braxton urged.

As suddenly as the pain had hit him, it evaporated, leaving Travis to sit up gasping and clutching his leg.

"Now, this is your very last chance," the man said, raising his cane and pointing it at Travis. "Madame Frost can stick pins in her voodoo doll all day long, but the thing about this dark magic is that it doesn't kill. Not directly, anyway. You might go into shock or suffer a heart attack I suppose, but these injuries you're suffering are purely in your head. Not pleasant, though, eh?"

Travis looked for the unicorn. She'd backed off and was watching from a shadowed section of the woods where the morning sunlight couldn't reach.

"And she can't help you," Mr. Braxton said, jerking his thumb toward the equine. "This corpse powder Madame Frost sprinkled all around is harmless to you and I, young Travis, but deadly poison to a pure-hearted unicorn. Or so I heard. Looks like it works, wouldn't you agree?"

He laughed, gesturing with his cane toward the wary unicorn. Next to him, Madame Frost had the long pin poised above the ragdoll, ready to jab.

Travis swallowed, fearful of that terrible pin. "What do you want from me?"

"What I wanted twenty-four hours ago," Mr. Braxton snapped. "I want you to persuade that unicorn—which you seem to be great friends with all of a sudden—to heal my leg so

I may walk again without the constant aches and this blasted cane."

"She'll never do it," Travis said.

"She might if it means saving you from torture."

"Unicorns can't heal injuries! They only heal sickness."

"And you know that for a fact, do you?" Mr. Braxton pursed his lips, thinking for a second. "You see, Madame Frost here isn't so sure. Perhaps the problem is that the unicorn is of no help *while she's alive*. It's well known that those magical horns, when cut off and ground into dust, possess great healing power for sickness *and* injuries—so perhaps the solution here is to put the unicorn to sleep and cut off its horn."

"No!" Travis shouted. He wasn't sure exactly how this man intended to catch the wary unicorn, especially with five dead men lying in the grass all around, but he wouldn't put it past him to have something up his sleeve.

"Yes," Mr. Braxton said firmly. "Look, I'll be frank with you. I have no control over that beast. I'm surprised she's still here, loitering in the trees around the lake. She could have run far away and found some lovely fields to graze in, but she stayed by the water. Madame Frost thinks she's confused without her herd, and so she stays. I don't believe unicorns are very smart."

He tapped his head and rolled his eyes.

"However," he went on, "what I *can* control is you, dear boy. Or rather, Madame Frost can. She's waiting for you to transform and try to fly away. Do you think you can do so before she has time to jab that needle into you again?"

Travis eyed the witch closely. She looked a little too eager to plunge the pin into the ragdoll. And he had no doubt that her hand would be far quicker than his ability to transform and fly out of range.

Mr. Braxton smiled again. "And so I will offer you a simple choice, Travis. Take away my pain, and I'll take away yours. Ask your unicorn friend to heal my leg, and Madame Frost will throw away this doll and you can be on your way. Your town is just thirty miles south of here, young man. Flying through the sky, I expect you'll make it home in twenty minutes. Think about it!"

Thirty miles, Travis thought with interest. *That's nothing for a wyvern!*

But he knew Mr. Braxton would never let him leave.

Movement in the bushes somewhere beyond the man caught Travis's attention. He glanced toward the unicorn, noting that she was looking in that direction as well. She nickered and trotted a few paces away, distancing herself from whatever was sneaking through the woods.

"I don't think there's any point in fixing your leg," Travis said slowly, his heart thumping.

Mr. Braxton frowned. "Why?"

"Because you won't be needing it much longer."

The man's frown deepened. "What's he talking about, Madame Frost?"

She spoke softly. "I don't know. But I could stick him again and—"

Travis heard the tiniest of *thwipp!* sounds. The witch dropped the ragdoll and slapped at her neck, and Mr. Braxton jumped and brushed at his shoulder. Both of them looked surprised, but then they looked at one another with strange expressions on their faces.

"What's happening?" he murmured.

Madame Frost held up something thin: a delicate needle. For a second, she looked quite comical—a voodoo pin clutched between the finger and thumb of one hand, and a manticore quill in the other.

Then she sagged to her knees.

Mr. Braxton's cane slipped from his grasp, and he staggered sideways and fell awkwardly. "Oh!" he said. "What the—"

Travis leapt to his feet and pounced on the ragdoll before the witch could grab it again. He backed up, turned, and threw it into the lake.

When he returned his attention to his enemies, he noticed the red-furred manticore slipping through the bushes toward them with barely a sound.

"Hello, Tiny Dragon," Lightfoot purred. "Thank you for keeping Mr. Braxton distracted. And I see you found the unicorn. Good for you. I hope you see to it that she makes it back home."

"I will," Travis said, a sense of renewed dread seeping into him. "Are you here to, um . . . ?"

"Devour Mr. Braxton? Absolutely."

Travis felt sick. With five dead guards and one soon-to-be dead millionaire, he wished he was far away from this place. "Look, what I said about him not needing his leg—"

"Was delightfully apt," Lightfoot said. He sat by a groaning Mr. Braxton and raised his scorpion stinger. "Now go, young man, and take the unicorn with you. Steer clear of the Braxton residence; the place is overrun by the authorities now. The mothman took flight just in time, but Varna is behind me somewhere. Hurry along now. I'll clean up here."

"You'll clean up—?" Travis started, then broke off.

There was nothing more to be said. But still, letting the manticore kill and eat Mr. Braxton was horrible. Travis could stop him if he wanted to. While the man was diabolical, being subjected to a savage execution just didn't seem right. It wasn't the way civilized people acted. It wasn't the way humans acted.

Travis drew himself up. "I can't let you do it."

Lightfoot sighed and lowered his stinger. "Go, boy, or our friendship and truce will be at a sudden end—as will you."

"I'm sorry, but I have to stop you."

With that decisive statement, Travis transformed and leapt forward with his wings spread and his tail whipping around—

And fell flat on his face.

He looked up, confused. He stared at his hands—his *human* hands—and wondered where his wings were. "What the heck?" he demanded.

As he climbed to his knees, he tried to transform again and failed.

A terrible sense of loss swept over him. Was that it? He was done with his wyvern shapeshifting? His immune system had finally overcome his ability and rendered him fully human once more?

"What's wrong with you, Tiny Dragon?" Lightfoot asked.

"Stop calling me that. I'm not a dragon anymore."

The manticore grinned, showing three rows of needlelike teeth. "Can it be that you find yourself unable to transform? If so, I heartily recommend you leave here at once. Leave me to my feast and take the unicorn home. Let us part on good terms, young human."

Defeated, Travis stood and brushed himself down. He gritted his teeth and trudged away from the clearing, trying not to look at the dead guard he stepped over. As he left, he glimpsed Madame Frost's pleading look where she lay on her back alongside her employer.

"What about her?" he asked nervously.

Lightfoot raised his stinger over Mr. Braxton. "I haven't decided. Truthfully, I'm rather full after last night's banquet. And I want to save all my venom for *this* one." He placed a heavy paw on the man's chest and elicited a moan of terror. "I may let her go after I'm done. Or, better still, hand her over to the naga, who will be along shortly if she hasn't lost the trail. Or perhaps the lamia; I believe she's been tracking me also, and she's a whole lot better at it. You do *not* want to run into her. Now go, boy!"

Travis shuddered. He had no choice but to sidle away. *Well, there was no way I could win that fight without being a wyvern*, he told himself. *A manticore versus an ordinary, puny, twelve-year-old human? I had no chance.*

He picked his way through the trees to where the unicorn stood. She seemed eager to see him, and it amazed him that she'd gone from a completely wild and flighty animal to what some might consider a loyal friend. He patted her on the nose and led her away, heading back toward the cabin.

As they walked, he heard a terrible howl of anguish somewhere behind him. He gritted his teeth and muttered, "Come on. Nothing left for us here."

* * *

When the enormous truck showed through the trees ahead, Travis realized Mr. Braxton might have more men waiting around, though he doubted it. The same five men had been with him since yesterday, along with their two Jeeps. But what about the truck driver? Assuming he was an extra, he would still be loitering in the area, now on high alert after Mr. Braxton's wailing.

And if the lamia were on the trail, she would hear that wailing, too.

Travis gave the cabin a wide berth, leading the unicorn around to pick up the lane farther out. He walked slowly, threading his way around dead branches and clumps of ferns, taking his time so that his faithful friend wouldn't lag behind. She stuck with him.

She's like a puppy dog, glad she's found someone to trust to take her away from this place.

He arrived at the main road and followed it out of the woods, sighing with relief that he hadn't run into any blood-thirsty reptilian cats. When the trees ended, he moved onto the grass bank alongside an overgrown hedge and a rickety fence.

A car approached from behind just then, and he jerked around in fright—but it was just a red family car. It sped past, but then the driver jammed on the brakes and screeched to a halt. He leaned out and shouted, "Is that a *unicorn?*"

The passenger door opened, and a woman emerged. "Oh, my gosh! It really is!"

The rear doors opened and three children spilled out, exclaiming and jumping up and down in excitement.

A little annoyed they were making so much noise, Travis looked out across the open fields and decided he and the unicorn would be far safer if they could just get through the hedge. And things would go a lot faster if she would allow him to ride her. "Any chance I can sit on your back?" he whispered.

She didn't react, but she seemed a little anxious about the rapidly approaching family of five. The Old Earthers had no qualms about overstepping boundaries; they just hurried toward Travis as though it were perfectly all right to come up and pet his equine friend without asking permission. *Bet they'll think twice when they see the blood on her horn.*

Travis looked for a way to mount her. Without stirrups, it seemed impossible for someone his size to climb up onto such a huge beast. But the fence might help.

"This way," he urged.

The family angled toward them, intent on cutting them off before they reached the fence. Travis shouted, "Stay back! She might attack! You can't just walk up to her like that. You'll scare her."

The mom immediately slowed the three children and told them to wait. The dad, however, was either completely deaf or willfully ignorant. He beamed and picked up his pace, his hand held out.

"Hi, I'm David, great to meet you. Are you from New Earth? You look like you are. Man, I've never seen a unicorn up close like this before. She's a beauty, right? How many hands, would you say? Twenty-one? Twenty-two? She's bigger than a Shire."

Travis quickly climbed the fence and waved the unicorn closer. She obliged, but she seemed restless.

"You need to stay back!" he shouted again. "See the blood on her horn? She just killed someone with that."

This stopped the man dead in his tracks. "*Killed* someone?"

"Some*thing*," Travis lied. "She killed an animal. Skewered it!"

His words distracted the man just long enough for Travis to throw himself onto the unicorn's broad back. She was much wider than he could have imagined. He moved forward and tentatively grabbed her mane, wondering if it would hurt if he clung on tight.

"Another thing," he called, suddenly worried. "Get your kids back in the car. I think there's a lamia around here somewhere."

The entire family looked blank.

"A silver, scaly vampire cat that craves the blood of kids," he clarified.

That seemed to do the trick. The mother hustled the kids back to the car.

"Let's go," Travis whispered, and made some tongue-clicking sounds he'd heard his granddad make when riding horses on the farm. He nudged with his heels, but he wasn't sure exactly how to—

The unicorn spun around, danced in place, then galloped along the grassy bank past the driver, past the mom and her excited children, and past the red car that sat abandoned in the road.

We're off, he thought jubilantly.

Travis clung tight to the unicorn's back as she picked up speed. Behind him, the family let out cries of disappointment, which infuriated him. This wasn't a petting zoo!

The roadside hedge petered out after a while, and the fence with it. Then the unicorn veered into the field and stampeded across the grass with Travis holding on for dear life. His teeth chattered with the constant bumping, and he knew he was going to be sore later. But for now, he forced himself to see past his fears about falling off and instead take in the scenery as he rushed along.

Thirty miles south, he thought, remembering what Mr. Braxton had said about the town of Carter. Riding through Old Earth was risky, likely to draw far more attention than he wanted, but he had no choice until he ran across a random portal. He looked around, trying to get his bearings. *The sun's behind me, and it rises in the east, which means I'm facing west, and so south is . . .* "That way!" he yelled, pointing to the left.

He knew a few basic things about steering horses, but without reins, he had only his voice and his legs to guide her with. He was pretty certain the unicorn didn't understand his shouted directions, and since he could barely straddle the massive animal, he doubted any of his leg cues would be noticed. As far as he could remember, he was supposed to apply pressure with his right knee to make the animal go left . . . or did that only apply to trained horses? Didn't untrained horses lean *toward* pressure points rather than away? Didn't they have to be taught to yield to the rider's cues? Or was he overthinking it? Besides, this was a unicorn, not a horse. Who knew what went on in their heads!

But with a bit of trial and error, shouting things like "Left! LEFT!" while frantically pointing and clumsily digging in with his knee, he got the two of them heading roughly south.

A thirty-mile journey for a creature that reportedly galloped at least sixty miles per hour? He grinned. He could be home in half an hour if he didn't get hopelessly lost.

Of course, first he had to find a portal.

Chapter 28
Riding the Unicorn

They made excellent progress across the open fields, but that didn't last long. Travis and his faithful mare came to an Old Earth town and ended up on private property. A surprised old man dropped his watering can and watched as Travis's unicorn hurdled a fence, tore around the side of a one-story house with a tin roof, and out into the road.

A car screeched to a halt, and Travis grimaced, urging the unicorn across to the other side of the road and through someone else's yard. He'd rather stay the course and skip around hurdles than gallop down a main road with cars and trucks everywhere.

Staying the course was kind of a joke, though. Keeping the sun to his left hardly qualified as accurate navigation. But this was Old Earth. It wasn't like he could ask anyone in the neighborhood where Carter was.

He hurdled more fences and galloped across several more yards, startling homeowners. He had a brief respite from staring eyes when his ride plunged through a small wooded area, but then they emerged in an even more built-up area with criss-crossing roads, a lot of traffic, and stores everywhere. He'd had classes in Old Earth once—Alter-Education, as it was called—and had grown accustomed to the concrete jungle, but it was still an ugly place.

Horns tooted, people cried out in amazement, and a police siren sounded as Travis steered his unicorn off the busy road and along the pavement, dangerously close to shopfronts.

"Not good," he muttered. "And I can't even see the sun now."

The way ahead looked worse, a set of traffic lights and four lanes of traffic. He frantically kneed the unicorn on the left-hand side and only just managed to help her understand that he wanted to turn into an alley. Though she moved slowly now, obviously not happy, she seemed pleased to be heading away from the crowds.

The alley was narrow and empty, but it let out into a huge parking lot. Apart from a cluster of parked cars at one end, presumably near a huge store, the lot was pretty much deserted, a flat expanse of space surrounded by buildings. It gave room to breathe and think. Travis allowed the unicorn to trot about in a random direction while he studied the various openings he could take.

And then a police car appeared, moving steadily toward him from the alley he'd used. It gave a single *whoop!* of its siren and went quiet, for which Travis was grateful. That noisy thing would likely scare his ride out from under him.

The police car eased to a stop some distance away, and two cops got out. One spoke into a handheld device, and his voice was amplified from the roof of the car. "Hold it there, sonny. Are you lost? Let us help."

Travis sighed with relief. With the unicorn continually trotting around in circles, he cupped his hands and shouted, "I'm trying to get home. Do you know Carter? It's somewhere south of here in New Earth."

The cops conferred for a second. Then: "Sure we know it. Carter's the only New Earth town in the area. It's the reason this city has grown so much in the past twenty years. But to get there, first you need to cross over. Can you control that animal?"

Travis couldn't help noticing the dried blood on the unicorn's spiral horn as she turned her head. "Uh, sort of."

"If you can follow us, I can lead you to a portal."

"Great!" Travis shouted, nodding. "I'll follow."

And follow he did. The police car pulled away and headed for one of the openings at the side of the parking lot. Travis urged his unicorn after it, and though she resisted at first, she finally relented and trotted after the slow-moving vehicle.

It seemed the cops had called ahead, because when they emerged back onto the main road, more police cars had arrived and blocked off several lanes, their blue lights flashing. With the traffic at a standstill and amazed drivers poking their heads out of windows, the friendly cops led Travis two blocks and then turned left. There, a sign pointed into a courtyard: PORTAL.

Travis had seen these official portal checkpoints before. Every town had one or more, and each required proper documentation—proof of identity, reason for visiting, and so on. It was hard to believe there had once been thousands of portals floating about across the land, free for anyone to pop from one land to another. Most had been closed now; the rest were heavily regulated.

The general public had been cleared back, and now a dozen policemen and other officials stood around, keeping their distance but making it clear this situation was out of the ordinary. In the background, Travis saw plenty of people taking pictures and recording the action with their phones while he tried hard to calm his nervous ride.

"Easy, girl," he whispered, leaning forward. "They're just trying to get us home. See the portal? The smoky black thing? Once we're through there, we'll be out in the fields again."

First, though, the portal had to be opened. Thick, super-strength glass walls surrounded it. The booth was hexagonal, some thirty feet across and twenty feet high. It had three doors around its perimeter, but the entire front section was hinged to allow official vehicles through. The spherical portal floated within, almost filling the space, pulsing in an out, tendrils of black smoke leaking off its surface. It was partially embedded in the concrete, making it ideal to drive through. Its location in the city, substantial size, and convenient positioning were all reasons this particular portal had been saved while others in the area had been closed down a decade ago.

The police officer Travis had spoken to earlier walked closer, taking his time and keeping an eye on the troubled unicorn. "I'm Officer Draydon. I'm going to need some information, son. Do you have any papers? ID?"

"I'm Travis Franklin. I don't have anything on me. I was kidnapped and taken to Old Earth, and I escaped and just want to go home."

The cop looked surprised. "Kidnapped? By whom?"

"A man called Mr. Braxton. He lives in a big mansion north of here."

Now Officer Draydon looked puzzled. "Wait—you mean Ted Braxton, the millionaire? Over in Littlehampton?"

Travis shrugged.

"The limping tycoon, as he's known?" the cop said.

"Yes! That's the guy."

A murmur spread through the crowd of police officers. Office Draydon raised an eyebrow. "That might explain something. His house caught fire last night. The flames were extinguished by the time police arrived early this morning, but there's lots of damage, much of it unexplained, like he was attacked by fireballs. Mr. Braxton is nowhere to be found. And we found seven bodies."

Travis swallowed. He knew a few had been killed, and now of course there were another five skewered in the woods near the cabin.

"Got a lot of reports about that place this morning. We tracked down other members of Mr. Braxton's staff, and they refused to talk. Littlehampton police said they looked pretty flustered, though, like something really bad went down. Care to shed any light on it?"

The unicorn snorted impatiently and stamped about.

"I'll tell you everything," Travis said. "But first, I have to get her home before she panics. If she throws me off . . ."

He left his words hanging, and Officer Draydon eyed the bloody spiral horn. "Did she kill someone?"

"She's a wild animal. If someone tried to trap a chimera, they'd get burned, right? If they went up against a manticore, they'd get eaten. And if they tried to hunt a unicorn, they'd probably get stabbed. Mr. Braxton's people were lucky. Did you see all those cages out in the warehouse? There's still a manticore about somewhere, and a lamia, and they're both dangerous."

He left it at that. The truth would come out—including that the unicorn had stabbed five armed men right in front of him, and Mr. Braxton had been devoured by a manticore—but right now he just wanted to get home. And get his nervous ride back to the herd.

The officer nodded. "Okay. So you're Travis Franklin from Carter? Make sure you go straight home. The police will be there waiting. We need to know *everything*, all right?"

After that, the huge glass doors hissed open, giving access to the smoky portal that floated within. With police standing all around, and crowds of spectators spread out around the courtyard, Travis urged the unicorn forward. "Go, go! Through the portal. Go on, girl, it's safe."

It took a few more seconds of gentle persuasion and digging in with his knees, but then she whinnied and bolted forward. She didn't *need* to leap into the portal, but she did anyway.

After a moment of blackness and curious silence, they shot out into a new landscape. The city buildings and police and concrete ground were gone, replaced by long grass for miles around. Even the air smelled better, the cool breeze invigorating.

With an excited nicker, the unicorn pranced around and bobbed her head as if to say, "Yes! This is more like it!" Travis couldn't help laughing, and he patted her with affection.

"I'm going to miss you. Anyway, do you know where we are now? I don't recognize the place, but you're used to running about in the wild. Can you find your herd? Hopefully it's still just outside Carter. Find your herd, girl. And then I can go home."

She took off galloping. Whether she sensed which way to go or was just excited to be moving again, she still headed south, and that was good enough for now.

Travis clung on tight and let out a whoop of joy.

"I should give you a name," he said when a familiar landscape finally opened up ahead. "Or maybe not. If I name you, that'll be like owning you. And I don't own you at all."

Indeed, the unicorn had obviously picked up the scent of her herd—or maybe she just magically knew where it grazed. Her direction all the way home had been straight as far as the terrain would allow. Not only that, as a cluster of tiny white specks in a distant field came into view, it appeared she'd made a beeline for the herd's *current location*, not where they'd been two days ago.

"It's your horn, isn't?" Travis said. "My mom—"

He stopped there. Telling her that his mom had a unicorn's severed horn stashed in a kitchen drawer at home didn't seem appropriate. In fact, it had once been owned by his grandmother, known to the village as Dotty Dr. Porter. She'd gotten it from Lady Simone, who had found it among a pile of bones several years earlier.

The horn had come in useful on the foggy island where Travis's parents and all their friends had grown up. Lady Simone had told Dr. Porter, "Blow into it when the children start to change. You won't hear anything, but I will, and I'll come as soon as I'm able." Or words to that effect. And she had done, nearly thirteen years later when the classmates had started showing signs of their first transformations.

"I bet you've been blowing your horn the whole time," Travis said. "Well, maybe not *blowing* it, because it's sticking out of your forehead, but something like that. Has your herd been answering?"

The unicorn didn't respond. She just galloped tirelessly onward, steam blasting from her nostrils. Her body felt almost unbearably hot now, and Travis couldn't wait to dismount and head home.

As they approached the herd, Travis spent a moment figuring out where he was, Yes, Carter couldn't be more than a ten-minute walk from here. He could see trails of chimney smoke over the trees. If he could fly, he would be home in thirty seconds. As it was, he'd have to trudge home on sore, weary legs.

His unicorn halted well away from the herd. She just stopped dead and waited, letting out little snorts and turning her head so she could see him. He took the hint and climbed down, almost crying out in pain at the cramps in his legs. He sat in the grass and groaned, stretching his toes and bending his knees.

"I'm fine," he told the unicorn, who stood looking down at him. "Go on."

She stepped closer and lowered her head. The spiral horn, still coated with dry blood, came within inches of his face and poised there. He looked at it in surprise. She waited, gazing at him through pink lashes.

"Uh," he said, reaching up. "What am I supposed to . . . ?"

He touched the tip of the horn—and in that brief split-second, all his aches and pains went away, and he felt renewed. Not only that, but the dry blood on the horn cracked and turned to dust, then drifted into the wind, leaving nothing but clean, gleaming ivory. A few muddy patches on her nose, which Travis had accidentally smeared there earlier back at the lake, seemed to fade away. Now she stood white and pure, positively glowing.

With that, she whinnied and galloped away to join her herd.

"Whoa," Travis muttered, watching as other unicorns welcomed her back. They all looked alike, all gleaming white, and pretty soon he wasn't sure which was his friend.

He stood up, feeling fit and ready for anything. The unicorn's magic had been subtle and unexpected, a sort of cleansing of them both. And if she could heal aches and pains, could she have healed Mr. Braxton's injury after all? It didn't really matter; he wasn't worthy of her magic.

He headed home.

Chapter 29
A Hero's Return

Travis passed the illegal portal. Centaurs were on site to close it down with their weird contraption, a set of mirrorlike screens stood up all around the portal and one very large dead geo-rock. He paused to watch.

In the old days, the only way to close a portal was to bury it or block it. In some cases, another portal opened right next to it would cancel it out, but that only worked in close quarters, like in a narrow tunnel. Walking through one would immediately entail walking through the second, bringing the traveler back to the exact same place.

But centaurs had been properly closing them for a very long time now. Travis didn't understand the science; he just knew the result. He could see the top edge of the pulsing portal from where he stood, and at that moment it vanished with a curious popping sound, its energy channeled into the dead geo-rock inside the downward-tilted mirrored screens. A centaur moved a screen aside, reached into the small clearing to pick up the geo-rock, and held it at arm's length. It glowed brightly now.

When Travis finally spotted his home at the base of the hills, he noticed a crowd outside and picked up his pace, wondering who was there and why. The police from Old Earth? He couldn't tell from this distance.

It was a while before anyone saw him, but when they did, a full-sized dragon suddenly shot upward. It approached at a rapid pace and descended. After thumping down, the dragon morphed into Travis's dad and shouted, "There you are! Are you all right?"

Before he had chance to answer, Travis was scooped up in his dad's arms and hugged tightly. Over his shoulder, his mom buzzed at top speed across the grass, her faerie wings a blur.

"Travis!" she cried, and her hug was even tighter. She even lifted him off the ground for a few seconds, her wings humming. When she put him down again, she glared at him with furious but moist eyes. "We've been *worried sick* about you. *Never* take off like that again."

"I was kidnapped!" he protested.

"I understand that," his mom said, gripping his shoulders, "but you literally took off and left us behind after you transformed the first time, and then you decided to tangle with dangerous hunters—and that was when you were kidnapped. So yes, you were kidnapped, but you wouldn't have been if you'd stopped to think for one second!"

She was out of breath by the time she finished. But she was right.

"Sorry, Mom. Sorry, Dad. I just saw them taking the unicorn, and I . . ." He trailed off as a mob came hurrying across the field. "Who are they?"

His dad shook his head and smiled. "Don't need them now that you're home. I was just organizing a team to come get you. We got word that a big house in Old Earth had caught fire and something weird had been going on. Remember what Simone told us? About what the soothsayer saw in his vision? We *knew* you were at that burning house. So I was about to head up there with a group of friends and tear the place apart looking for you."

The group of friends turned out to be exactly that—Lady Simone plus all his mom and dad's shapeshifter buddies, the ones they'd grown up with on the foggy island. Though they were all in human form, Travis identified them one by one as they approached: Robbie the ogre, Lauren the harpy, Darcy the dryad, Dewey the centaur, Thomas the manticore, Emily the naga . . . and finally Fenton, who Lady Simone insisted on calling an ouroboros even though everyone else simply called him a giant lizard monster.

They didn't look like much in human form, just a bunch of thirty-somethings like his parents, but what a team! Travis felt proud to know that these fearsome friends had gathered on his behalf, to find and save him.

Only they hadn't needed to. Travis had saved himself and everyone else.

They all crowded around and made a lot of noise asking questions while clapping him on the shoulder, patting his back, and ruffling his hair. They pulled and pushed him in every direction until, finally, his mom said loudly, "All right, give him room to breath! Fenton, don't you dare mess with his hair again. You know he hates that."

"Why else would I do it?" the big man retorted, looking puzzled.

Lady Simone cleared her throat. "Travis," she said, and everyone hushed. "I understand you transformed successfully and took off flying straight away. That's wonderful."

"It was easy," he said. Then he pursed his lips and reconsidered. "Well, flying was easy. It was easier to fly than stay on the ground. I felt like a kite! But the transforming part was hard. It took me a while to learn how to do it at will."

"Me too," his dad grumbled.

"But you figured it out," his mom said with a smile.

"Now, shush," the dark-haired woman named Emily said. "Travis, tell us *everything* that happened." She'd always been bossy. *Typical naga*, Travis thought.

With everyone listening, he launched into his tale. He'd expected to go home first, tidy up, get something to eat, then sit down to a table with a rapt audience and spend three hours recounting his tale. Instead, he summed everything up in about ten minutes.

"Don't feel too bad about Mr. Braxton and his staff," Lady Simone said. "I know that's probably going to weigh on you."

"You think?" Travis's mom said, looking irritated. She kissed him on the forehead. "I'm so sorry you had to deal with that. Mr. Braxton brought it all upon himself, though. He must have known that trapping deadly animals was going to backfire one day—but worse, he trapped deadly and *intelligent* beings, ones who would harbor a grudge and make it their mission to come after him. If it wasn't the manticore, it would have been the naga—or the mothman—or even the centaur."

"I like how his house was torched," Thomas snickered. "Go chimera and cherufe. And I hope Lightfoot enjoyed his meal."

"Stop it, Thomas," Darcy scolded. "This isn't funny. People died at that house."

"Only because they were idiotic enough to stay behind."

Funny, Travis thought. *That's pretty much what Lightfoot said.* "I hope everyone makes it home okay," he said, thinking of the variety of creatures he'd released from the cages. Some were smart adults, able to figure out where they'd ended up. A few probably wouldn't even care. Others, though . . . "The ogre was so young, like a small kid. He might be lost!"

Robbie shook his head. "No way. Ogres have a fantastic sense of direction. I guarantee he'll have no trouble finding his way. The troll, though? They're hopeless. But he'll probably follow the ogre. I bet they're wrestling right now!"

This elicited a few chuckles, and Travis felt better.

"Well, anyway," Darcy said with sigh. "Hal, Abigail—you have a hero for a son."

"I'm not a hero," Travis protested. "I just escaped, that's all. And only because I was finally able to shapeshift. Now I've used up my ability."

Everyone looked uncomfortable. His dad shook his head and looked a little annoyed—not at Travis but at the unfairness of it all.

Lady Simone narrowed her eyes. "Are you saying you think you used up your ability by shifting too many times?"

Travis nodded. "Yeah. I used it up. I wanted to change one last time, but I couldn't. It just stopped working. Maybe if I'm more careful next time and spread it out over weeks—"

The blond-haired woman held up her hand and cut him off. "I'm sorry, but that's not going to help. Your story correlates with my tests in the lab over the last couple of days. I've been watching samples of your blood. Fascinating stuff. In the end, your immune system fought hard and overcame your shapeshifter power. I checked when I woke early this morning, and the power was gone. So I'm not surprised to hear you confirm this. You see, it's not about how many times you shifted. Your ability just expired."

"But in two days?" his dad exclaimed. "His power lasted *two days?*"

A silence fell, and it felt to Travis like everyone was mourning the loss of a great friend—in this case a wyvern.

"But he can undergo the treatment again," Lady Simone said. "I see no reason why not. In fact, I'm keen to study his blood. Maybe his immune system will weaken after time, and he can remain a shapeshifter for longer periods. Or maybe it will grow stronger. Or maybe it depends on what he's shifting into; some creatures may put up more of a fight than others."

"But two days?" Travis's dad said again. "I thought he'd have weeks or months! Two days is just . . ."

He stopped when Aunt Lauren nudged him. At that point, Uncle Robbie said, "Don't worry, Travis, this just means you'll get to experience more than any of us. Imagine it! A wyvern one day, an ogre the next, then a griffin, and whatever else you want!" He looked wistful. "I kind of envy you. It gets old being the same thing all the time."

Travis smiled. "I guess so. But I wish I had more than two days each time. That's not enough to do anything useful."

His mom put her arm around him. "Not enough time to do anything *useful*? So rescuing twenty prisoners and getting them back to New Earth isn't enough for you? Putting Mr. Braxton out of business for good isn't enough? Taming a unicorn and riding it home isn't enough?"

Everyone laughed, and Travis shrugged. "Well, I guess. I felt sure she'd never let me get close. I wouldn't have even tried if Nitwit hadn't suggested it."

He noticed a shared glance between several of the adults, something he'd noticed earlier when telling his tale. "About that," his dad said. "Son, are you sure Nitwit is real?"

Rolling his eyes, he said, "Look, I know you've never seen her, but I keep telling you she's shy. I tried to get her to meet you the other morning, and that's why she ran off." Seeing all the disbelieving faces, he felt indignation rising. "She's been with me the whole time, watching from a distance and showing up whenever it was safe. She *helped* me."

"Hmm," his dad said. "Did she? Did she really?"

Well, no, not really.

Travis thought about how the imp had failed to look for the cage keys, and she could have dashed back to Carter to fetch help if she'd really been looking out for him. In truth, she hadn't helped at all except to be there for him.

His mom and dad looked at each other again. Then his dad said, "Nobody's ever seen her but you. Imps do exist, of course, and there are cases where one has latched onto a particular youngster and formed a connection, but it's very rare. All this research you've been doing . . . Is it possible you just imagined her?"

Flabbergasted, Travis opened his mouth to argue. But what if his dad was right and Nitwit didn't exist? What if the imp was nothing but an *imaginary friend*?

He shook his head. "Nice try, Mom and Dad. She's real. And I'll prove it one of these days, just you wait and see."

Chapter 30
Nightmare

Travis dreamed of a young ogre rushing into its parents' arms, a unicorn herd galloping away across the plains, and a squonk shuffling around in the bushes with barely a sniffle, probably the happiest squonk in the land. He dreamed of Portal Patrol officers showing up, and lots of pats on his back for saving everyone.

But then his dreams soured. Portal Patrol wasn't overly happy about everything. Travis should have gone home for help and let the authorities deal with the situation. Instead, the soothsayer's vision had come true, and Mr. Braxton's mansion had burned, and deadly creatures roamed Old Earth. In his dream, he saw a manticore eating Mr. Braxton, and Madame Frost jabbing pins into a miniature Travis while an imp sat there laughing. Odd noises permeated his nightmare—a tiny creak, a sinister whispering noise, warm and unpleasant-smelling breath on his face . . .

He jolted awake in the darkness of his bedroom.

Just a dream, he told himself. *It was just—*

Two figures leaned over him, and he jerked in fright. At first, he thought maybe it was his mom and dad coming to check on him. They'd probably heard him calling out during his nightmare. But he knew immediately the shadowy figures weren't his parents at all.

Both were female. One leaned close to his face, breathing on him, her breath foul. The other stood by the open bedroom door, a tall, long-haired woman wearing robes. It was hard to discern their features in the darkness; Travis saw only their silhouettes in the soft glow of a lantern the tall woman held by her hip.

Madame Frost, he thought in horror.

He struggled to sit up, but whoever it was by his bedside thumped an arm down on his chest. Before he could cry out, she clamped a powerful hand over his mouth. Or clamped *something* over his mouth, anyway. It felt weird, and it had claws that dug into his left cheek.

"Hello, sweet thing," she purred in a low voice.

Though her face was utterly black in the feeble light, Travis suddenly knew who she was. And she wasn't human.

The lamia.

He moaned, certain she was about to bite into his neck and drain him of blood. And without his shapeshifting power, there was nothing he could do about it.

The witch took a couple of steps forward and brought up the lantern to reveal her face. "Be quiet now, boy. We're all going to step outside without any trouble. Do you understand?"

He nodded, eager for a chance to avoid the lamia's fangs or at least delay her feeding.

When he was allowed to get up out of bed, he shuddered at the sight of her silver-scaled body and serpentine tail. Though the lamia was fairly small in size, he knew those claws could rip him to shreds if she pounced on him in a rage.

Her silvery hair hung loosely, framing a freakishly human woman's face. She smiled at him, revealing her fangs. "So nice to smell you again," she whispered.

With the witch nudging him along, Travis crept into the hall and toward the front door. He passed his parents' room and prepared to shout out. He was confident he could burst in and wake them, and his dad could transform and deal with the intruders even while Travis lay on the floor with the lamia biting his neck.

"Don't," the witch murmured in his ear, gripping his arm. "Nox will snap your neck in a heartbeat and drink your blood before your father blinks himself awake. Just keep moving."

Whether that was true or not, her warning delayed Travis enough that he was already past the bedroom and all the way to the front door before he knew it. The door stood ajar, and he pulled it open and stepped outside into the crisp nighttime air. His pajamas were about as thin as smart clothes only without the inherent magical warmth. He shivered and walked barefoot down the cold, stone-paved path, the lamia nudging against his side.

"This will do," the witch said, her voice a little louder now. She rummaged in her robes and pulled out a small bottle filled with an innocuous-looking liquid. Without a word, she placed this bottle carefully in the middle of the path and stepped away, ushering Travis and the lamia a little farther toward the gate at the end.

"What's going on?" Travis asked.

Nox the lamia immediately jumped up at him, threw her front legs around his neck, and twisted sharply. Off-balanced, Travis tumbled to the ground, and she straddled him with her jaws poised around his neck, her fangs touching his skin.

Breathing hard, he closed his eyes and held very still. He felt so powerless. As a wyvern shapeshifter, he could have transformed in an instant and thrown her off, then whacked her with his poison-tipped tail. As a mere human, he was useless.

"Hal Franklin!" the witch yelled. "Come out here!"

From where he lay on his back on the path, Travis could see the witch and the house, though most of his sight was blocked by an extreme close-up of the lamia's pale face and silvery hair.

His dad slept fairly heavily, and it took several more outbursts from Madame Frost before a light came on in the hallway. After a few more seconds, the geo-rock-powered porch light came on, and a sleepy man in nighttime smart clothes appeared in the doorway. "What's going on out here?"

Then he froze, his eyes widening.

"Hal?" another voice called from behind him.

Travis's mom came into view, also dressed in smart clothes, in this case a knee-length nightgown. His parents had learned a long time ago that trouble could brew at any time—and tonight proved their point.

Hal's dad dashed forward and transformed, and suddenly a massive dragon filled the space in front of the house, giant clawed paws thudding as he roared with anger.

"Stop!" the witch screeched. "Stop, or your son will die in an instant!"

As the screaming and roaring continued, Travis felt the fangs press harder into his neck. He froze, trying to control his panting. He had no chance of rolling out from under the lamia. She would sink her teeth in. And if what the witch said was true, Nox could easily crunch and twist, breaking his neck in an instant.

The dragon had paused. Travis's mom came running around him, her dark-brown hair tousled and hanging loose. "Leave my son alone!" she yelled. "What do you think you're—"

Madame Frost held up her hands. "Quiet! Listen to me, and listen good." Her voice dropped in volume a few notches but also hardened. "I'll make this very simple. I'm taking Travis. You will *not* come after me. And to ensure I have a good head start, I require that you, Mr. Franklin, drink the contents of that small bottle on the path before you."

The enormous dragon glanced down. There it was, the tiny glass object standing a few feet beneath his chin. The idea that a dragon this size—or any size—could take a swig seemed ridiculous.

The witch pointed at Travis's mom. "Mrs. Franklin, pick up the bottle and pour the potion into your husband's mouth. Save a drop for yourself."

"I'm not doing anything of the sort. Do you really think we're just going to *fall asleep* while you take our son away?"

"Yes, I do," Madame Frost said. "Because the alternative is that Nox here will snap his neck like a twig, and his life will be ended before you can blink. Then it will be too late to ruminate on poor decisions." She placed her hands on her hips. "Go ahead. Drink and sleep. When you wake, feel free to come after us. Your son will be fine. We just need to borrow him for a while, that's all."

She spoke so calmly that even Travis felt a sense of calm assurance. *Go ahead and take the potion, Dad*, he thought. But he didn't say it aloud. He wasn't sure the fangs digging into his throat would allow it.

"One word," Madame Frost said, sounding almost bored now. "One word from me, and young Travis is dead. Of course, I'll also be dead after that, and so will Nox, because I have no doubt your enraged husband will burn us where we stand. But we're fairly confident you'll be sensible and drink the potion before any irreversible harm is done. Am I wrong?"

Travis's mom and dad looked at one another. Their expressions were unreadable, but they probably shared an entire conversation in that single glance.

"Change back," his mom finally told him.

Madame Frost took a step forward. "No!" She paused, then added, "Just stay in dragon form, Mr. Franklin, so I can see you from a distance. Take the potion and fall asleep right here on the path. Take it *now*."

Suspicion crept into Travis's mind then. He had no idea what the witch wanted with him, but he'd assumed it was some kind of follow-up to the Mr. Braxton case. Whatever she wanted, Travis had been certain it was between him and her.

But now he wondered. *Stay in dragon form*, he repeated in his mind. *Why does she want him to stay in dragon form?*

With a shock, he realized his mom had picked up the potion and was, very slowly, edging closer to the dragon's jaws while keeping her eyes on the witch.

"All but a drop," Madame Frost said. "Save some for yourself."

"How do I know this won't kill us?" Travis's mom said.

"If I'd wanted you dead, I could have killed you in many different ways while you slept. All I want is a simple assurance you won't follow us until you wake several hours from now."

They'll be in a trance, Travis thought. *Just like the unicorn and I were. It's safe, but I'll be on my own for sure. And without a shapeshifter power.*

As his mom hesitated, the witch gave an impatient sigh and turned to Nox. "Perhaps we need to hurry things along."

Without a word, the lamia dug her teeth in just a little bit. Travis cried out, trying to bat her away with his hands. She simply clung tight, her claws digging into his chest.

"All right, all right!" his mom shouted. "Look, I'm doing it!"

As the pain in his neck eased, Travis shifted his gaze to his parents. His mom had removed the lid and was gently pouring the liquid into his dad's mouth as he held his jaws open. With great reluctance, he swallowed and licked his lips.

"Now you, Mrs. Franklin," the witch said, relief evident in her voice.

She'd held back a drop or two. Now she took a swig and threw the bottle aside, a look of angry defiance on her face even though she'd done exactly what the witch demanded.

Madame Frost clicked her tongue and turned away. "Finally. All right, now we'll wait a few minutes."

Her hand crept inside her robes, and Travis glimpsed the handle of a knife. His suspicion deepened. She had no intention of running away with Travis. She had other plans, though he couldn't fathom what. Like she'd said, she could have killed both his parents while they slept if she'd wanted to. Instead, she'd forced them outside, provoked his dad to transform, coerced them to sleep, and seemed keen for his dad to stay in dragon form throughout.

Travis sucked in a breath. A cold dread seeped into his chest, and he almost wailed with anguish. But he forced himself to lie absolutely still, waiting for the lamia to loosen her grip just a fraction so he could leap up and . . .

And what? He was no match for Madame Frost, nor the lamia. With his parents in a spaced-out stupor, he was literally on his own, just an ordinary twelve-year-old boy against a powerful witch and a vampire cat.

He remembered something the witch had said to Mr. Braxton outside the cabin at the lake. "You promised to trap dragons for me," or words to that effect. And then: "I'm here for one thing only—a dragon's fire gland."

Travis watched her closely, noting how she fingered the knife under her robes, and how she stood there patiently, watching the dragon grow sleepy.

Waiting.

Chapter 31
Under the Knife

Madame Frost pulled the knife from her robes. It had to be a foot long, its blade gleaming in the moonlight. She held it up and closed her eyes, her lips moving.

Appalled and fascinated, Travis lay on his back on the cold path with the lamia straddling him, her fangs still at his throat. For the moment, he was distracted by the witch's silent utterings. Whatever she was saying, whatever evil spell spouted from her lips, it had an effect on the knife. The blade started glowing a faint green color, and flecks of light danced off the steel.

When the spell was finished, the witch smiled and bent over, placing the tip of the glowing blade against the paved path. Without any effort, she pushed the point into the stone slab.

"The knife is ready," she said, casting a look back at Travis. "It will slice through your father's scales and cut deep without pain, and it will seal the flesh with magic. He'll live—just without his fire gland." She straightened and tilted her head. "No hard feelings, boy. I truly wanted Braxton to trap a *real* dragon. He showed great promise with the griffin and chimera and others, and I expect a dragon was next on his list. Alas, you spoiled it all."

Travis gritted his teeth. "Let me up."

The lamia didn't move. But the witch said, "Go on, release him," and Nox grudgingly eased off so that Travis could sit up and rub his neck. She remained inches away, though, her gaze fixed on him, her expression clearly indicating she intended to suck his blood very soon.

"You can't do this," Travis pleaded the witch. "That's my *dad*. He's not just some dragon—"

"You brought this on yourself, boy," she interrupted, approaching the oddly quiet reptilian giant. "And truthfully, I don't know if the fire gland of a dragon shapeshifter will work. It might not *stay* in dragon form after I cut it out. It might shift back to human form, and I have to wonder what it will become. Something utterly useless, I should imagine. A pound of flesh, perhaps. But it's worth a try. Fire glands offer *tremendous* power to an experienced witch like me."

She ducked under the dragon's chin and stood under his broad chest. She lifted the blade, which glowed even more in the shadows.

"Stop!" Travis shouted. The lamia growled and bared her fangs.

Madame Frost spoke softly. "There's a jengu shapeshifter who spends her time in a wheelchair by the Lake of Spirits. She lost her tail when she tried to cross through a portal just as that portal closed down. Her fishtail was severed at the waist. From what I hear, her tail remained in that form afterward even though the jengu's true form was human. So perhaps the fire gland cut from your father's throat will *remain* a fire gland."

She lifted the blade, aimed at a point dead center of the dragon's throat, and—

"Stop!" a small, female voice cried.

Travis, the witch, and the lamia looked around with equal surprise. A figure stood there on the grass as if she'd been there all along, a tiny imp with floppy ears and large, glistening eyes.

"Nitwit," Madame Frost said, sounding irritated. She stepped out from under the dragon's chin. "Go away. You can't interfere. Your curse won't allow it. Make yourself scarce."

"My curse won't allow me to help Travis," she said to the witch. "But there's nothing to stop me helping his parents."

"Nitwit?" Travis said, bewildered. A dozen thoughts rushed through his head, primarily the idea that the witch could *see* her. So she was real after all, not just a figment of his imagination. And they spoke as though they *knew* each other.

"I'm sorry, Travis," the imp said, turning to him. Tears formed and rolled down her cheeks. A flood of words rushed from her lips. "The witch trapped me a few weeks ago. She's been spying on you for ages, and she caught me one day and put me in a cage and interrogated me, found out you would be a shapeshifter one day soon, and she wanted to know what *kind* of shapeshifter, and I didn't know, and she asked if you would be a dragon like your dad, and I said I didn't know, and she told me to find out, and I told her I would never lie to you, and she cursed me and made me keep tagging along but never to help you if you were in trouble, and I really *couldn't* help you even though I tried, or even *tell* you why—"

"Imp!" the witch roared. She snapped her fingers. "Nox, get her."

The lamia tore off across the lawn and pounced—but the imp lifted one foot and vanished, then reappeared fifteen feet away. It was as though she took a huge, impossible step sideways.

She turned again to Travis. "I couldn't even *talk* to you about this, because my throat closed up every time I tried. But the curse is wearing thin. It started wearing thin yesterday, at the lake shore. I could feel it. I told you about the unicorn."

The lamia leapt again, and the imp neatly stepped away, reappearing next to Travis.

She spoke quietly now. "I can talk to you now, but I still can't *help*. Not directly, anyway. But you can help *me*. Get the witch to lift my curse, and then I can help *you*."

"H-how?" Travis cried. "I—"

Again the lamia came running, and this time when she leapt, Nitwit barely moved in time. She ducked down and vanished, reappearing several feet to one side, and the lamia thundered past Travis, almost bowling him over.

Nox spun around and shook her head, snarling with fury. She glared at Nitwit, her muscles bunching up as she prepared for another pounce.

219

Nitwit backed away, looking at Travis. "Help me—or I might as well let the lamia get me."

The witch was busy fumbling in her robes with one hand while holding the glowing knife with the other. She finally pulled out a ragdoll, and as she turned it around and held it up, Travis made a frantic run for her across the lawn.

She laughed. "No more pins, boy. This knife has a much more *devastating* effect."

Time seemed to slow. He knew in an instant he would never make it to her in time, and the one person that could—Nitwit—couldn't attack her either, because that would be directly helping him.

Two things happened at once as Travis sprinted across the lawn.

First, his mom sprang into action from just a few feet away, grappling with Madame Frost.

Second, the lamia leapt for Nitwit.

Seeing an extra two seconds of time opening up before him, Travis launched himself at the witch and his mom, and the three of them went down in a flurry of limbs. His mom had one hand clamped around Madame Frost's knife-arm, and Travis grabbed for it, too. With nothing but the sounds of panting and scuffling on the cold grass, he wrestled with her locked fingers and thumb, trying to pry the deadly knife loose.

He had no idea what was going on in the background, what the lamia was doing to Nitwit, but he couldn't break away now. Gritting his teeth and digging his knees into the writhing witch's stomach, he tore her fingers loose from the handle, one by one until the knife tumbled free and fell on her.

She let out a gasp as the glowing blade slipped easily through her torso to one side, passing all the way through to the hilt. Green sparks flew, and a glow enveloped that part of her body. It probably wasn't a fatal wound by any means, but it shocked her to the core.

Rather than leave the knife embedded in her, Travis grabbed it and pulled it out, eliciting another gasp. He rolled away, then made a savage slash for her other hand, which still gripped the ragdoll. His aim was bad, but still he cut the ragdoll in half and took one or two of her fingers with it.

She cried out again, clutching at her hand. No blood welled up; the green glow surrounded her two stumpy fingers, sealing the wound.

As Travis's mom retreated, he again leapt at the witch and held the knife to her throat.

Panting and trembling, he said, "Take away Nitwit's curse. Now!"

The witch, also out of breath, peered at him from behind her tangle of long, grey hair. "It's too late. She's already dead."

Travis stiffened. He didn't want to look. He gripped her hair with one hand so she couldn't roll away from him. "You're lying. Take away her curse."

He touched the knife to her throat, his hand shaking. He saw his own silhouette reflected in both her eyes, illuminated by the blade's green glow.

She refused to say or do anything, so he pressed harder. The steel tip eased into her neck, and green sparks flashed.

"I can't!" Madame Frost cried out. "But the curse is about to expire anyway. I can't lift it. It just fades away. You heard what she said—it's nearly done with. It'll be gone tomorrow, maybe the next day. That's if she's still alive, which I doubt."

"You're lying," he snarled.

"Travis," his mom murmured from where she knelt in the grass. Her eyes were wide. "What's happening to you?"

He assumed she was shocked by the anger that boiled away inside, but he couldn't help that. "Is she dead?" he whispered. "Tell me she's not dead."

Then he realized something strange. The backs of his hands were a curious blood-red color, a little scaly. His pajama sleeves were stretched tight because he had half-formed wings underneath. He blinked, aware that his face had altered, a partial snout pushing outward.

A half-transformation? But how—?

The witch sneered. "That's it? That's all you have?"

He relaxed his grip on her, feeling defeated. Even if he'd fully transformed, what then? He couldn't have forced the witch to do anything. He had no power over her. Even at the height of his anger moments ago, he'd still been unable to do anything beyond threaten her with the blade. Stabbing her in the side had been her own fault, the missing fingers an accident. Despite his wyvern rage, he was still human.

Travis climbed to his feet, his anger ebbing. The blood-red coloring of his hands faded, and his sleeves loosened. Whatever weird partial shift had occurred, it was over.

Madame Frost glared at Travis's mom. "How are you awake? Even a few drops of that potion should have knocked you out for hours."

"The drops I spat out, you mean?"

Travis held up the green-glowing knife, then spun around to face the lamia, fearing for the worst.

Nox was gone. So was Nitwit.

Confused, Travis stared at the ground. He saw no signs of a struggle, no traces of blood. Both had disappeared. "Where are they?"

The witch huffed a laugh and struggled to her feet. "The stupid little imp jumped away with the lamia's fangs in her neck. Nox took in the imp's blood, so they *both* jumped." She looked round in the darkness. "Wherever they are, I'm sure the imp is sucked dry by now."

Travis began trembling again. The horror of what Madame Frost had said was too much to accept. He dropped the glowing knife, and it embedded itself up to the hilt in the grass.

"Well, I'll bid you all goodnight, then," the witch said. "I can't say it was fun, but it was certainly interesting. Maybe we'll meet another time."

At that moment, Travis's mom sprouted insectoid wings out of her back and lifted off the ground with a fierce buzzing. She grabbed the witch under the arms and shot upward with her, clearing straining under the weight.

Madame Frost shouted and kicked, but the two of them were thirty feet up in a matter of seconds. Startled, Travis watched as his mom flew slowly and steadily across the lawn toward one of the trees standing around the back of the property.

The trunks of these trees were thick and tall, bare of branches for the first thirty or forty feet. His mom rose to a solid-looking bough and dumped the witch on it. Madame Frost screamed and held on for dear life with both hands, one leg over the branch and the other dangling. She pulled herself up and lay there, clinging tight.

The witch continued screaming and hollering as Travis's mom buzzed back to the ground, looking decidedly worn out.

"She can stay there until your dad wakes up," she said stiffly. "Awful woman. We've met her before, several times over the years. She lives outside the village. I think she'll be heading to the Prison of Despair after this."

Travis went to her. They hugged and stood there a while, listening to the witch's complaints. He looked over at his dad, who sat quite calmly in dragon form, his wings half spread, his jaws hanging open. *So much for my big, strong dad,* he thought. *Turns out being a fearsome dragon doesn't mean a thing if the bad guys are smart enough. Madame Frost just showed up tonight and controlled all of us without breaking a sweat. She nearly took his fire gland!*

The knife, still embedded in the dirt, had sunk a little more. Travis disengaged from his mom and walked over to it. Using his bare foot, he pressed it down farther, finding it shockingly easy. He finished the job with his big toe, gently pushing until the entire handle had vanished and earth caved in over the top.

He turned back to his mom—and found her staring at a tiny figure with a bloodstained neck.

Travis's mouth dropped open. "Nitwit! Are you okay?"

She smiled weakly. "Just tired. I took the lamia a long way from here, at least fifteen hops. I think my curse must be fading, because . . ." She teetered, and Travis rushed to hold her up. "Because I helped you, right? I stopped the lamia from attacking you again."

"You did, Nitwit, you did. The curse is fading. And anyway, you helped me already just by showing up here. You distracted the witch." He pointed up at the tree, where the witch flailed helplessly. "And she's not a problem anymore, either."

The imp nodded. "So everything's fine, then." She sagged, and Travis stooped to lift her up in his arms. She was as light as a feather.

Nitwit grinned at his mom. "Hello, Mrs. Franklin."

"Uh . . . hello." She blinked a few times. Then she shook her head and smiled, offering her hand. "It's nice to finally meet you, Nitwit."

**A SNEAK PEEK AT THE NEXT BOOK IN
THE ISLAND OF FOG LEGACIES . . .**

"You don't know what you're talking about, Rez," Travis said, getting annoyed now. "It's probably a good thing you don't ever want to be a shapeshifter. You wouldn't know what to do with your power. It'd be wasted on you."

Rez laughed. "Probably. Hey, shouldn't we be out of this mess by now? Feels like we've been walking for ages."

The narrow path wound on ahead, trees and prickly bushes crowding in from both sides. Travis slowed, puzzled. His friend was right. They should have emerged from the forest by now.

"Did we take a wrong turn?" he wondered aloud.

Rez looked back the way they'd come. "We took a left at that gnarly old tree just like it says on the map. There's nowhere else we could have gone wrong."

Travis fished in his pocket for the folded piece of paper and smoothed it out. "Maybe the map's wrong."

But it looked pretty clear. The forest path meandered for miles, then forked. It was marked *Left at Gnarly Old Tree*, and they'd gone left. They should have made it to the valley shortly after. It actually said *Fifteen Minutes' Walk to Valley* from the fork, but they'd been walking much longer.

"Are we lost?" Rez said with a scowl.

At that moment, a deep, booming moan sounded from the trees to one side. . .

SINISTER ROOTS

ISLAND OF FOG LEGACIES #2

OTHER SCI-FI AND FANTASY NOVELS
BY THE SAME AUTHOR . . .

In *Island of Fog*, a group of twelve-year-old children have never seen the world beyond the fog, never seen a blue sky or felt the warmth of the sun on their skin. And now they're starting to change into monsters!

What is the secret behind the mysterious fog? Who is the stranger that shows up one morning, and where did she come from? Hal Franklin and his friends are determined to uncover the truth about their newfound shapeshifting abilities, and their quest takes them to the forbidden lighthouse . . .

There are nine books in this series, plus a number of short stories available for free at islandoffog.com. It's an expansive saga set in a parallel Earth with plenty of magic and familiar creatures from myth and legend.

In *Sleep Writer*, everything changes for twelve-year-old Liam when a girl moves in next door. Madison is fifteen, pretty, and much weirder than she seems. Sometimes when she's sound asleep, she scrawls a message on a notepad by her pillow. She finds these cryptic words when she wakes the next morning—a time and a place.

But a time and a place for what? Liam and best friend Ant join her when she goes hunting around a cemetery late one night, and life is never the same again.

This fun science fiction series is ongoing, with at least one new novel each year.

In *Fractured*, the world of Apparatum is divided. To the west lies the high-tech city of Apparati, governed by a corrupt mayor and his brutal military general. To the east, spread around the mountains and forests, the seven enclaves of Apparata are ruled by an overbearing sovereign and his evil chancellor. Between them lies the Ruins, or the Broken Lands—all that's left of a sprawling civilization before it fractured. Hundreds of years have passed, and neither world knows the other exists.

Until now.

We follow Kyle and Logan on their journey of discovery. Laws are harsh. In the city, Kyle's tech implant fails to work, rendering him worthless in the eyes of the mayor. In the enclaves, Logan is unable to tether to any of the spirits, and he is deemed an outcast. Facing execution, the two young fugitives escape their homes and set out into the wastelands to forge a new life.

But their destinies are intertwined, for the separate worlds of Apparati and Apparata are two faces of the same coin . . . and it turns out that everyone has a twin.

There are two books in this series, with a possible third (a prequel) planned for the future. This series is co-written with author Brian Clopper.

In *Quincy's Curse*, poor Quincy Flack is cursed with terrible luck. After losing his parents and later his uncle and aunt in a series of freak accidents, Megan Mugwood is a little worried about befriending him when he moves into the village of Ramshackle Bottom. But incredibly good fortune shines on him sometimes, too. Indeed, it turns out that he found a bag of valuable treasure in the woods just a few months ago!

As luck would have it, Megan has chosen the worst possible time to be around him.

This is a fantasy for all ages, a complex and rewarding tale, a little dark in places but also a lot of fun.

Go to **UnearthlyTales.com** for more information.

Made in the USA
Monee, IL
13 October 2020